MIKE BARTLETT

Mike Bartlett is a multi-award-winning playwright and screenwriter whose most recent plays include *Wild* (Hampstead Theatre); *Game* (Almeida Theatre); *King Charles III* (Almeida Theatre/West End/Broadway; Critics' Circle Award for Best New Play, Olivier Award for Best New Play, Tony Nomination for Best Play); *An Intervention* (Paines Plough/Watford Palace Theatre); *Bull* (Sheffield Theatres/Off-Broadway; TMA Best New Play Award, Olivier Award for Outstanding Achievement in an Affiliate Theatre); *Medea* (Glasgow Citizens/Headlong); *Chariots of Fire* (based on the film; Hampstead/West End); *13* (National Theatre); *Love, Love, Love* (Paines Plough/Plymouth Drum/Royal Court Theatre; TMA Best New Play Award); *Earthquakes in London* (Headlong/National Theatre); *Cock* (Royal Court/ Off-Broadway, Olivier Award for Outstanding Achievement in an Affiliate Theatre); *Artefacts* (nabokov/Bush Theatre); *Contractions* and *My Child* (Royal Court).

Bartlett has also written several plays for radio, winning the Writers' Guild Tinniswood and Imison Prizes for *Not Talking*. He has received BAFTA nominations for his television series *The Town* and *Doctor Foster* for which Bartlett won Outstanding Newcomer for British Television Writing at the British Screenwriters' Awards 2016. Bartlett's adaptation of his play *King Charles III* aired on BBC television in 2017.

T0322504

Mike Bartlett

DOCTOR FOSTER
THE SCRIPTS

NICK HERN BOOKS

London

www.nickhernbooks.co.uk

A Nick Hern Book

Doctor Foster: The Scripts first published in Great Britain in 2017 as a paperback original by Nick Hern Books Limited, The Glasshouse, 49a Goldhawk Road, London W12 8QP

Doctor Foster: The Scripts copyright © 2017 Drama Republic
Foreword copyright © 2017 Suranne Jones
Introductions copyright © 2017 Mike Bartlett, Roanna Benn and Jude Liknaitzky

Mike Bartlett has asserted his right to be identified as the author of this work

Front cover: Suranne Jones as Doctor Gemma Foster and Bertie Carvel as Simon Foster; back cover: Suranne Jones; photography by Phil Fisk; © Drama Republic Ltd

Suranne Jones photo on page vii: photography by Liam Daniel; © Drama Republic Ltd

Designed and typeset by Nick Hern Books, London
Printed in Great Britain by Ashford Colour Press, Gosport, Hampshire

A CIP catalogue record for this book is available from the British Library

ISBN 978 1 84842 570 5

MIX
Paper from
responsible sources
FSC
www.fsc.org   FSC® C011748

Contents

Dear Reader

You are in the position I was a few years ago when I was first sent these scripts.

You hold in your hands a story that will take you on a real journey; that tests your moral compass, and challenges your ideas of a marriage, a professional woman, a community, love and betrayal…

It took me a long time to read the scripts as I wanted to really put myself in Gemma's head at every turn, even on the first reading (and trust me, that doesn't always happen with scripts and screenplays – but this one is special).

Enjoy! And once again, thank you, Mike.

Suranne Jones

Introduction
Mike Bartlett

Why publish a screenplay, when these days the finished film or TV series is so readily available? If one only thinks of them as working documents then perhaps there is little point, beyond the academic. But reading screenplays has always been as interesting to me as reading plays; an activity in its own right. Now I think about it, I may even have read a screenplay before I properly read a play. It was the script for *Pulp Fiction*. I was technically too young to have seen it, only fourteen when it came out, but I think I must have watched it at a friend's house on video. What I remember is loving the sound of the dialogue and being fascinated by the structure itself. I wanted to know how it was made, and I wanted to be part of it, so when I saw the screenplay in the bookshop I bought it, and read it again and again – hearing the rhythm of the dialogue in my head, imagining the scenes, and how I might shoot them. I saw that dialogue looks completely different on the page to transcribed speech – especially Tarantino dialogue. A world away from naturalism, it's got artistry, form, music and structure. Reading that screenplay inspired me to write my first real scene – about two people meeting on a bench, thinking they might fall in love with each other, and then realising they hated each other. It was very Tarantino-esque, but it was, at least, dialogue.

In the years that followed I read many screenplays: William Goldman, *The Godfather*, *American Beauty*, TV shows like *The West Wing* and *The Sopranos*, recently the screenplay to *Lincoln* by Tony Kushner. All films and TV I'd already seen, but wanted to re-experience myself, from the script upwards. I was learning, but also enjoying and imagining. If there's a theatrical version of film, and maybe later a director's cut, then the version in your head as you read a screenplay is *your* cut. You choose the shots, and the cast. You imagine the world yourself.

What I had no idea about, until I started working in television myself, is that the script you read at the end of the process is not a pure literary document, crafted by a writer in isolation. Some plays are this, but, I would bet, hardly any screenplays. They've had notes upon notes given and acted on, both artistic and logistical. They've been revised as shooting has progressed, and they may reflect what has happened in the edit. In my experience, plays are revised and rewritten but tend to settle down around halfway through rehearsals. Screenplays, however, are in flux all the way through, for one reason or another. But despite this, I always try to make sure that the script is the document we return to – the centre point around which everything revolves. Even in the edit, when some people (quite legitimately) say that one should throw away the script and start again, I'm drawn back to it, believing that the best way to stay true to the project that everyone wanted to make in the first place is to look for the intentions in that script – even if you end up achieving them in a very different way.

So for *Doctor Foster* we're never that far away from a script, in pre-production, through shooting, and afterwards. And just as there's a creative tension between the part as it was written before it was cast, and the actor that finally plays it, I also think there's a similar tension between the yet-unshot, utopian, platonic screenplay, full of potential, and the inevitably flawed, pragmatic, money-bound production that ends up on screen. The unrealistic utopia of the original pushes the project further than it might otherwise go, and equally the pragmatism of having to make it real and tangible can help it discover greater truth.

So in that sense the process of writing continues for me long after shooting has finished, right up until we lock the episodes in the edit, with new lines being added in ADR (additional dialogue recording), reordering of the scenes, and occasionally even creating new scenes. These scripts therefore reflect as best I think they can, what a *final* script would look like. The end of a writing process. It's been fascinating for me to see some of the original descriptions of sequences and locations, and how the dialogue looks on the page. Although mostly it reflects the words you'll find in the finished episodes, one can see the decisions that have been made by actors, designers and directors as they make it real. Reading the scripts, you're aware that there are always other routes one could have taken. Performing a line in a different way, shooting a scene in a different style. As we've established, that's part of the fun of reading the script. But of course it also makes very clear how much everyone brings to the production. What Suranne Jones adds to the Gemma Foster on the page, and how she interprets the role. How much of the tone is established through music, direction, or cinematography. The screenplay, like a play, is an invitation to collaborate, and this production had amazing artists come to work on it throughout, who were simultaneously very faithful to the scripts you're about to read, but knew it was a jumping-off point for something potentially greater.

Doctor Foster: The Road to the Small Screen
Roanna Benn and Jude Liknaitzky (Executive Producers)

Contrary to what one might imagine, as producers in television drama, it is not *ideas* that we struggle to come up with. Finding brilliant writers, and persuading them to work with us, is the real challenge.

We had long been devoted fans of Mike Bartlett's writing – having seen or read all of his plays. What we loved most of all is the way Mike collides characters: people who shouldn't come together, who shouldn't say those things to one another, *do* come together and *do* say those things, and the result is electric. His writing is fearless, he take things to the extreme in the most thrilling, unpredictable and dramatic ways. However, it only works if there is an underlying truth in the writing – otherwise who cares? But with Mike there is always truth at the heart: a couple at war fighting over their child (such as in his play *My Child*); a couple arguing over the ambiguous sexuality of one of them (*Cock*); a family in disarray over the legacy left by one generation to another (*Love, Love, Love*); the struggle in the workplace to survive when others are determined to destroy you (*Bull*), etc. To sum up: we wanted to be involved in capturing what Mike does best and make it work on television for millions of people to enjoy – and we didn't want to screw it up!

We were thrilled when we eventually got the opportunity to meet Mike, although it took a long while. We had to persuade his agent, Nick Quinn, and this was no easy feat. Everyone wanted to meet Mike, and he was *very* busy. When we finally succeeded in squeezing an hour out of him before his rehearsals at the Royal Court for *Love, Love, Love*, we talked about our shared passions and, to our delight, our connection felt very natural.

Sometimes TV developments feel like wading through treacle: trying to attach the right writer to the right idea and then to match both to the right channel and the right commissioner, and everyone trying to work out what the audience might like. Far too much second-guessing and not enough coming from the heart. And therein misery lies. But on this rare occasion the elements came together surprisingly easily.

Once we hit on the notion of betrayal and revenge, and making this a very intimate story about marriage, we got very excited. Of course, affairs are

ten-a-penny in television drama, not least in the soaps. But we talked about
how infidelity can destroy lives and push people to the very edge. Isn't the
loss of a person's love and devotion, their gross betrayal, akin to a death?
We really believed in those high stakes and they were core to the idea. This
may be a rare drama with no dead body, but in our eyes the marriage was
'the body' and there *was* a murderer to pursue.

The next step was to convince a commissioner at one of the channels that
this was a good idea. Our commissioner was Matthew Read at the BBC
who, fortunately for us, is one of those brilliant commissioners who trusts
the writer to be their best selves. The idea we pitched was a simple and
dynamic one: what happens when a woman finds out her husband is having
an affair? Matthew liked it. What's more, he confirmed that there was
nothing else on the BBC slate that was dealing with this most universal of
subject matters.

Mike wrote a fantastic first episode. Of course, there were a number of
drafts, as there always are in development, but the process was particularly
creative and streamlined. Mike seemed to relish notes and collaboration,
whilst at the same time being very clear about what he wanted to write and
the pitfalls he wanted to avoid. He discovered that whilst he wanted there to
be lots of story, the script never worked if plot took precedence over the
emotional journey of the character.

Matthew Read contributed his notes, which Mike took on board, and then
the script went on its journey upwards to the Head of Drama – then Ben
Stephenson – into the hands of the Head of BBC One, Charlotte Moore, and
after one full of year in development the show was green-lit. This is an
extremely quick result in television!

We cast Suranne Jones as Doctor Gemma Foster before we had any other
crew or cast on board. We knew it was crucial to have the best and most
particular lead actor, someone the audience would love and follow on this
roller-coaster journey. We knew Suranne was a remarkable actor, but we
had no idea how her fearlessness would match Mike's – an incredible
pairing.

The BBC gave us a year for Mike to write all five episodes before we
started filming. This was a wonderful luxury as it meant Mike was able to
write the whole series and then go back and rewrite with hindsight so that it
felt like a complete and wholly authored piece of work. The way we – as
producers – worked seemed really to suit Mike: he would relish the story-
lining process traditionally used in television where we all sit in a room for

days and bash ideas around. We spent a lot of time in a grotty pub in North London covering the walls with sticky white paper. We each felt we could say whatever we wanted, and it was a 'free' space to talk about the stories and characters. Even if Mike would occasionally tell us an idea was 'neither original nor interesting'!

Once Mike felt he had enough to go off and form an episode, he would write up an informal story outline for himself, and for us producers and Matthew Read to get on board. This was a working document written in prose, rather than a piece of work in itself, but it was a crucial stage in the process that worked so well for *Doctor Foster*. It meant there wouldn't be any huge surprises when the script arrived, therefore Mike could completely throw himself into writing a script knowing it was unlikely he would later get a note that would pull the episode apart. It has to be said that, whilst Mike stuck broadly to the story he outlined in each of these working documents, the scripts would always surprise and delight us with things he did not describe in the prose version, things we could never imagine.

Once we got into production, every detail was pored over. In such a detailed and intimate relationship drama we knew that the setting, design, costume, make-up would all be utterly crucial in building the right 'world' for the characters. So every decision was scrutinised and carefully thought through by every department. Mike is not only an extraordinary writer, but a true show-runner, an executive producer who genuinely earns that credit, broad-shouldered and interested enough to take on all these considerations: the logistics of scheduling, casting, costumes, title sequence, grade, and so on. The best of writers find the practical challenges creative rather than restrictive. After all, what mug a character drinks from, or what dress a character wears is just as relevant to their character as what they say and, of course, no one knows this character as well as the writer. It is such a joy – and relief – to work with a writer in this way.

We had no idea how audiences would respond to the show. And every week was nail-biting waiting for the overnight ratings to come in. Would people stick with Gemma's story? Would they continue to care? We were blown away by the response, and particularly that audiences felt compelled to watch on the night. When we asked people why they liked the show, the overwhelming response was that they loved not having a clue what Gemma was going to do next...

Thanks
Mike Bartlett

The writing and preparation of these scripts has involved a large group of people, to whom I'm hugely grateful:

Matt Applewhite
Roanna Benn
Miranda Boscawen
Greg Brenman
Bertie Carvel
Lauren Cushman
Nick Hern
Polly Hill
Suranne Jones
Jude Liknaitsky
Clare Lizzimore
Charlotte Moore
Phil Mulryne
Nicola Sangster
Ben Stephenson
Matthew Read
Sarah Liisa Wilkinson

And the cast and crew of *Doctor Foster*.

EPISODE ONE

INT. FOSTER HOUSE. GEMMA'S BEDROOM. DAY

Early morning. We see details around a room, as sex
goes on in the background. A discarded suit on the
floor, a suitcase, the curtains letting in the
morning light. We can hear the sex is good - the
sex noises are slightly hushed, but clearly
enjoyable.

On to a pillow on a bed. In profile.

Suddenly Gemma falls back into shot, beaming. She's
thirty-seven, very bright. She smiles -

                    SIMON
      You miss me?

                    GEMMA
      Yeah, I did.

Simon leans down. He's forty, young looking,
sincere. They kiss passionately, then roll over so
she's on top -

CUT TO -

TWENTY MINUTES LATER.

It was great sex but now they're late. Gemma's
getting dressed but looking for her jacket. Simon
emerges from the en suite bathroom in his shirt and
underwear.

                    GEMMA
      There's only a few days to go and
      there's a lot to arrange.

                    SIMON
      You didn't need to, it's just a
      few friends. And we've got Neil
      and Anna tonight?

                    GEMMA
      It's all under control.

Gemma moves Simon's still-packed suitcase, picks up
his trousers from the floor. As she does, some
coins fall out, along with a red lip salve. She
picks it up, and looks at it.

>   GEMMA (CONT'D)
>   (holds up the lip salve)
>   Is this yours?

>   SIMON
>   Yes, actually. Dry lips.

>   GEMMA
>   (teasing)
>   Bit girly.

>   SIMON
>   Red? Nothing wrong with that, and
>   it was the only one they had.

>   GEMMA
>   (not listening)
>   Remember you're taking Tom to
>   school.

>   SIMON
>   I'm late.

>   GEMMA
>   (finds her jacket)
>   Me too.
>   (smiles)
>   Worth it though.

He smiles as she leaves. Loves her.

INT. FOSTER HOUSE. HALLWAY/KITCHEN. DAY

A radio plays Bon Jovi - 'Living on a Prayer'. We
pan across the front of a fridge, where various
things are pinned up with magnets. A photo of
Simon, Gemma, Tom, and an older woman in a
wheelchair (this is Helen). A list of names with
the heading 'Simon Birthday', and a calendar.

As we come off the fridge, Gemma rushes in, to find
Tom, her son, already eating cereal. We see the
kitchen - it's the working hub of the home. Piles
of paperwork on the table, and the side. Unwashed
mugs in the sink. It all works, but only just.

Gemma's not happy with her hair.

>   GEMMA
>   (to herself)
>   No one's going to notice, it
>   looks fine.

>   TOM
>   What does?

>   GEMMA
>   Nothing.

>   TOM
>   Morning, Mum.

>   GEMMA
>   Morning, darling.

>   TOM
>   You know we're late.

>   GEMMA
>   The form for the trip is in your
>   bag.

>   TOM
>   Thanks.

                    GEMMA
        No problem. Don't forget your
        coat.

                    TOM
        Yeah, okay.

She picks up her car keys, puts on her coat just as
Simon enters in his suit, holding some papers and
blueprints.
                    SIMON
        All ready mate?

                    TOM
        Nearly.

Tom gets down from the table and goes into the hall
to get his stuff ready.

                    GEMMA
        Where's my scarf?

                    SIMON
        Have mine.

                    GEMMA
         (picking it up from the chair)
        It's black. I'm wearing blue.

                    SIMON
        I think you'll manage.

She wraps it round her neck. Kisses Tom as he comes
back in, in his coat.
                    GEMMA
        Bye.

                    SIMON
        Bye.

Then she turns to Simon. Kisses him too.
Then leaves.

                         TOM
           Dad, did you drive back last
           night?

                         SIMON
           Yeah. Got meetings this morning.

INT. FOSTER HOUSE. HALLWAY. DAY

As she goes Tom and Simon are still talking.

                         TOM (O.S.)
           What happens in a meeting?

                         SIMON (O.S.)
           What do you mean?

                         TOM (O.S.)
           What do you do?

                         SIMON (O.S.)
           You sit and drink coffee and
           discuss things.

Gemma opens the front door and goes out.

                         GEMMA
           See you later!

                         SIMON (O.S.)
           Bye!

                         TOM (O.S.)
           Bye, Mum!

The front door shuts.

EXT. PARMINSTER. DAY

Parminster in morning sun. It's a medium-sized town, a few miles away from the nearest city. Old buildings, mixed in with new-build and sixties housing estates.

Aerial shot as Gemma's blue car makes its way up a street. On speakerphone in the car, she's talking to Anna.

> GEMMA (V.O.)
> Right, we're on the food, the cake... like, you're doing the decorations.

> ANNA (V.O.)
> Not a problem. What would you like?

INT. GEMMA'S CAR. DAY

Gemma drives and talks on the phone.

> GEMMA
> Balloons, bunting...

> ANNA (V.O.)
> Absolutely.

As she stops at some lights, on the pavement, a mum with two toddlers points her out. The toddlers wave. Gemma waves back -

> GEMMA
> Oh, we talked about putting something behind the bar?

> ANNA (V.O.)
> Very generous.

                         GEMMA
          Enough so that they'll have a
          good time...

A woman crosses the road in front of the car, and
spots her.

Gemma mouths 'You okay?'. The woman holds up her
bandaged hand, and mouths 'Better'. Gemma thumbs-up
back. Winks.

                    GEMMA (CONT'D)
          Not so much that I'll need a
          stomach pump.

                       ANNA (V.O.)
          You know what Neil's like. I'll
          speak to the landlord.

                      GEMMA (V.O.)
          You're a life-saver.

                       ANNA (V.O.)
          We'll catch up tonight.

                         GEMMA
          Lovely. Speak then Anna. Bye.

Gemma hangs up. The lights change and she drives
on. As she does, it reveals an old school building.
In front a hoarding for a redevelopment of the
site. 'Academy Green - 14 Luxury Flats.' Pictures
of what it will look like - and the name of the
company: 'Simon Foster Property Developments Ltd.'

CUT TO -

EXT. THE SURGERY CAR PARK. DAY

Gemma walks from her car to the surgery. She's
joined by Gordon Ward, fifty-three, glasses,
hypochondriac, also just parked.

>   GEMMA
>   Gordon. How are you?
>
>   GORDON
>   Not good at all - that's why I'm
>   here. Back pain.
>
>   GEMMA
>   Okay, well we'll deal with that
>   inside, I was just saying hello
>   really.
>
>   GORDON
>   Oh, right. Well. How are you?
>
>   GEMMA
>   Good. Bit of a disaster with the
>   hair this morning but...
>
>   GORDON
>   Yes I can see that.

They enter.

INT. THE SURGERY. RECEPTION. DAY

Pan across a board of photos of the practice GPs.
Gemma (Senior Partner) at the top. We see Jack
Reynolds (Partner), Ros Mahendra (Partner), Luke
Barton (Salaried GP), Nick Stanford (Practice
Manager) and a couple of others.

INT. THE SURGERY. RECEPTION. DAY

Gemma heads into the reception. Behind the desk are
Ros - forty, bright, big hair, her colleague and
best friend, Luke Barton - twenty-nine, dark,
handsome, and Nick - forty, efficient, precise.
Also there is Julie - the receptionist (thirty-
nine, blonde, no sense of humour).

> GEMMA
> Good morning, Julie.

> JULIE
> Not really.

> GEMMA
> What's happened?

> JULIE
> Jack's ill. Not coming in.

> ROS
> Oh why?

> NICK
> That's his final warning -

> ROS
> What did he say?

> JULIE
> Gastroenteritis.

A sceptical reaction from Nick and Ros.

> LUKE
> I saw him in the pub last night.

They go through into the office.

> GEMMA
> Alright, how many on his list
> this morning?

> JULIE
> Twelve.

                    GEMMA
Julie see what you can do.
          (to the doctors)
Take the appointments down to
eight minutes.

                    JULIE
Okay.

                    LUKE
Eight minutes is impossible.

                    GEMMA
Talk faster.

He leaves.

                    ROS
              (flirty)
See you later, Luke.

Ros watches him go.

                    ROS (CONT'D)
Not a flicker.

                    GEMMA
He's too young for you.

                    ROS
Maybe but I accidentally on
purpose brushed up against his
shirt the other day and he is
toned like a bastard.You would if
you could.

                    GEMMA
Shall we make a start.

12

INT. THE SURGERY. WAITING AREA. DAY

Gemma emerges into the full waiting room, smiles at
the patients. They smile back. She's popular. We
follow her out, down the corridor, to a door which
she opens.

INT. THE SURGERY. OFFICE

Gemma enters. Her office is as functional and as
everyday as her home. It works but there's paper
everywhere, a few medical textbooks on shelves.
Along with her desk, which has a computer on it.
There's two chairs for the patients, and a couch
ready - for examinations. She puts her bag by the
chair, takes off her coat, hangs it up with Simon's
scarf.

She's about to carry on when she notices something.
On the scarf is a hair. It doesn't look like hers.
It's blonde - against the black. She stares at it.
Worried.

CUT TO -

TITLE SEQUENCE

INT. THE SURGERY. GEMMA'S CONSULTING ROOM. DAY

Close-up of a picture of Gemma, Simon and Tom on
Gemma's desk.

Gordon's opposite Gemma. He's been going a while.
As he talks we see Gemma - listening, really <u>trying</u>
to be kind and not interrupt. Willing him to get to
the point - but the clock is ticking.

> GORDON
> As you know, I live on my own and
> once a week my sister comes

> over... bit of a drive for her,
> but she brings the shopping.
> Meals - soup, tomatoes, meat,
> onions...

> GEMMA
> Yes -

> GORDON
> She was there on a Thursday, I
> had a headache that day, which
> isn't the primary reason I'm here
> but now I mention it - I've had
> them for years, it's on your
> notes...

> GEMMA
> Hmmm...

Gemma looks at her watch.

> GORDON
> Last weekend I saw a documentary,
> they said headaches have
> histor...

> GEMMA
> (interrupts)
> Gordon can we get back to the
> specific symptoms that brought
> you in?

We hear the voice of another patient...

> CARLY (V.O.)
> I lay there with my eyes open...

We now CUT TO later. Close-up on Carly,
twenty-eight, black hair, high street but nothing
overstated. She's intelligent, but not had much
support in her life. Dropped out of school after
A levels. Learned to look after herself.

                    CARLY (CONT'D)
...all night. I only get a couple
of hours, and then I'm falling
asleep in the day.

                    GEMMA
Have you had any recent big
changes? Moving house? New job?

                    CARLY
No.

                    GEMMA
Do you have a partner?

                    CARLY
          (getting impatient)
Aren't there pills?

                    GEMMA
Sleeping pills yes but I wouldn't
prescribe them in your case.

                    CARLY
You wouldn't prescribe sleeping
pills for someone who can't
sleep?

                    GEMMA
Only if we'd tried everything
else or if there was a medical
condition, and that's rare.

                    CARLY
You think I'm lying?

                    GEMMA
No -

                    CARLY
Yes, because you're not giving me
the pills, even though they do
exist and would help my problem.

                    GEMMA
                   (firmly)
          I think we should try some other
          things first.

We hear the voice of a new patient...

                    SUSIE (V.O.)
          We're opening a new restaurant
          tomorrow...

We now CUT TO later. Gemma finishes examining Susie
Parks, forty-six, blonde, glamorous. She's middle
class and eloquent, six months on from treatment for
breast cancer. She's putting her clothes back on her
top half, after an examination - and in comparison
to the other two patients, slightly takes over the
room. She's full of energy, life - almost too many
thoughts...

                    SUSIE (CONT'D)
          I would love it if you could come
          so I can say thank you.

                    GEMMA
                   (smiles)
          Oh, it's fine.

                    SUSIE
          No, no please! Look, I'll send
          through the details.

Gemma hands Susie a prescription.

                    GEMMA
          Okay.

                    SUSIE
          So I don't need to do anything?

                    GEMMA
          Keep taking these, but other than
          that, no.

                    SUSIE
          Good.

They get up and walk to the door. At the door, Susie pauses.

> SUSIE (CONT'D)
> Gemma, thank you, so much.

> GEMMA
> No problem.

Gemma opens the door.

She goes. Gemma closes the door and notices the scarf hanging up. The hair is still there. She looks at it again. Against the black of the scarf. Blonde.

She picks it up. It's long.

We hold on it a moment. Stillness as Gemma wonders where it came from...

> POPPY (V.O.)
> *Doctor Foster went to Gloucester*
> *in the pouring rain!*

CUT TO -

INT. HIGHBROOK SCHOOL. DAY

Close-up on Poppy. She's an eight-year-old with her arm in a plastic sling. She is with her mother and Gemma.

> POPPY (CONT'D)(V.O.)
> *She stepped in a puddle right up*
> *to her middle and never was seen*
> *again!*

> GEMMA
> (smiling, slightly weary)
> Well... I hope not! It's good to
> see you Poppy. You're very brave!

> POPPY
> Thanks!

Gemma smiles as Poppy skips back to her mum.

We realise Gemma is one of a number of parents, waiting to collect their children at the end of homework club.

Tom's one of the first to come out, with a few friends. He walks towards Gemma.

>   TOM
>   I did my science and Harry
>   checked it so I know I got it
>   right.

>   GEMMA
>   Is Harry good?

>   TOM
>   He's a genius. He did his IQ and
>   got a hundred and forty which is
>   loads.

>   BECKY
>   Gemma?

Gemma turns. It's Becky, thirty-four, happy, open, with Isobel, her daughter. She's high energy. Maybe a little _too_ high energy.

>   BECKY (CONT'D)
>   Hi! How are you?

>   GEMMA
>   Sorry, I... don't -

>   BECKY
>   Becky. Simon's assistant?

>   GEMMA
>   (noting Becky's blonde hair)
>   Oh... yes.

>   BECKY
>   You didn't recognise me. It's
>   fine, been a while! Hi Tom!
>   Haven't seen you in ages!

>   TOM
>   Hi.
>
>   GEMMA
>   So your daughter goes to
>   Highbrook?
>
>   BECKY
>   Isobel! Yes, just started. Me and
>   her dad broke up middle of last
>   year -
>
>   GEMMA
>   Oh sorry.
>
>   BECKY
>   Yeah. We just thought Isobel
>   might like a new start. The
>   homework club is a blessing!
>   I can do the whole day, finish
>   off, lock up and be here at five-
>   thirty to pick her up myself!

An awkward pause. Then...

>   GEMMA
>   I'm so sorry I didn't recognise
>   you.
>
>   BECKY
>   (reassuring)
>   Oh no! No one does any more.
>   After the split I wanted a new
>   start too. So I went blonde. Mum
>   wasn't happy, said I looked like
>   Tess Daly, as if that's a bad
>   thing. But I like it. And Mum's
>   mad so - anyway, see you soon!
>
>   GEMMA
>   Bye.

Gemma and Tom get in the car. As they do, Gemma
watches Becky, she hadn't remembered her being so
attractive...

INT. FOSTER HOUSE. HALLWAY. DAY

Gemma comes down the stairs, changed into more
comfortable clothes for the evening.

She catches herself in the mirror. Looks at her
face. Is she attractive? Tired maybe...

> TOM
> (from the kitchen)
> Mum?

Thinking of Becky, she roughs up her hair a little,
then feels stupid, puts it back as it was -

> TOM (CONT'D)
> (from the kitchen)
> Mum!

She snaps out of it, and carries on to the kitchen.

> GEMMA
> Yes?

INT. FOSTER HOUSE. KITCHEN. DAY

Gemma enters and goes straight to the oven to check
the food - a little anxious. Tom's at the table
eating pasta, reading a biology textbook.

> TOM
> You know how many bones there are
> in the human foot?

> GEMMA
> Twenty-six. And thirty-three
> joints. And more than a hundred
> muscles, tendons and ligaments.

Off - the front door opens.

> TOM
> Mum, you're a geek.

                         GEMMA
                        (proud)
          I know.

Gemma smiles at him as Simon comes in with his work
bag, and a carrier bag with some bottles.

                         SIMON
          I was stuck in traffic for twenty
          minutes but bearing in mind I
          started late today, I think I've
          done pretty well. What's more,
          I have wine.

                         GEMMA
          Perfect.

                         SIMON
                (taking his stuff off)
          Can I do anything?

                         GEMMA
          You can pour me a glass. Oh,
          before I forget -

She picks up his scarf from the chair and gives it
to him.

                         SIMON
          Did you cope with the colour?

                         GEMMA
                (glances at him)
          The colour was fine.

                         SIMON
          (turning to get a beer from the fridge)
          Mate, you gonna come and say
          hello tonight?

                         TOM
          No.

                         SIMON
                (pouring Gemma a glass)
          Why not?

                    TOM
Mum said I don't have to.

                    SIMON
You're not a kid any more.

                    TOM
Yeah, but you never let me leave
and you tell these stories.

Simon gives the wine to Gemma.

                    SIMON
Up to you mate.

                    TOM
Right.

                    GEMMA
          (still preparing the food)
So tell me about your weekend.

                    SIMON
          (stirring the food)
Well it's a conference. A load of
men gather in a cheap hotel, talk
about planning legislation.

                    GEMMA
What about the evenings? Did you
go out?

                    SIMON
Occasionally.

                    GEMMA
Every night in the casino?
Roulette, cocktails, beautiful
women...

                    SIMON
It's Hemel Hempstead.

                    TOM
What's so fun about casinos? In
the end you always lose.

                    SIMON
        Ah well, now let me explain.

                    GEMMA
        No I don't think you will.

There's a ring at the front door.

                    SIMON
        Aha!

Simon goes to open the door. Tom immediately gets
down from the table.

                    TOM
        Okay, see you later Mum.

                    GEMMA
        Do you want a juice to take up?

                    TOM
                  (going)
        No, thanks.

He leaves. Gemma stands with her wine, looking
through the doors out into the hall. Tom just gets
up the stairs as Simon opens the front door to
Neil, forty-four, an attractive, well-dressed
accountant, and his wife Anna, forty-three, blonde,
an occasional Pilates teacher. No coats, as they
live across the road from the Fosters and visit
quite often.

                    NEIL
                  (to Simon)
        Good timing. Just got in?

                    ANNA
        We saw you pull up.

                    SIMON
        I had to stop for booze.

                    NEIL
        (holding up two bottles of wine)
        No need!

INT. FOSTER HOUSE. DINING ROOM. NIGHT

The four of them are around a table having dinner.
The conversation's in full flow.

                    NEIL
          It was a resort, but it really
          wasn't bad. You open the door and
          you were right there on the
          beach.

                    ANNA
          Yeah and they have activities for
          children -

                    SIMON
          I'm sure Tom would love it -

                    ANNA
          There's kids everywhere.

                    NEIL
          Screaming...

                    ANNA
                 (to Neil)
          They were just having fun! He
          told them to shut up.

                    NEIL
          I did not -

                    ANNA
          'Pipe down.' Like an old man!

                    NEIL
          It's an expression.

                    ANNA
          You can imagine how popular that
          made us...

                    SIMON
          Gem hates feeling trapped so I'm
          not sure a resort's / really our
          kind of -

                    GEMMA
It's not me! I'd be fine. There's
no point in us staying near the
sea. You don't like water! He's
even nervous in the shower.

                    NEIL
What?

                    GEMMA
He can't swim, is the issue.

                    SIMON
I can.

                    GEMMA
Barely.

                    ANNA
Didn't you learn at school?

                    SIMON
I had asthma so -

                    ANNA
                  (teasing)
Aw -

                    SIMON
Yeah, I grew out of it.

                    GEMMA
I rescued him once.

                    SIMON
Jesus, really? I don't think we
need to...

                    ANNA
I think we do.

                    GEMMA
I must've told you?

                    ANNA
Don't think so!

Gemma smiles at Simon. He smiles, gestures. Go on
then.

                    GEMMA
          We were on holiday in Greece. On
          the beach, and he goes in for
          what I can only assume was meant
          to be a paddle -

Neil smirks.

                    GEMMA (CONT'D)
          ...two minutes later I look over,
          realise he's been swept out, and
          he's drowning. So I leave our
          stuff, run to help -

                    NEIL
          Baywatch.

                    GEMMA
          Baywatch, right - exactly -

                    NEIL
          Slow motion.

                    ANNA
                  (to Neil)
          You can stop thinking about it
          now.

                    GEMMA
          I swim over, get him back to the
          shore, and he's fine. But of
          course he's coughing, wheezing,
          playing it up -

                    SIMON
          It was real, actually. And very
          humiliating. We'd only been
          together a month or two -

                    GEMMA
          Three months.

> SIMON
> Yeah right, but here's the thing,
> I can hardly breathe, I nearly
> died –

> ANNA
> (mocking)
> 'Nearly died'?

> SIMON
> Yeah, but what happened made me
> realise she was the one. This is
> her and I don't ever want to let
> her go. Clever, funny –
> (to Neil)
> Hot in a bikini –

Anna shoots a look at Neil.

> SIMON (CONT'D)
> – but also back then: Bright.
> Red. Hair.

> ANNA
> You didn't!

> GEMMA
> It was a phase.

> SIMON
> That night I proposed.

> ANNA
> Right! So that was –

> SIMON
> Yeah.

> GEMMA
> And for some reason I said yes.

> NEIL
> (to Simon)
> You did well.
> (to Gemma)
> You didn't.

                    GEMMA
          You should learn to swim
          properly.

                    SIMON
          I'm fine.

                    ANNA
          Yeah! I'll teach you! Arm bands!

She laughs.

                    NEIL
          Don't bother, mate. When I hit
          forty I gave up on a whole load
          of stuff. Never gonna. Don't
          wanna.

                    ANNA
          So how are you feeling about your
          birthday party?

                    SIMON
          Good, I think. I'm not being told
          any details so -

                    NEIL
          I'm in charge of the barbecue
          mate, so that's all you really
          need to know.

                    ANNA
          Alert the authorities!

Simon and Anna laugh together. Complicit.

                    NEIL
          Yeah yeah...

Anna laughs more, and touches Simon's arm. Gemma
notices this... a closeness between them.

INT. FOSTER HOUSE. KITCHEN. NIGHT

In the background we see the dinner continuing in
the dining room - everyone a little more drunk now.
Gemma comes into the kitchen, picks up her wine
glass from the table, opens the fridge, takes a
bottle and fills it up. She stands for a moment.
Worried. Rubbing the fingers on her left hand
together. Then shuts the fridge door - revealing
Anna, who's come in from the dining room.

                    GEMMA
                  (shocked)
          Oh! I didn't see you.

                    ANNA
          The canapés are my first priority
          now I'm back, so if it's the
          canapés that were bothering you,
          it, it's all fine.

                    GEMMA
          It's not the canapés.

                    ANNA
          No.

Gemma looks at Anna. It's all she's thinking about
and she can't help but say it...

                    GEMMA
          I found a long blonde hair on
          Simon's scarf.

                    ANNA
          A long blonde hair?

                    GEMMA
          Yeah.

                    ANNA
          And you think he's been with
          someone else?

                    GEMMA
          I don't...

                    ANNA
          A long blonde woman?

                    GEMMA
          Paranoid. I know.

                    ANNA
          Lots of people have blonde hair.

                    GEMMA
          It's just I've never -

                    ANNA
                (dead straight)
          I mean I'm sleeping with Simon,
          it's probably mine.

Gemma stares at her. Is she actually admitting...?

                    ANNA (CONT'D)
          I'm joking! God you are worried.
          Look, I mean, it doesn't even
          have to be a woman. Men can be
          blond.
                    (beat)
          Horses?

Anna smiles. More sympathetic now.

                    GEMMA
          It's just once you have the
          thought...

                    ANNA
          Do you trust him?

                    GEMMA
          Yes. Yes.

                    ANNA
          Then trust him, otherwise you'll
          start checking his phone, his
          pockets. You two are fantastic.
          The hair... is just a hair.

Gemma smiles, and Anna hugs her.

> ANNA (CONT'D)
> (releasing the hug)
> Now I see what you've done with
> your wine glass and I approve.
> You work too hard. Wine is good.
> Come on.

Anna goes back through to the dining room. Gemma
notices Simon's mobile phone on the side. She looks
at it and then at the other three in the dining
room. As Anna sits, she reaches into her bag, takes
out some lip salve and applies it, as she joins the
conversation. Gemma watches her interact with Simon
for a bit. Gemma glances down at the phone again...
then leaves it, goes through to join the others.

INT. FOSTER HOUSE. KITCHEN. NIGHT

From the kitchen, Gemma and Simon say goodbye to
Neil and Anna, then shut the front door. Gemma turns
and wanders back to the kitchen. Simon follows.

> SIMON

Fun.

> GEMMA

Yeah.

She goes to the dishwasher and starts loading it.
Not the reaction Simon was expecting. He puts the
kettle on.

> SIMON
> Have I done something?

> GEMMA

What?

> SIMON
> You're acting like I've done
> something wrong.

Gemma stops and turns back to him.

>   GEMMA
>   Tired.

He goes to her.

>   SIMON
>   Love you.

>   GEMMA
>   (smiles)
>   You go up. I'll make tea.

They kiss and after a second he kisses her hand.

He looks at her, then goes, unsure.

Simon's mobile is on the side. She looks at it, sat there.

She gets some mugs out, and the sugar.

...The mobile is still there.

She puts teabags in the cups. Stands for a moment as the kettle boils. Nothing else to do...

She's tempted by the mobile.

She goes to it, swipes it... and reveals:

A photo of her and Simon, completely in love. It's the background on the phone. She feels self-conscious and idiotic, puts it down.

We stay focused on it, as in the background, she takes the tea out, turns off the light, and closes the door. A beat - is it the end of the scene?

Then the door immediately reopens, the lights back on, she puts the tea back down, and picks up the mobile.

She starts properly looking through it...

INT. THE SURGERY. OFFICE/STAFFROOM. DAY

Gemma makes coffee. Ros has a sandwich.

> ROS
> I've got lip salve.

> GEMMA
> Yeah I know.

> ROS
> And what else? A blonde hair, and
> nothing on his phone. That's it.

> GEMMA
> Of course there's nothing. I
> shouldn't have even looked but -

> ROS
> What?

> GEMMA
> His assistant went blonde
> recently.

> ROS
> So you're saying -

> GEMMA
> Yeah, they're either definitely
> sleeping together or she once
> hung up his scarf.

> ROS
> This isn't like you.

> GEMMA
> Simon's never home until half-
> seven, he says that's when he
> finishes work...

> ROS
> (humouring her)
> Okay...

                    GEMMA
But I met his assistant at the
school gate and she said she
locks up the office at five to
pick up her daughter. So what is
he doing in those two and a half
hours?

                    ROS
Well he's not with her if she's
picking up her daughter.

                    GEMMA
Yeah, I know. Then I thought it
could be Anna.
          (beat)
I know. It's just a feeling.

                    ROS
Are you drinking more coffee than
usual?

                    GEMMA
No.

                    ROS
You're acting like you're
drinking more coffee than you
should.

                    GEMMA
     (smiles, reassuring Ros)
I'm sorry. I'm fine. Crisis over.

                    ROS
Good.

As Ros turns and walks away, Gemma's smile drops.
She's not reassured at all.

INT. THE SURGERY. GEMMA'S CONSULTING ROOM. DAY

Close on Gemma glancing at the clock. It says
4.30 p.m.

She's opposite Gordon who has come back.

> GORDON
> I googled for rashes.

He hands her a small pile of A4 sheets.

> GORDON (CONT'D)
> And as you can see, skin
> irritations can look very
> different but none of them are
> anything like what I've got.

> GEMMA
> I only gave you the cream
> yesterday.

> GORDON
> It doesn't work.

> GEMMA
> You're supposed to allow a week.

> GORDON
> Okay but if it's going to have an
> effect in a week I should see
> some improvement by now and
> there's nothing.

Gemma turns away, frustrated.

> GORDON (CONT'D)
> I've also stopped using the
> washing powder as you advised,
> but there's no evidence so far
> that -

Gemma suddenly sighs very loudly and very
pointedly. Gordon stops. Surprised.

                    GEMMA
          You'll have to leave, I'm afraid
          I'm not feeling very well.

                    GORDON
          But you're a doctor.

                    GEMMA
              (packing up her things)
          Ironic.

                    GORDON
          What is it? What's wrong with you?

                    GEMMA
          I'm running a temperature, and
          I feel quite sick, and... to be
          honest, I've got a suspicion that
          whatever it is... it's probably
          contagious...

Gordon's horrified.

INT. THE SURGERY. WAITING AREA. OFFICE. DAY

We see Gordon hurriedly leaving. Gemma follows him,
now in her coat, bag in hand and a pile of folders.
She comes past the reception desk, and speaks to
Julie.

                    GEMMA
          Got to head off - problem with
          Tom at school. I'll catch up on
          paperwork at home. Can you call
          the last few, reallocate or put
          them off?

                    JULIE
          No problem.

Gemma leaves. As she does, Ros looks up from the
back office having heard the whole thing...

EXT. THE SURGERY CAR PARK. DAY

Gemma comes out, in a hurry, heading for her car,
but she bumps into Carly who's on her way in.

>   CARLY
>   Oh, are you leaving? I wanted to
>   see you. It's urgent.

>   GEMMA
>   Then you need to call first thing.

>   CARLY
>   The not-sleeping is medical. I've
>   got back pain.

>   GEMMA
>   Tried paracetamol?

>   CARLY
>   I have but I need something
>   stronger.

>   GEMMA
>   How about a benzodiazepine? That
>   sound like the right sort of
>   thing?

>   CARLY
>   (acting innocent)
>   I don't know... yeah, what's a...

>   GEMMA
>   It's a muscle relaxant.
>   Essentially a <u>sleeping pill</u>. You
>   didn't mention this back pain
>   yesterday Carly, I think you've
>   been on the internet. Why do you
>   really need the pills?

>   CARLY
>   I can't. Sleep.

Gemma stops and looks at her. Even now she'll give
her time.

> GEMMA
> You can tell me anything at all.
> You know that.

Carly wants to be honest, but doesn't reply.

> GEMMA (CONT'D)
> Book an appointment when you're
> ready to trust me.

Gemma gets in her car, leaving Carly annoyed.

EXT. SIMON'S OFFICE BLOCK. DAY

Gemma is in her car, on the phone, across the
street from the office block. Her voice on the
phone is light, and casual, in contrast to her
clear physical anxiety.

> ANNA (V.O.)
> Hello?

> GEMMA
> Anna. It's me. Hi!

> ANNA (V.O.)
> Hey...

> GEMMA
> I don't know if you're... around
> or what you're doing at the
> moment? But Tom needs picking up
> from school, I'm stuck at work.

> ANNA (V.O.)
> You mean this afternoon?

> GEMMA
> Yeah.

> ANNA (V.O.)
> I'm sure I can. What time exactly?

> GEMMA
> Half-past?

As Gemma talks, Becky and Simon come out of the office, say goodbye and head towards their respective cars in the car park.

> ANNA (V.O.)
> Just outside the front?

> GEMMA
> Yeah.

Gemma stares at Simon as he goes to his car - suddenly emotional - has he really been lying to her?

> ANNA (V.O.)
> No problem. I'll take him back to mine.

> GEMMA
> You're a star.

> ANNA (V.O.)
> I'll see you later.

> GEMMA
> Yeah.

> ANNA (V.O.)
> Bye.

> GEMMA
> Bye then, bye.

As Becky's car drives past Gemma slumps down in the seat a little, to hide.

She sits back up, as Simon's car leaves the car park. She starts her engine, pulls out, and follows him, at a distance.

CUT TO -

EXT. PARMINSTER STREET. DAY

Simon's car drives through the town. A couple of
cars behind, Gemma follows.

EXT. PARMINSTER STREET. DAY

Simon pulls up on the road outside a supermarket.

Gemma slows, then pulls up further up the road, and
watches as Simon gets out of the car, and goes into
the supermarket.

Gemma sits and waits.

She looks at the time. Taps the dashboard. Checks
her phone.

She tries to relax, sits back in the seat -

Suddenly a <u>bang</u> on the car window! She looks round.

It's Jack - the absentee doctor. He's sixty, in an
old jumper and coat. He's been shopping. Gemma
lowers the window, worried Simon might come back
out of the supermarket and look over because of the
noise.

> JACK
> You want me gone.

> GEMMA
> I'm not getting into it now.

> JACK
> Why not?

> GEMMA
> Because we're talking through a
> car window. We're due to have a
> meeting, let's have that meeting.

> JACK
> I saved someone's life last night
> in the pub, this young man was in

                    pain. I examined him, he had
                    appendicitis. He's alive because
                    of me.

                              GEMMA
                    I'm pleased to hear it.

                              JACK
                    I'm still a doctor.

Gemma sees Simon come out of the supermarket, with
a bunch of flowers. She turns.

                              GEMMA
                    Shit.

                              JACK
                         (following her eyeline)
                    What?

Gemma presses a button, the window rises.

Jack watches her as she starts to well up. She
wipes her eyes quickly, starts the engine, and goes
after Simon's car, which has pulled away.

Jack watches her go.

The sound of thunder –

EXT. PARMINSTER ROAD. DAY

It's started to rain. Gemma has the windscreen
wipers on. She's thinking...

FLASHBACK:

INT. FOSTER HOUSE. GEMMA'S BEDROOM. DAY

Gemma picks up the lip salve that has fallen out of
Simon's pocket.

FLASHBACK:

INT. THE SURGERY. GEMMA'S CONSULTING ROOM. DAY

Gemma touches the blonde hair on Simon's scarf. She twists it round her fingers.

BACK TO PRESENT:

INT. GEMMA'S CAR. DAY

Gemma's remembering, panicking.

FLASHBACK:

EXT. HIGHBROOK SCHOOL. DAY

Gemma meets Becky outside school.

FLASHBACK:

INT. FOSTER HOUSE. DINING ROOM. NIGHT

Anna looking at Simon.

FLASHBACK:

INT. FOSTER HOUSE. GEMMA'S BEDROOM. DAY

Simon and Gemma make love.

INT. GEMMA'S CAR. DAY

Simon turns off. Into a private drive. A sign says 'Bridewell – Residential Care Home for the

Elderly'. Realising, Gemma pulls up and doesn't
follow his car down the drive. Ridiculous. She
should have known! She rests her forehead on the
wheel. <u>Idiot</u>!

INT. BRIDEWELL. LOUNGE. DAY

Bridewell is a well-run nursing home, as
comfortable as somewhere like this could be.
Helen, Simon's mother, is sat in a wheelchair.

Helen is suffering after having a stroke. It
paralysed much of her left side. It has no
noticeable effect on her speech, but causes huge
amounts of pain - like a migraine - all the time.
Recently, it's been getting worse. She's very
still, quiet - keen for interaction but we can see
it's a <u>real effort</u>.

Simon sits with his mum. The flowers on the side
nearby. There's no one else in the lounge at the
moment.

Gemma enters, wet from the rain, and stands by the
door.

> GEMMA
>
> Hi, Helen.

Simon turns. Surprised. Gemma goes to Helen, kisses
her.

> HELEN
> (smiles a little)
> I didn't know you were here.

> GEMMA
>
> Just arrived.

> HELEN
>
> Alright?

> GEMMA
> Yeah, absolutely. How are you?

                    SIMON
    Not a good night, was it Mum?

Helen wells up, she can't bear to think about it.

                    GEMMA
    I'll speak to Doctor Barton and
    maybe we can make you more
    comfortable.

                    HELEN
              (takes her hand)
    Thanks.

                    GEMMA
    I'm sorry, Helen, I don't mean to
    be rude. But would you just give
    us a minute? I need to check
    something.

Helen stares at her, smiles a little.

                    SIMON
              (to Helen)
    I must be in trouble.

Simon stands, and moves out, with Gemma into the
corridor –

INT. BRIDEWELL. CORRIDOR. DAY

Gemma and Simon move a little away from Helen's
room.

                    SIMON
    Shouldn't you be picking up Tom?

                    GEMMA
    Anna's doing it.

                    SIMON
    Why? What's the matter?

                    GEMMA
                    (beat)
          The thing is you don't get home
          till half-seven and Becky says
          that she locks up at five, so I
          couldn't work out what you were
          doing for two and half hours each
          day.

                    SIMON
          What I was doing?

                    GEMMA
          So I followed you.

                    SIMON
          I come here, that's what I do.

                    GEMMA
          Every day?

                    SIMON
          Most days at the moment yeah,
          last couple of months, she's
          worse so -

                    GEMMA
          Why didn't you tell me?

                    SIMON
          It's not a secret.

                    GEMMA
          But you never mentioned it.

                    SIMON
          Okay. Sorry.
              (as if it's just sinking in)
          You _followed_ me?
                    (beat)
          What did you think I was doing?

Gemma doesn't reply.

                    SIMON (CONT'D)
          Is everything alright?

                              GEMMA
          I just got worried. I... it
          doesn't matter. We should...

She goes back to Helen's room. Simon looks at her a
moment, then follows.

INT. BRIDEWELL. LOUNGE. DAY

As Simon and Gemma enter they both put the smiles
back on.

                              HELEN
          All sorted out?

                              GEMMA
          Absolutely! I've got to head off.

                              HELEN
          Alright.

                              GEMMA
          Got to pick Tom up.

INT. BRIDEWELL. RECEPTION DESK. DAY

Gemma makes her way from the lounge heading out.
She stops at the reception desk. There's no one
there at the moment, but she knows the drill. She
takes the visitors' book, and writes the time she's
leaving. She then turns to go –

Almost does, but then has a thought. She can't
resist.

She goes back to the look at the book – sees
Simon's name today, then looks over the last week –
around 5.30 p.m. The previous day – he's not there.
The day before, nothing. The day before... nothing.

Pages and pages and she can't find his name.

She keeps looking, until a nurse comes out to sit at the desk and smiles.

> NURSE
> Alright?

> GEMMA
> Does everyone have to sign in and out here?

> NURSE
> Absolutely. Fire regulation. We got pulled up on it last year. You done it?

> GEMMA
> Yeah. Yes. I'm... Thanks.

She turns and walks out of the home, devastated. He's been <u>lying</u> to her.

EXT. BRIDEWELL

The rain is pouring down. Gemma dashes to the car and gets in. Switches on the engine, and gets the windscreen wipers going.

As the windscreen clears, she can see Simon and Helen in the lounge, through the window. Simon is talking to Helen passionately, about something. Helen just listens.

She could go and confront him right now. But she has an idea, makes a decision, puts the car in gear, and drives off, fast.

We CUT TO -

INT. SIMON'S OFFICES. RECEPTION. DAY

An unlocking - then the door opens. Gemma's with
a security guard (Dennis) who's just unlocked the
door for her - which says 'Simon Foster Property
Development Ltd.'

The reception has Becky's desk, a few chairs to
wait, a water cooler and some generic Ikea art on
the walls.

> GEMMA
> Nightmare! He's such an idiot!
> Thanks Dennis. Sorry.

INT. SIMON'S OFFICES. PRIVATE OFFICE. DAY

The door to Simon's reception closes behind Gemma.
It's amazing how rarely she's been in here. A new
computer, with Post-it notes on top. Filing
cabinets in the corner. On the wall, a large set of
designs for Academy Green. Some concept pictures,
a prototype sales document. Pictures and drawings
of ideas, other potential developments - Simon's
dreams.

A photo of the family on the desk. The three of
them.

We jump cut as Gemma searches - opens drawers,
looks on the wall. But she doesn't find anything
unusual.

On the desk is a pad - with doodles - Simon
designing buildings himself -

She sits and wakes up the computer.

She sees an icon entitled 'Simon Schedule'. Clicks
on it. Looks through it. There are sections in red
- at the end of each day between 5 p.m. and 7 p.m.,
but also other times, including tomorrow at 3 p.m.
- labelled 'Simon unavailable'. This worries Gemma
- a lot.

She clicks print, then collects the printed schedule from the printer, folds that up, and puts it away.

Then she goes back out to Becky's office -

INT. SIMON'S OFFICES. RECEPTION. DAY

- and looks around. On the coat hook, by the door, she spots a black laptop bag - she goes over, searches the main compartment, there's nothing inside.

She opens a side pocket - feels something...

She takes out some condoms.

Looks at them.

Proof. No question about this.

Suddenly the door opens. She thrusts them back in the bag, just as Becky appears - surprised. With her, is her daughter, Isobel.

>BECKY
>Oh. Hi.

She sees Gemma with her hand in the bag. She looks over and sees Simon's door unlocked. Gemma's not sure if Becky saw the condoms...

>GEMMA
>Hi, I was looking for Simon's
>schedule. Couldn't find it
>anywhere. Sorry - is this his
>bag?

>BECKY
>...it's mine.

>GEMMA
>Yours?
>(sceptical)
>Sorry.

She puts it back where she found it.

                    BECKY
          I only came back cos I left some
          notes -

                    GEMMA
          Dennis let me in.

                    BECKY
          I pick up Isobel and Simon...
          he's normally gone by five so -

                    GEMMA
               (confidentially)
          To be honest, that's what I was
          counting on.
               (getting into her stride)
          We haven't been away in ages as
          a family and I thought I could
          book a surprise holiday, but I
          need his schedule to know when
          he's free so that's why I'm
          sneaking around. I didn't want
          him to find out.

A moment. Does she believe her...?

Then Becky smiles, relieved.

                    BECKY
          That's really nice.

                    GEMMA
          Well...

                    BECKY
          Well I'll tell you what - I'll go
          through, and email you some weeks
          that might work. Is that okay?

                    GEMMA
          Perfect.

                    BECKY
          Just saves you going through the
          whole thing.

> (beat)
> I assume you'd rather I didn't
> mention it?

                    GEMMA
              (smiling, persuasive)
          Is that okay?

CUT TO -

EXT. PARMINSTER. TOWN CENTRE ROAD. NIGHT

Simon, Gemma and Tom are walking from the car to
the restaurant. Simon's effusive. Gemma's a little
short with him.

                    SIMON
          I'd love to open a restaurant one
          day. We'd serve just two things,
          but do them really well, like
          lamb and carrots.

                    TOM
          Dad, that's a really bad idea.

                    SIMON
          Why?

                    TOM
          What if you didn't like lamb or
          carrots?

                    SIMON
          Then you don't come.
                    (to Gemma)
          What's this place called?

                    GEMMA
          Ciao.

                    SIMON
          And it's owned by a patient?

                    GEMMA
Yes, Susie Parks. She's nice, and
I didn't think I could -

                    SIMON
Susie Parks?

                    GEMMA
Yeah.

                    SIMON
Her husband is Chris Parks?

                    GEMMA
Yes, yes I think so.

                    SIMON
Chris Parks, he's... I've told
you about him, he's given me
advice, helped me out.

                    GEMMA
Right... well this is their new
place. Opening tonight.

                    SIMON
Amazing!

Gemma smiles a little and turns to walk on, but
Simon takes her hand - suddenly intimate, and
sincere.

                    SIMON (CONT'D)
I'm sorry.

                    GEMMA
What for?

                    SIMON
I know I'm working long hours at
the moment, away a lot, but I
really appreciate you supporting
me. And once this project's up
and running, I promise, it'll be
worth it.

Tom's walked on ahead. He turns round and calls to
them.

> TOM
> You coming?!

> GEMMA
> (to Simon)
> Don't worry about it. Come on,
> we're late.

He smiles and they walk on.

Gemma's heard everything he's said, but she's not
placated at all.

CUT TO -

INT. CIAO RESTAURANT. NIGHT

Simon, Gemma and Tom are sat with Ros, at a round
table in the very busy restaurant. It's the
official opening. Decorations. Buzzy atmosphere.
Ros is slightly more dressed up than most and is
sat between Gemma and Tom. Gemma's edgy, her
emotions close to the surface now.

Chris and Susie come over, dressed up. Everyone
stands, smiles.

> SIMON
> We only just made the connection!

> SUSIE
> Me too! Foster and Foster. Really
> should've worked that one out.
> Gemma this is my husband Chris.
> Chris this is the Doctor Foster.

> CHRIS
> Susie's told me everything you've
> done. Thank you so much.

                    GEMMA
              (shakes it off)
Oh. Well... This is Ros Mahendra,
my colleague.

                    ROS
Hello.

                    SUSIE
Yes, I've seen you a few times.

                    GEMMA
And Tom.

                    TOM
Hi.

                    SUSIE
Make sure you stay for pudding,
chocolate cake's to die for!

                    SIMON
              (flirty)
Did you make it yourself Susie?

                    SUSIE
              (laughing)
I might've helped with the
recipe...

                    SIMON
   (to both of them, trying hard)
You've worked wonders with this
place, I don't recognise it.

                    CHRIS
(slightly performing. He's done this
  speech a number of times tonight)
Yes, we want that family feel,
obviously it's not our first one
- we've got five now - but it's
where we live, it's our home, so
it's important it has that
personal touch. We're all mucking
in. I'm out front, Susie's
keeping an eye in the kitchen.

                    SUSIE
        Best as I can!

                    CHRIS
        And this is our youngest Andrew
        who's serving food...

We see Andrew, a young teenager in a Ciao uniform
(black polo shirt, black jeans) delivering a dish
to a table.

                    CHRIS (CONT'D)
        And Kate's about somewhere...

We, and they, through some tables, see Kate on the
far side of the room. She looks about seventeen,
stroppy, also in a uniform, hair tied back,
awkwardly pouring some water out. Meanwhile Gemma
is watching Chris, Susie and Simon, suspicious of
all of them.

                    ROS
        Child labour. I thoroughly
        approve.

                    SUSIE
        Absolutely!

                    GEMMA
        You should all come tomorrow, so
        we can return the favour.

                    SUSIE
        Tomorrow?

                    GEMMA
        Simon's fortieth, tomorrow
        evening at The Artichoke.

                    SUSIE
                (surprised)
        You're forty?

                    SIMON
        Unfortunately...

                    SUSIE
Oh, we'd love to!

                    CHRIS
Absolutely. Why not! We'll be
there.
          (he needs to move on)
Anyway, have a great evening.

                    SUSIE
          (looking at Simon)
So good to see you.

                    SIMON
Thanks Susie. You too. Love this
place.

                    SUSIE
You're a sweetheart.

Susie reaches out and touches Simon's shoulder.
Familiar.

                    SUSIE (CONT'D)
Bye.

They leave to continue mingling. Simon eagerly
watches them go. Gemma notices this - her anger
building.

                    ROS
This used to be a pub. And it was
nasty. What was it? The Honey...

                    SIMON
The Beehive.

                    ROS
The Beehive! That was the only
place that you could get served
if you were underage. Landlord
didn't care. We came here quite
a bit, didn't we, back then?

                    GEMMA
          (standing up)
Excuse me.

EXT. CIAO RESTAURANT. A SIDE ALLEY. NIGHT

Gemma is outside. As the fresh air hits her, she
breathes deeply. She's finding it very difficult to
be at the same table as her husband.

She can see across the town square - The Rose and
Crown pub.

Outside are smokers. One of them looks familiar -
it's Carly who's in a uniform for the pub.
Obviously she works there. Gemma turns away to go
back inside, but -

>   CARLY
>   Hey!

Close on Gemma as she stops. She's got no choice -
she has to turn back. Carly's coming over to her,
smoking a cigarette.

>   CARLY (CONT'D)
>   Are you alright?

>   GEMMA
>   Yeah, fine thanks.

>   CARLY
>   What's all this?

>   GEMMA
>   New restaurant. You work at The
>   Crown?

>   CARLY
>   Yeah.
>   (beat)
>   You look stressed mate.
>   (holds up a packet of cigarettes)
>   Want one?

Gemma looks at the packet. Tempted. Carly sees.

>   GEMMA
>   Haven't for years.

                         CARLY
          Used to though?

                         GEMMA
          My husband helped me stop.

But she's still looking at it.

                         CARLY
                        (knowing)
          Won't kill you.

Gemma lights a cigarette easily and habitually.
Enjoys it - calms down.

Behind them, across the square, we see a lad
(Daniel) outside the pub - shouting, standing on
a chair hugging another man. He shouts 'Have it!'

                    CARLY (CONT'D)
          That's Daniel. My boyfriend. He's
          got a new job. Celebrating.

Carly looks at her for a moment, and can see
Gemma's opinion of him.

                    CARLY (CONT'D)
          And yes he's a twat, but not a
          bad one as they go.

Gemma's enjoying the smoke - full of thoughts.

                    CARLY (CONT'D)
          You alright?

Gemma looks at her - she genuinely seems to care.
Gemma breathes out. What the hell? Why not?

                         GEMMA
          I'm pretty sure my husband is
          sleeping with someone else.

                         CARLY
          Oh.
                        (beat)
          Why? Have you seen him out with
          her?

                         GEMMA
          No -

                         CARLY
          Found emails or whatever?

                         GEMMA
          No.

                         CARLY
          Only cos you better be sure
          before you say something. My mate
          Bromley threw her boyfriend out
          cos he lied about where he was
          one afternoon. Only thing was,
          he was shopping for her birthday
          present. Two weeks later they
          split up. Couldn't trust each
          other after that.
                         (pause)
          You going back in?

                         GEMMA
          Yeah.

                         CARLY
          Then you'll want one of these.

She gives Gemma some gum. Gemma chews it.

                    CARLY (CONT'D)
          And some of this.

She takes out some perfume and sprays. Gemma's
startled for a moment, then smiles. She likes
Carly. She's surprising.

                         GEMMA
          Thanks.

                         CARLY
          No worries.

Carly turns and walks back across the square.
Daniel spots her.

> DANIEL
> Where the fuck have you been?

She gives him the finger, and carries on into the pub. Gemma watches for a moment, then turns and goes back in the restaurant.

EXT. STREET OUTSIDE FOSTER HOUSE. NIGHT

The house that night. A couple of lights on upstairs.

INT. FOSTER HOUSE. TOM'S BEDROOM. NIGHT

Tom's room is reasonably tidy. Posters of footballers on the wall, also posters from films, computer games. Gemma sits on the bed, saying goodnight to Tom.

Simon appears in the doorway.

> SIMON
> Night mate.

> TOM
> Night.

> GEMMA
> Sleep well.

> TOM
> Already asleep.

> GEMMA
> Dream good then. Love you, Tom.

> TOM
> Love you too.

He turns over in bed. Gemma looks at her son - sad.

INT. FOSTER HOUSE. GEMMA'S BEDROOM. NIGHT

It's quiet now. Gemma comes in. Simon's in bed.

She gets in. He kisses her. She tries to engage but something's stopping her... and he notices.

> SIMON
> What?

> GEMMA
> Nothing.

We CUT TO –

Gemma and Simon having sex. Him on top. A similar shot to the opening scene – of her head on the pillow. But this time, we move closer in on her eyes, watching him.

Then close on him, from her POV. His eyes closed. What's he thinking? Who's he thinking of?

Later – he turns over and goes to sleep, switching off his side light, but Gemma's wide awake, leaves her light on – she's angry – she wants to know <u>the truth</u>.

Later – Gemma still not sleeping. She gets up.

CUT TO –

INT. FOSTER HOUSE. LIVING ROOM. NIGHT

Gemma's sat on the sofa with her laptop. The light from the screen on her face. Her fingers typing lightly on the keys.

We see what she's typing into a search engine.

'Cheating Husband'

We see the results. 'The truth about cheating husbands' /'How to tell if your husband is cheating'

In the pictures section at the top, we might notice a small picture of a car with 'HOPE SHE WAS WORTH IT' spraypainted on to it.

But Gemma's attention is drawn to a line which just says – 'Is it my love? Ask again that question.'

She clicks on it, and we find a page titled *The Mourning Bride* – and underneath a quote –

We go back to Gemma as she reads – closer and closer on her –

A V/O as she reads, which continues into the next scenes.

She takes it down, opens the top of the box.

> GEMMA (V.O.)
> *Is it my love? Ask again that question.*

INT. FOSTER HOUSE. KITCHEN. NIGHT

Gemma opens a cupboard. In the cupboard is a large white box. In pen, written on it – 'Don't Touch'.

She takes it down, opens the top of the box.

> GEMMA(CONT'D)(V.O.)
> *Speak again in that soft voice.*

It's Simon's birthday cake – in icing 'HAPPY 40th BIRTHDAY.' She stares at it.

> GEMMA(CONT'D)(V.O.)
> *And look again with wishes in thy eyes. Oh no. Thou can'st not.*

INT. FOSTER HOUSE. BEDROOM. NIGHT

Gemma stands with the door open, watching Simon, on his back, asleep in bed.

> GEMMA (CONT'D)(V.O.)
> *Can'st thou forgive me then? Wilt*
> *thou believe so kindly of my*
> *fault, to call it madness? Oh*
> *give that madness yet a milder*
> *name. And call it passion.*

INT. THE SURGERY. GEMMA'S CONSULTING ROOM. DAY

Gemma, the next day, at her desk. She's looking at pictures on her phone - continuing from the feel of the previous scene - pictures of her, Simon and Tom, in different places, the last ten years in pictures. The voice-over continues.

> GEMMA (CONT'D)(V.O.)
> *Then be still more kind and call*
> *that passion love.*

A knock on the door, and Gemma puts her phone down.

The door opens and Carly comes in, sits down, apprehensively. She looks very tired, strung out.

Gemma glances at the framed picture of her, and Simon on her desk.

> CARLY
> Is everything okay?

> GEMMA
> Yes, it's nothing to worry about.
> I know we called, said it was
> urgent, but it's because I wanted
> to speak to you this morning.

                         CARLY
          Nah, I meant you. Your eyes are
          red.

Gemma looks at her for a moment. Then continues.

                         GEMMA
          Are you still having difficulty
          sleeping?

                         CARLY
                    (sad)
          Yeah.

                         GEMMA
          Well I'm going to give you the
          pills that you've asked for. Only
          a few. See if it helps.

                         CARLY
                    (some life now)
          Oh.

                         GEMMA
          But I need something in return.

Gemma gets out the schedule and puts it on the
table. An entry marked 'Simon unavailable' is
ringed in pen - for 3 p.m. today.

                         GEMMA (CONT'D)
          A favour.

EXT. SIMON'S OFFICE BLOCK. DAY

Carly waits at the wheel of an old Fiat. She's got
the window down and is smoking.

Simon emerges from the office block. Carly looks
down at her phone where there's a photo of Simon.
She checks it - same person. She starts the engine -

EXT. SANDBRIDGE HOUSES. DAY

Simon's car has pulled up outside some new-build, relatively posh houses. Each with their own front door.

Carly parks a little way off. She watches as Simon gets out, opens the boot, grabs a backpack from inside, then runs to one of the houses, opens the door with a key, and goes in.

Carly gets her phone and texts.

INT. THE SURGERY. GEMMA'S CONSULTING ROOM. DAY

Gemma is examining a serious man's elbow. She gets the text, keeps one hand on the elbow, and picks up her phone with the other. Reads it.

'He's gone into a house near Sandbridge, by the river'

The serious man clears his throat, pointedly.

>   GEMMA
>   Sorry...

She puts the phone down, and continues with the examination... but now very concerned...

INT. CARLY'S CAR. SANDBRIDGE HOUSES. DAY

Carly watches the house, as the curtains upstairs are drawn.

She reaches into her bag, grabs her phone, opens up a game, sits back, and waits.

INT. THE SURGERY. MEETING ROOM. DAY

Ros and Nick are sat behind a table, like in an interview. There is a chair for Gemma in the middle, which she heads for, and unpacks her stuff.

                    ROS
          I assume you'll lead?

                         GEMMA
          Sure.

Nick goes out of the room. Ros turns to Gemma, who's looking at the paperwork, and occasionally checking her phone.

                    ROS
          Are you okay?

                         GEMMA
          Yeah.

She smiles and goes back to the papers. Ros is worried.

A moment, then Nick comes in. Jack behind him.

                    NICK
          Jack, come in please. Would you
          take a seat.

Jack sits down - staring at them across the table. Hostile.

                    JACK
          Enjoying this?

                         GEMMA
          Of course not.

                    JACK
          Why do you need three of you?

                    NICK
          We're the partners in the
          practice, it's standard procedure.

                    JACK
Who makes the decisions?

                    ROS
We all do.

                    JACK
But who do I talk to?

                    GEMMA
Jack, you know full well. I'm
senior partner.

                    JACK
I've been a family doctor thirty-
five years. I am respected in
this town.

                    GEMMA
Of course -

                    JACK
And I have seen this place change
from a <u>practice</u> where the doctors
knew the patients, and had time
to look after them, to an
<u>institution</u>, where it's just
about efficiency, management. We
are supposed to work to the maxim
first do no harm. Well let me
tell you, harm has most certainly
been done -

                    GEMMA
Can I interrupt?

                    JACK
No, you wait.

                    GEMMA
I have a question.

                    JACK
I've told you, I'm going to speak -

                    GEMMA
Have you been drinking today?

                    JACK
        What?

                    GEMMA
        Because I can smell it.

A moment. For the first time Jack's a little
uncomfortable.

                    JACK
        Don't see why I shouldn't, I'm
        not at work. The fact is I
        disagree with the way things are
        run -

                    GEMMA
        No -

                    JACK
        What?

                    GEMMA
        You don't disagree with the way
        things are run, you disagree with
        me, you're offended because I'm a
        thirty-seven-year-old woman, not
        from round here, good at my job,
        and when our former senior
        partner retired he chose me
        rather than you to take over.

                    NICK
        Shall we stick to the procedure?

                    GEMMA
            (to Jack)
        You don't like me.

                    JACK
        That's right. But it's not
        because you're a woman, or from
        somewhere else. When you arrived
        I was happy to give you a chance.
        But I've gone off you, Gemma,
        because it's all gone to your
        head - you think you're so
        <u>clever</u>.

A moment.

> GEMMA
> We have to let you go.

> JACK
> No shit.

> GEMMA
> You've had three formal warnings -

> JACK
> I'll tell you what happens to
> arrogant people -

> GEMMA
> - you are suspended immediately
> pending a formal dismissal.

> JACK
> They end up alone.

A beat - Gemma looks at him - shocked - the others
look to her to reply - but she doesn't...

> NICK
> Alright, let's just calm down -

> JACK
> It's alright. I've got the idea.

> NICK
> Jack!

He leaves. Gemma is upset.

> ROS
> Never seen you like that.

Gemma's mobile rings, she looks at it - Carly.

> GEMMA
> Excuse me.

She answers it and leaves the room.

> GEMMA (CONT'D)
> Yes.

INT. THE SURGERY. CORRIDOR. DAY

Gemma comes out into the corridor. We stay on
Gemma, only hearing Carly's voice now.

> CARLY (V.O.)
> He was in there half an hour,
> with the curtains closed and now
> they've both come out. He's
> saying goodbye -

> GEMMA
> Get a picture.

> CARLY (V.O.)
> I'm too far away. They're...
> they're kissing.

Gemma tilts slightly against the wall - runs her
hand down it, looking for something to hold on to -
to steady herself. It's really hitting her now.
She's having this <u>huge</u> moment of betrayal in a GP
surgery corridor.

> CARLY (CONT'D)(V.O.)
> You still there?

> GEMMA
> What does she look like?

> CARLY (V.O.)
> Your height. Blonde. She's getting
> in her car. He's gone to his -

> GEMMA
> How old?

> CARLY (V.O.)
> I can't see.

> GEMMA
> Take a picture.

> CARLY (V.O.)
> <u>I can't.</u>

                         GEMMA
          You <u>can</u>. <u>Take a picture</u>. Take a
          picture of <u>anything</u>.

                         CARLY (V.O.)
          Okay.

And suddenly she's hung up. Gemma's left in the
corridor, absolutely shocked. Puts a hand to her
head - runs it through her hair. A moment. The life
she thought she had is now completely over - blood
rushing - panic -

Nick comes out of the meeting room. Gemma pulls
herself together quickly.

                         NICK
          I'm going to do the minutes now.
          I wasn't sure if we'd finished?

                         GEMMA
                    (hurried)
          Yes, I think so.

                         NICK
          Okay.

Nick walks away. The phone buzzes. A text. She opens
it - a picture. A green car driving away. We can't
see who's driving but the number plate is clear.

The phone rings again. Carly.

Gemma answers.

                         GEMMA
          Yes.

                         CARLY (V.O.)
          It was all I could get. Sorry.
          Looks like you were right.
                    (beat)
          You want to know who it is?

                         GEMMA
          What?

                    CARLY (V.O.)
        I can find out.

CUT TO -

EXT. STREET OUTSIDE FOSTER HOUSE. DAY

Gemma pulls up at her house, in her car. Carly is
across the road in her car. As Tom gets out, Gemma
opens the front door.

                    GEMMA
                  (to Tom)
        You go inside, love. I, I just
        need to speak to my friend...
        Don't forget the cake, it's on
        the table.

Tom goes inside. Carly walks over, another fag, and
with her phone out.

                    GEMMA (CONT'D)
        Well?

                    CARLY
        I've got a mate down the pub,
        he's a desk sergeant so he can do
        the number plate.
                  (reading)
        Susan... Parks.

FLASHBACK:

INT. DOCTOR'S SURGERY. GEMMA'S PRIVATE OFFICE. DAY

Susie smiling at Gemma.

BACK TO PRESENT:

EXT. STREET OUTSIDE FOSTER HOUSE. DAY

Gemma stares. Of course.

> GEMMA
> What?

FLASHBACK:

INT. CIAO RESTAURANT. NIGHT

Susie smiling at Simon.

BACK TO PRESENT:

EXT. STREET OUTSIDE FOSTER HOUSE. DAY

> CARLY
> You know who that is?

FLASHBACK:

INT. CIAO RESTAURANT NIGHT

Susie and Simon touch. Flirty.

BACK TO PRESENT:

EXT. STREET OUTSIDE FOSTER HOUSE. DAY

> CARLY
> What you gonna do?

> GEMMA
> It doesn't make sense...

Gemma reaches into her pocket, and pulls out
a prescription she's written.

>   GEMMA (CONT'D)
>   Here. Seven, for now. See how you
>   go.

Carly takes it.

>   GEMMA (CONT'D)
>   I assume that he wakes you up?

>   CARLY
>   (beat - realising Gemma understands)
>   I come back from work, and every
>   night he is rowdy, up till the
>   early morning. If I can get in
>   and go straight to sleep... it
>   makes it easier.

>   GEMMA
>   You don't have to stay with him.

>   CARLY
>   Yeah, I know.

She turns to go, and Gemma sees something on the
back of her arm, just appearing beneath her short-
sleeved shirt.

>   GEMMA
>   Carly... show me.

Carly rolls up her sleeve to reveal bruise marks
where clearly someone has grabbed her.

>   GEMMA (CONT'D)
>   Did he do this?
>   (beat)
>   Carly?

>   CARLY
>   Last night. Yeah. He won't leave
>   me alone.

Gemma examines the bruise again. Anger rising. She
snatches the prescription back.

> CARLY (CONT'D)
No wait! I need that...

> GEMMA
Where is he?

EXT. CARLY'S HOUSE. DAY

Gemma's car arrives, and parks in a side road made
up of small terraced houses. Carly parks behind
her. Gemma gets out of her car. Tom's in the front,
a birthday cake on his lap.

> TOM
I thought we were going to the
party?

> GEMMA
I need to do something first.

> TOM
We'll be late.

> GEMMA
Can't be helped.

Carly comes across and they walk away from the cars
a little.

> GEMMA (CONT'D)
Number 7?

> CARLY
What are you going to do?

> GEMMA
Have a word.

> CARLY
You don't know him.

> GEMMA
It's your house? You want him to
leave?

Carly doesn't answer for a moment - upset.

> GEMMA (CONT'D)
> Right then.

Gemma runs her hand through her hair - roughing it up. She goes to the boot of her car and opens it. She gets a text on her phone - picks it up. It's from Simon - *'Where are you? x'*. She throws the phone down and grabs her doctor's bag.

> GEMMA (CONT'D)
> What's his full name?

> CARLY
> Daniel Spencer.

Gemma closes the boot of the car.

> GEMMA
> Any problems, drive away, take Tom, call the police. Back in a minute.

> TOM
> Mum! What are you doing?

> GEMMA
> House call.

CUT TO -

INT. CARLY'S HOUSE. LIVING ROOM. DAY

Daniel Spencer, twenty-seven, is sat in the living room with a bottle of beer, playing a video game. The doorbell rings.

It rings again. He pauses the game reluctantly and stands, goes over to the door, and opens it to find Gemma.

The iconic shot of the show. On the doorstep. With her doctor's bag. Her hair roughed up. Piercing eyes.

                        GEMMA
            Daniel Spencer?

                        DANIEL
            Who are you?

                        GEMMA
            I'm your doctor.

                        DANIEL
            No, you're not.

                        GEMMA
            I'm the senior partner so I have
            overall responsibility. Could I
            come in?

                        DANIEL
                    (letting her in)
            Is this normal? Doctors calling
            round randomly?

                        GEMMA
            Not at all.
                    (she comes into the room)
            Perhaps you'd like to sit down?

                        DANIEL
            Why?

                        GEMMA
            I think you should.

        Something in her tone makes him sit, empty beer
        cans around his feet.

                        GEMMA (CONT'D)
            You know what medical records
            are?

                        DANIEL
            What?

                        GEMMA
            We record every conversation that
            you have with your doctor and it

                    stays on file. They can be
                    extremely revealing. How's the
                    new job? Responsibility.

                              DANIEL
                    What you talking about?

                              GEMMA
                    Occasionally these records get
                    leaked and the wrong people get
                    their hands on them - employers
                    for instance. And they're full of
                    the sorts of things that you
                    wouldn't want people knowing -
                    history of drug use, mental
                    instability. I'm having one of
                    these okay?

Gemma picks up some cigarettes from the arm of the
chair. There's a lighter inside..

                              DANIEL
                    Who are you?

                              GEMMA
                    I'm Doctor Gemma Foster, head of
                    Parminster Medical Practice. I'd
                    let me finish.
                         (lights the cigarette)
                    I've seen Carly's arm.

                              DANIEL
                         (defiant)
                    Accident.

                              GEMMA
                    It's a very deep bruise.

Daniel stares at her. Threatening, but unsure.

                              GEMMA (CONT'D)
                    You're going to leave. Get out of
                    her house.

                              DANIEL
                    None of your fucking business.

> GEMMA

You should get help, come and see
me if you like. That's up to you,
but if, once you've left, you go
near her, if she even sees you
again, your employers will receive
a copy of your medical records,
and if they don't contain anything
compromising already, I will
ensure that they are altered -
drug problems, injuries suggesting
a history of violence. I'll go to
the police and I'll mention what I
saw on your girlfriend's arm and
this new career of yours will
stop, very suddenly.

> DANIEL

They won't believe you.

> GEMMA

I'm a doctor with ten years
experience. I'm a senior manager,
a school governor. In this town
Daniel, people take me at my word.

> DANIEL

You fucking bitch...

He steps forward and grabs her arm. She grabs his
arm back, quickly takes the cigarette with the
other hand, turns his hand over, and holds the tip
just over his skin. He screams, scared and
surprised -

> GEMMA

You think it's okay to call women
words like that: IT IS NOT.

A moment where she might burn him. Then she lets
him go. He's terrified.

> GEMMA (CONT'D)

Daniel.

He's breathing, shocked.

> GEMMA (CONT'D)
> She'll send your things.
> (beat)
> Leave. Now.

EXT. STREET OUTSIDE CARLY'S HOUSE. DAY

Daniel walks off quickly down the road.

Gemma watches him. Carly approaches.

> CARLY
> He'll come back.

> GEMMA
> Doubt it. If he does, give me
> a call - I'll set the police
> on him.

Gemma makes her way back to her car where Tom is
waiting patiently.

> CARLY
> (aware of Tom)
> About the other thing? Your thing.

> GEMMA
> What?

> CARLY
> You said you looked everywhere
> and never found anything... Well
> when I saw... what I saw earlier,
> he kept on going to his boot, in
> the car. So maybe, if you want to
> know what's been going on, look
> there.

Carly goes back to her house.

EXT. THE ARTICHOKE GARDEN. DAY

Gemma and Tom walk towards the party, from the
parked car. Gemma's holding the cake, which is in
a white box. The sun is shining - music plays -
there's a big banner up, a barbecue, manned by Neil
- who waves to her. She forces a smile back.

There's also an outside bar, and already quite a
few people milling about. Tom sees a couple of his
friends and runs off.

Gemma quickly removes one of her earrings, just as
Simon hurries over. He's stressed, whispering.

>   SIMON
>   Where've you been?

Gemma trying really hard not to cry.

>   SIMON (CONT'D)
>   What?

>   (beat)
>   What?

>   GEMMA
>   Could you give this to Anna?

She holds out the cake box. He takes it - a little
touched.

>   SIMON
>   Right. Sorry... I just thought
>   you'd be here...

>   GEMMA
>   Have you got the keys to your
>   car? I'm missing an earring.

>   SIMON
>   Why do you need...

>   GEMMA
>   I've searched everywhere else.

>   SIMON
>   You look fine.

>   GEMMA
>   I know it's in there, I need it.

He looks at her for a second. She's resolute.

>   SIMON
>   Okay. Just... come back quickly,
>   yeah?

He gets the keys out of his pocket, gives them to
her and then sees across the garden - Chris Parks
arriving with Susie. Behind them are the two kids -
but we can't see them clearly. Simon smiles
broadly, and quickly makes his way across the
garden to greet them. Gemma watches him with
them...

He shakes hands with Chris, but then gives Susie
a kiss, and a close hug - he says something in her
ear, and she laughs, loudly.

Gemma wants to destroy her.

EXT. THE ARTICHOKE CAR PARK

Gemma walks up to Simon's car, and presses the
button to open it. Then she goes straight to the
boot. She opens it.

Nothing. Just an umbrella, an old map.

She shuts the boot, then opens the other doors -
we cut quickly - her searching and searching -
desperate. But the car is very clean. There's
clearly nothing there.

She's about to give up. Then she has another
thought.

She goes back to the boot. Opens it again, reaches
down and pulls up the floor. Underneath, next to the
spare wheel, is a backpack. She unzips it, and tips
out what's inside. She quickly goes through it.

A T-shirt. A wallet with some cash, a single debit card in Simon's name, and a condom.

Then, underneath the T-shirt she finds a mobile phone.

She picks it up and presses to wake it up.

It works - immediately there's a picture - Simon and... Kate.

Chris and Susie's daughter - but now she doesn't look seventeen at all. She's in her mid-twenties. The picture is of Simon and her outside a beautiful house, in the sun, clearly on holiday.

Gemma looks over at the party, and sees Chris Parks, with his children - Andrew, as before, and... Kate. But now she's wearing her own clothes, she looks her real age (twenty-two). She's with her mum, Susie.

Gemma looks back down - flicks through the pictures... there's lots of them. Simon and Kate as a couple in different places, fields, the beach, at the zoo. The next picture on the phone, with Kate and Simon, is Becky, with blonde hair, in a loose top - clearly on holiday. Gemma looks up - there at the party: Becky, chatting.

The next photo - around a wooden table in what looks like a big house in the warm countryside - there's Simon and Becky and... a couple looking relaxed - it's Neil and Anna, Simon's accountant and his wife, from across the road.

Gemma looks over at the party and sees Neil at the barbecue, with Anna, laughing.

Gemma doesn't know what to do. Suddenly feels very alone. She's about to put the phone away - then she thinks -

Opens text messages. A list of recipients. Amongst them -

From yesterday - Kate.

And... <u>Ros</u>.

She opens Ros's messages – the most recent is:

'*Gemma's left work early. I think she's going to follow you.*' (Before that we might see other messages. All very short and non-descript: '*You have to tell her.*' '*Simon call me.*') There are other non-descript messages beforehand.

Gemma looks up and sees Ros handing a burger carefully to Tom.

She's seen enough. Devastated, she puts the phone, the T-shirt and wallet, back in the backpack, and zips it up.

She's crying now - almost convulsing, but aware she's in public. She doesn't know what to do. Panicking, she puts the backpack back in the boot compartment and shuts it. Then she shuts the boot, locks it and staggers over to her own car.

She opens it and opens her doctor's bag. Inside is a very sharp pair of scissors. She looks at them for a second, then slips them into her pocket.

Gemma puts her earring back on and walks into the garden. It's now packed full of people. Ros, from across the crowd, shouts very loudly -

                    ROS
        Hey! Where have you been?

Everyone turns to look at her. Expectant. Happy. She looks across them all. Neil and Anna, tanned, standing together, Ros, looking expectant, Chris and Susie, with Andrew, and Kate.

                    ANNA
        You alright?

Near the barbecue: Simon. He's staring at her. Wondering what she's doing, why's she being so weird -

Suddenly the cloth that Simon's holding catches
fire.

                    SIMON
          Shit -

He grabs it instinctively - throws it on the floor
but has burnt his hand. He screams and everyone
moves to help him.

CUT TO -

Gemma slowly finishing pouring water over his hand.
He's acting like it really hurts.

                    SIMON (CONT'D)
          I'm an idiot. Sorry.

He turns his left hand over. It's red from the
burn, but not too bad.

                    GEMMA
          I'll have to take this off.

She takes his wedding ring off, and gives it to him.
Then she takes out a dressing and starts to apply
it. Simon finds this extremely painful, and makes a
noise. She cuts the dressing with the scissors.

                    GEMMA (CONT'D)
          There.

                    SIMON
          Maybe I'll leave the food to
          Neil. You alright?

Gemma puts the dressing back in her bag, but keeps
the scissors in her hand, manoeuvring them round so
they could be used to stab someone.

She stares at Simon. Real hatred... she might...

                    NEIL
          Mate, if you've finished in the
          sick bay we need your attention
          over here for two seconds. Come
          on, best smile.

Neil taps him on the shoulder -

Simon stands, moving away from Gemma because appearing from the pub is his birthday cake - now with forty candles on it. Applause from everyone. Gemma watches him approach it - leave her behind. She still holds the scissors but the moment's gone, for now...

Simon blows out the candles. A cheer from everyone. Then calls for 'Speech!'

> SIMON
> Forty! Jesus! I would say thanks
> for coming but there's free
> booze, so I know why you're here.
>> (he points at Neil)
> Especially you!

Everyone laughs a little. Neil holds up his beer and drinks.

> SIMON (CONT'D)
> I'm not really into speeches but
> I have to thank two people. At
> least want to do that. Firstly
> Tom - he's smart, he's well-
> behaved - most of the time - but
> better than that, and he won't
> like me saying this, but he's
> kind. He always wants people to
> be happy and he does his best to
> make that happen. Sorry Tom! I'm
> embarrassing you I know, but I'm
> really so proud to be your dad.

More laughter. Tom's shy. Over the next section we favour Gemma, noting her reactions to what Simon's saying...

> SIMON (CONT'D)
> And the other person... Well...
> As you'll know I've lived most of
> my life here. Apart from five
> years in London, which I hated!
> But even so, I'm glad I went.

Because in London I found Gemma
and since then, I've never looked
back. I'd be nothing without her.
She's a wonderful mother, a
talented doctor, and not a bad
little earner! All my dreams,
what I want, she never laughs,
she just asks how she can help.
And in return she's stuck with a
middle-aged man. So, in sympathy
and admiration, please be
upstanding for a toast. To Gemma!

Everyone raises a glass and looks at Gemma.

                    ALL
        To Gemma!

A round of applause, and more calls for a speech!

We go close on Gemma - what's she going to do?

Gemma turns around and stands in front of the
people who have betrayed her. Simon looks at her
expectantly.

She glances at Kate, who is not smiling, instead -
applying some lip salve...

Then Gemma turns back to Simon. She looks strangely
alone and vulnerable...

Gemma breathes out - swallows - looks like she's in
pain - the crowd look worried, for the first time -
is she okay?

Then she suddenly breaks into a smile, grabs Simon
and passionately kisses him. The crowd cheers
approvingly and applauds!

The party starts again - Simon walks away,
mingling. Gemma watches him merge into the crowd.
We move closer and closer in on her eyes -`

                    GEMMA (V.O)
        Hell! Hell. Yet I'll be calm. Now
        the dawn begins... and the slow

hand of fate is stretched to draw
the veil, and leave thee bare.
Heaven has no rage, like love to
hatred turn'd...

She stares - as everyone parties around her - no
love in her eyes any more - something hard, and
very different...

                GEMMA (CONT'D)(V.O)
Nor hell a fury, like a woman
scorned.

CUT TO BLACK.

EPISODE TWO

EXT. THE ARTICHOKE GARDEN. DAY

The same action as the end of Episode One but now
it looks different. We see all of this through
Gemma's eyes. Whereas the end of Episode One was
more held, still. Now it's unsteady, moving,
swimming - real.

Close on Gemma. The sound of her own breathing.
We move across the faces of these people who have
betrayed her - Ros, Becky, Neil, Anna... and Simon.

They're all looking at her. Expectant. But she's
not responding - is she okay?

Now we move back, seeing her alone amongst them.
Betrayed.

A woman scorned...

CUT TO -

Thirty seconds later. The party's started again.
We see it as Gemma does: loud. Gemma's putting on
a front now - outwardly the same genial host as
before, but we notice her fingers rubbing together
- her hand touching her head -

She starts to walk through the party, looking
around, for Kate - bumping into people. From the
left, Ros bumps into her, holding three full
champagne glasses. She offers one, but Gemma turns
back in the direction she was heading - to find
Susie, Chris, Kate and Andrew, who have in fact
come over to her.

Gemma's staring at Kate, about to tell her what she
knows, but just as she's about to -

> SIMON
> (to Gemma)
> There you are! We ought to cut
> the cake really. I thought you'd
> want to be there.

>   GEMMA
>   (tiny beat)
> Of course.

>   SIMON
> Excuse us.

>   CHRIS
> Yeah, sure!

He leads Gemma away towards the cake. But Gemma
can't hide it much longer - the tears rising. She's
going to lose it - in front of everyone. She stops
walking.

>   GEMMA
> Sorry I'm not feeling well.

>   SIMON
> You've only been here half an
> hour.

>   GEMMA
> Not drunk, I just, feel sick.
> I could be sick. I should go
> home.

From across the party, where the cake is, a group
of people, including Neil and Anna, are looking at
them. We also start to notice music playing now -
from an outdoor sound system, tinny pop ('Face to
Face' by Gary Barlow and Elton John) but slowly
getting louder - some people are even starting to
dance now - the party's tipping into the evening...

>   NEIL
>   (shouting)
> Come on you two!

>   SIMON
>   (shouting back)
> Yeah, yeah!

>   NEIL
> Come on!

                    SIMON
                 (to Gemma)
          You wanna go now?

                    GEMMA
          I'm really suffering.

                    SIMON
          Is it serious?

                    GEMMA
          No, I'm sure it'll be fine, I
          just... I just want to lie down.

                    SIMON
                 (disappointed)
          After everything you've done?

In the background Neil...

                    NEIL
          I'll do it myself!

Anna shushes him. The others around them laugh -

                    GEMMA
          You carry on. There's no point in
          spoiling it all. I'll take Tom
          back. So you can enjoy yourself.

                    SIMON
                 (beat)
          Are you sure?

                    GEMMA
          Absolutely.

She kisses him.

                    SIMON
                 (close and intimate)
          I meant every word by the way.

He smiles, then goes off to Neil and Anna and the
others. Jokes with them. They laugh! The music
louder now -

We're close on Gemma - as she watches him with Neil
and Anna, who've betrayed her. How many more know?
She turns and we –

CUT TO –

EXT. THE ARTICHOKE CAR PARK. DAY

Tom follows Gemma to her car.

> TOM
> What now? You said we could stay.
> I want to go back with Dad. Mum?
> Mum!

Gemma starts the engine.

The car lurches back. Then shoots forward - roars
out of the car park. The left wing mirror smashes
into a post, and tumbles to the ground.

Through the dust, we find Ros, at the edge of the
car park.

Watching. Concerned.

EXT. GEMMA'S CAR. PARMINSTER. DAY

Engine sound - the streets rushing by. Tom looks at
where the wing mirror was.

> TOM
> You broke the mirror.

> GEMMA
> Yeah.

And now we're close on her. Determined and
focused –

TITLE SEQUENCE

INT. FOSTER HOUSE. KITCHEN. NIGHT

Gemma enters with Tom. He automatically takes off
his coat and hangs it up. She puts on the kettle,
turning away -

                    TOM
          - a girl there, Isobel, her mum
          works for Dad, she said her
          parents got divorced last year.
          Her mum cries all the time.

                    GEMMA
          What?

                    TOM
          She was talking to me about her
          mum -

                    GEMMA
          Why are you talking about divorce?

                    TOM
                    (beat)
          I... don't know. We talked about
          loads of stuff.

Tom looks over at his mum, who's now staring at the
front of the fridge - the montage of their life,
that we saw at the beginning of Episode One.
A photo of the three of them smiling, with Helen.
A calendar of dates, stretching into the future.

                    TOM (CONT'D)
          What are you doing?

                    GEMMA
                    (snapping back to the room)
          Making a cup of tea. D'you want
          something?

                    TOM
          Can I have a Coke?

                    GEMMA
          No. Squash?

                              TOM
          Yeah, okay.

                              GEMMA
          I'll bring it up.

                              TOM
          Okay, thanks.

He turns to go.

                              GEMMA
          Tom...

He turns back.

                          GEMMA (CONT'D)
          Love you.

He smiles, a little confused, then goes.

Leaving Gemma on her own. She circles for a moment.
No idea what to do next. Then she calmly goes to
the fridge front and takes down the photo, the
calendar - then all the bits and pieces of their
life, gathers them up, and puts them in the bin.

INT. FOSTER HOUSE. BEDROOM. NIGHT

Gemma enters their room with two suitcases. Simon's
stuff on the bedside table. She goes to the
wardrobe. Gets out a suitcase, and starts to remove
all Simon's clothes and put them in the case.
Folding and scrunching them roughly. Maybe we jump
cut through this - to get a sense of the volume of
clothes - another suitcase. The rest of the
clothes. The stuff from the side table.

The wardrobe ends up practically empty.

The only thing left is a suit - still in the
wrapping from the dry cleaner.

She takes it, about to put it in the case, but has
another thought. She takes the wrapping off. It's
pristine.

Looks at it for a moment, then tears at a sleeve,
trying to rip it off. It's not easy, as she has to
prise the stitching apart - we should see the
difficulty of this, but she perseveres, and
eventually it rips apart. Then takes the trousers
and more easily now, rips them in two.

She grabs the two suitcases, zips them up, puts the
torn suit over her shoulder, lifts them up –

CUT TO –

INT. FOSTER HOUSE. HALLWAY. NIGHT

Gemma has lugged the two suitcases down the stairs,
and leaves them just to the right of the front
door. She throws the torn suit on top. She then
stops for a minute, out of breath. So upset.

INT. FOSTER HOUSE. TOM'S BEDROOM. NIGHT

Tom is playing a game on his tablet in bed, looking
a little worried. Gemma enters and gives him the
squash. He takes it.

                    TOM
          What was that noise?

                    GEMMA
          I'm just throwing a few things
          away.

He looks serious. She strokes his head.

                    TOM
          Isobel said that when the divorce
          was happening she thought she'd
          have to live with her dad in
          Reading. She said it was horrible.

                         GEMMA
     I don't know. Good shopping in
     Reading.

                         TOM
     I mean the <u>divorce</u>. The <u>divorce</u>
     was horrible.

                         GEMMA
     Tom. What's the matter?
          (she kneels by his bed)
     Where has this come from?

                         TOM
     Isobel.

                         GEMMA
     Has Dad said anything?

                         TOM
     Dad? Is that why you're annoyed?
     Have you had an argument?

                         GEMMA
     No.

                         TOM
     Mum, if you do get divorced I
     don't want to move. I like it
     here.

                         GEMMA
     Tom, we're not...

She looks straight at him.

                    GEMMA (CONT'D)
     This is your home. You'll live
     here as long as you like.
               (beat)
     I promise.

                         TOM
     Okay.

Strokes his head again. He smiles. Then there's a
knock at the front door.

>   TOM (CONT'D)
>   Is that Dad?

>   GEMMA
>   It's a bit early.

>   TOM
>   Maybe he's drunk.

>   GEMMA
>   Don't be silly.

She gets up and goes downstairs.

INT. FOSTER HOUSE. HALLWAY. NIGHT

Gemma comes down the stairs slightly cautiously.
Through the front door glass, she can see who it
is. Ros.

She opens the door, and sees Ros is holding her
wing mirror.

>   ROS
>   I've never seen you drive like
>   that before.

>   GEMMA
>   I'm ill.

Gemma takes the wing mirror.

>   ROS
>   Can I come in?

Gemma looks at her, then lets her in. Shuts the
door behind her.

>   ROS (CONT'D)
>   Is Tom upstairs?

Gemma nods, turns and goes into the kitchen. Ros
sees the suitcases, and the torn suit, then follows
her.

INT. FOSTER HOUSE. KITCHEN. NIGHT

Gemma goes straight to a cupboard. Ros enters, still bothered by the suitcases in the hall.

> GEMMA
> I'm having a rum and Coke. You?

> ROS
> I'm fine.

Gemma starts making her a gin and tonic anyway. Ros looks at the suitcases in the hall.

> ROS (CONT'D)
> Is that Simon's stuff?

> GEMMA
> How long have you known?

> ROS
> (beat)
> What?
> (beat)
> Known what?

> GEMMA
> I found his other phone in the boot. Pictures of them together. Your <u>texts</u>. You need to be honest with me NOW before I get really fucked off. How long have you known?

Ros stares at her. Horrified.

> ROS
> Oh God, Gemma.

> GEMMA
> (she puts ice in the glass)
> Yeah.

> ROS
> Did you tell him?

                    GEMMA
I haven't said anything except
I'm ill. Answer my question -

                    ROS
He came in with something, maybe
four weeks ago?

                    GEMMA
Four weeks?

                    ROS
I thought it might be an STI so I
asked him about sexual partners.

                    GEMMA
Today just gets better and better -

                    ROS
Oh no, it's okay, in the end it
was fine, it's just that when I
asked him the question he paused
and so I guessed.
                    (beat)
And since then I have been telling
him every week, texting him - you
deal with this or I will.
                    (getting up)
I'm so sorry! Can I give you a...

                    GEMMA
What?

                    ROS
A hug -

                    GEMMA
No. I don't know who you are.
                    (beat)
Neil, Anna. His assistant. You.
Who else?

                    ROS
If that's who was on the phone
that's probably it.

                    GEMMA
Her parents presumably?

                    ROS
I don't know.

                    GEMMA
Why didn't you tell me? And don't
say it's because you didn't want
to take sides.

                    ROS
Well technically I'm not allowed
to tell you anything - he's my
patient -

                    GEMMA
He's my <u>husband</u>.

                    ROS
            (calmer now)
I thought it would be better if
he told you himself. He promised
me he would.

A moment.

                    GEMMA
How long has it been going on?

                    ROS
I'm not sure -

                    GEMMA
No, you've asked, he's told you.

                    ROS
            (beat)
Three months. I'm sure it's not
serious. I mean it's serious for
you.

                    GEMMA
You warned him. Yesterday. When I
talked about the blonde hair.

                              ROS
              Sorry.

                              GEMMA
              You should be.

Ros stands to go to Gemma.

                              ROS
              Gemma, please...

Gemma turns back, sharp.

                              GEMMA
              No.

Ros sits back down.

                         GEMMA (CONT'D)
              Anyway I've decided. When Simon
              gets back, he'll move out.

                              ROS
              What, forever?

Gemma looks at Ros - she just hasn't thought any of
this through.

                         ROS (CONT'D)
              Cos I mean, it's probably just
              sex isn't it? A midlife crisis?

Ros clearly has no idea what a marriage is.

                         ROS (CONT'D)
              He probably knows he's made a
              mistake, still loves you and -

                              GEMMA
              Whose side are you on?

                              ROS
              I don't want to be on a side.

                              GEMMA
              Wrong answer.

                         ROS
          Yours.

Gemma looks at her.

                         GEMMA
          Go back to the party. He should
          have a good time and really enjoy
          himself.

                         ROS
          I don't think -

                         GEMMA
          Don't tell him that there's
          anything wrong. I want him to
          come in and see those suitcases
          and understand in that second
          exactly what he's lost.

                         ROS
          I'd like to stay here with you.

                         GEMMA
          No.

                         ROS
          I don't think that you should be
          on your own.

                         GEMMA
          I think if you want us to stay as
          friends, you should do exactly as
          you're told.

                         ROS
          Of course.

Ros goes towards Gemma and before she can stop her,
she hugs her. Gemma doesn't really respond. After a
moment, Ros lets go, and leaves.

A moment. Gemma drinks her rum and Coke.

CUT TO -

INT. FOSTER HOUSE. KITCHEN. NIGHT

Close on a computer screen, images and information
from a Google search on 'Kate Parks Parminster'.
Picture of Kate on a night out, a charity party at
university, where she seems young, reckless, and in
this picture, bitchy.

A couple of others where she's clearly younger.

INT. FOSTER HOUSE. KITCHEN. NIGHT

It's two hours later - Gemma has finished on the
computer, left it open, but is now stood in the
kitchen pouring another rum and Coke. Headlights,
and an engine sound from outside. A car door slams.
Gemma gets ready - closes the laptop, grabs her
drink and walks through into the hall.

INT. FOSTER HOUSE. HALLWAY. NIGHT

The suitcases stand by the front door. Simon won't
be able to miss them.

After a moment, a shape appears through the glass
of the door - a key in the lock. A fumble.

He's dropped the key.

He reaches down for it. Scrabbles around. Finds it.
Stands back up. Opens the door.

And stumbles in - he's really drunk. He shuts the
door behind him.

                    SIMON
          Hi -

He then heads straight for the downstairs toilet,
not noticing the suitcases at all.

Gemma stands - waiting - the sound of Simon pissing.

She looks at the suitcases. Waits for him to finish.

A moment. Then he comes out of the downstairs toilet, and turns to Gemma. Smiles.

                    SIMON (CONT'D)
          I loved that. It was amazing.
                    (beat)
          The party. Not the piss.

                    GEMMA
          Simon -

                    SIMON
          You should be in bed. You're ill.

                    GEMMA
          Couldn't sleep.

                    SIMON
          I'm really tired.

He turns and falls over the suitcases.

                    SIMON (CONT'D)
          Sorry, drunk.

He picks them all up and places the suit back on top. Gemma watches as he doesn't register exactly what it all is.

                    SIMON (CONT'D)
          Can you bring some water up
          please?

Simon turns and heads up the stairs to bed. He didn't notice the suitcases at all.

INT. FOSTER HOUSE. GEMMA'S BEDROOM. NIGHT

A dark room. The door opens - it's Gemma, holding a pint of water. The light from the hall means we can see Simon, face down, passed out on the bed, snoring, sprawled across both sides.

The door is still open on the empty wardrobe. He clearly hasn't noticed.

Gemma looks at him, then goes in, puts the water on the side, turns and leaves.

INT. FOSTER HOUSE. TOM'S BEDROOM. NIGHT

Another dark room. The door opens, similarly. Gemma comes in and checks Tom is asleep. We catch a glimpse of her eyes - full of tears.

Gemma looks at him - thinking through what's about to happen to his life...

She leaves.

INT. FOSTER HOUSE - HALLWAY - NIGHT

Gemma comes down the stairs, passing the suitcases in the hall. All ready to go. She glances at them, then keeps going into the kitchen.

INT. FOSTER HOUSE. KITCHEN. NIGHT

She sees, out of the top of the bin is the calendar she took off the front of the fridge -

A moment. She thinks.

She retrieves it, and looks at it - 'Simon B'day Party' is clearly marked, and then marked for the next day 'Football Trip'.

She stares at this. She'd forgotten.

FADE TO -

INT. FOSTER HOUSE. BEDROOM. DAY

Simon slowly wakes to an alarm buzzing. It's 7.30
a.m. and he's really hungover. He lifts his head to
find a mug of coffee on the side table.

He smiles, gets up, winces with a terrible
headache. Drinks the coffee.

Slowly he goes to the wardrobe. The door to his
side is now closed, and he looks at himself in the
in-built mirror. He's a mess.

He reaches out and opens his side - to reveal - all
his clothes magically back in place. He casually
grabs a towel from the shelf, and heads for the
bathroom -

INT. FOSTER HOUSE. KITCHEN. DAY

Simon enters dressed in weekend clothes, having had
a shower.

We notice that behind him the suitcases have <u>gone</u>.

Gemma is in her work clothes, emptying the
dishwasher. Tom is sat having cereal and fruit at
the table.

> GEMMA
> Morning.

> SIMON
> I forgot to turn off the alarm.

> GEMMA
> It's a good job you didn't. You
> need to be up.

                           SIMON
         Why?

Without Tom seeing, she points to the calendar on
the fridge.

Everything's come out of the bin and gone back up,
exactly how it was. On this Saturday on the
calendar it says 'Football Trip'.

                    SIMON (CONT'D)
                 (for Tom's benefit)
            Right! Yes! Tour of the ground,
            meet the players. Are you
            excited?

                           TOM
         Dad, were you drunk last night?

                          SIMON
         Don't know what you're talking
         about mate.
                    (cheeky)
         I didn't touch a drop.
                    (to GEMMA)
         How are you?

                          GEMMA
         Better.

                          SIMON
         What was it?

                          GEMMA
         What?

                          SIMON
         You didn't feel well.

                          GEMMA
         I don't know. There was a pain.
         In my stomach.

                          SIMON
         You should get it checked out.

                    GEMMA
Yeah I will if it carries on.
          (she kisses Tom)
Enjoy it.

                     TOM
Yeah, I will.

                    GEMMA
  (to Simon, without kissing him)
Bye.

                    SIMON
Er...

She stops, turns and kisses him, quickly.

INT FOSTER HOUSE. HALLWAY. DAY

She goes to the front door. He follows.

               SIMON (CONT'D)
Was I alright last night?

                    GEMMA
Were you <u>alright</u>?

                    SIMON
I didn't say anything to upset
you?

                    GEMMA
You didn't have a chance. You
came in, went to the loo then
passed out.

                    SIMON
Sorry.

                    GEMMA
Don't be. It was your birthday.
You're supposed to have a good
time.

                        SIMON
                        (warmly)
            Thanks.

EXT. FOSTER HOUSE. DAY

Gemma comes out of her house. Takes a breath to
gather herself. It's all a huge effort today.

                    NEIL (O.S.)
            Your wing mirror's off.

Across the street is Neil with the garage door
open, polishing his car (a classic MGB V8
Roadster).

As Gemma walks to her car she looks at him. Years
of friendship, betrayed. She tries to ignore him.

                        GEMMA
            Yeah.

                        NEIL
            What happened to you last night?
                    (he smiles, cheeky)
            You hit the champagne a bit hard?

She stares at him. Hates him.

                    NEIL (CONT'D)
            I know what you doctors are like.

                        GEMMA
            I was ill.

                        NEIL
                    (sceptical, annoying)
            But better this morning...?

                        GEMMA
                (she _fucking_ hates this)
            I'm in a hurry.

Gemma gets in the car. Neil watches her go, still
cheeky, then goes back to polishing his car.

INT. THE SURGERY. OFFICE. DAY

Gemma and Ros in the office situated behind
reception. Lots of noise. She's stressed, and
preoccupied. Julie, the receptionist is there.

Nick's working on a computer. The place looks
a mess. Ros speaks quietly to Gemma.

> ROS
> Gem, now you know, you can't just
> let this –

> GEMMA
> They're going to Villa Park to
> see a game, a special tour, Tom
> won it in a school raffle so...

> ROS
> Gem, you <u>need</u> to tell him.

> GEMMA
> (sharp)
> He's been looking forward to it.

Julie comes over to her.

> JULIE
> So update on this morning –
> locum's here, so is Doctor
> Barton, Doctor Mitchel's ill, and
> Jack –

> GEMMA
> Jack doesn't work here any more.

> JULIE
> He left a message saying he was
> going to sue.

> ROS
> What for?

> JULIE
> He sounded drunk.

                    LUKE
                  (entering)
          My computer's packed up.

                    GEMMA
          Already? That has to be a record.

                    ROS
                  (to Luke)
          Morning!

                    GEMMA
                  (to Julie)
          Call the man, check it's not the
          whole system.

                    NICK
             (his computer's frozen)
          It's the whole system.

                    GEMMA
          This place is a joke -

The others notice - look at Gemma, a little
surprised, offended. Ros looks at her
sympathetically.

                    GEMMA (CONT'D)
          Sorry. Let's just start.

Ros goes back and picks up her list. Luke heads
back towards his room. Gemma follows. She gets to
the door into reception. Takes a breath. This is
going to be a long day - big smile.

INT. THE SURGERY. RECEPTION. DAY

Gemma heads out, professionally, into the waiting
area - lots of patients - including Gordon, who's
on the other side of the waiting room.

                    GORDON
          Doctor...

She avoids him, pretending not to hear.

>   GEMMA
>   Anwar Shamsi!

Anwar stands up. He's forty, affable, good suit.

>   ANWAR
>   Yeah.

>   GEMMA
>   Hi.

>   GORDON
>   Doctor, it's urgent.

>   GEMMA
>   Gordon, we have to stick to
>   appointments, you know that. Mr
>   Shamsi, if you'd like to come
>   with...

Gemma looks up as the toilet door opens. Suddenly in front of her is...

Kate.

They stare at each other for a second.

Gemma can't believe it. Kate's surprised too.

>   KATE
>   Hi.

She smiles a little and hurries past.

Gemma watches, as Kate goes back to her seat in the waiting area. She's dressed for the gym - wearing her kit, headphones, her hair tied back, she drinks from a bottle of water. She's in really good shape.

>   ANWAR
>   Sorry, should I...

>   GEMMA
>   Could you give me a second?

Gemma turns and makes her way back to the reception desk. She can't just ignore Kate. She's almost panicking. Should she - Ros appears from the office area with her list - she just has enough time to see Kate, before Gemma ushers Ros out through a door -

INT. THE SURGERY. CORRIDOR. DAY

Gemma and Ros get through the door, and face each other.

> GEMMA
> What is she doing here? Is she here to confront me?

> ROS
> No, I've just seen, she's on my list. It's a normal appointment. She booked it a couple of days ago.

Gemma runs her hand through her hair.

> ROS (CONT'D)
> Come here.

> GEMMA
> This is <u>hard</u>. I'm good at keeping my head together but today...

> ROS
> Talk to Simon.

> GEMMA
> I will, but before I do I need the facts. What is this relationship? Three months, is that a fling -

> ROS
> Yes. He's never suggested it's anything -

                    GEMMA
          What about her? What does he see
          in her? Apart from -

Gemma's had an idea. She turns and goes back
through the door.

                    ROS
          Gemma, wait - stop. What are you -

INT. THE SURGERY. RECEPTION. DAY

Gemma strides into reception, pretending to look at
a patient list -

                    GEMMA
          Kate Parks. If you can come with
          me?

Kate stands up, unsure, as Ros appears from the
corridor.

                    ANWAR
          Sorry, I thought -

                    KATE
          I'm here to see Doctor Mahendra?

                    GEMMA
          Doctor Mahendra has too many
          appointments today. Mr Shamsi if
          you can wait five minutes. Kate,
          you don't mind swapping, do you?
          It speeds things up for everyone
          else.

Kate looks at them both. Unsure. All the other
patients waiting, including Anwar, and Gordon, look
at her -

CUT TO -

INT. THE SURGERY. GEMMA'S CONSULTING ROOM. DAY

Kate and Gemma sit opposite each other.

Gemma just looks at this girl - flicking her hair, legs crossed, drinking water. Bitchy, privileged, overconfident.

From Kate's point of view - she won't be intimidated.

> GEMMA
> So Kate, how can I help?

> KATE
> I've been feeling tired recently, like a cold and it's not going away.

> GEMMA
> How long?

> KATE
> Couple of weeks?

> GEMMA
> Alright, so if you take off your top and trousers we'll have a look.

> KATE
> Top and trousers? Why do I need -

> GEMMA
> To examine you.

Kate's suspicious but gets up and goes behind the curtain.

Gemma puts on sterile gloves. Kate draws back the curtain and stands confident, in her underwear.

> GEMMA (CONT'D)
> You're in good shape.

> KATE
> I'm heading to the gym. I go every morning. I've got a trainer.

                    GEMMA
          Sounds wonderful.

                    KATE
          You should try it.

Zing. Gemma smiles, and puts a paper over the couch.

                    GEMMA
          Maybe I will. You just lie on
          here for me please.

Kate lies down. Gemma takes Kate's pulse.

                    GEMMA (CONT'D)
          So you work at your dad's
          restaurant?

                    KATE
          Sometimes. Just for a bit of
          money but I'd rather - OW!

Gemma puts her hand on Kate's abdomen, examining
her - pushing hard. It's uncomfortable.

                    GEMMA
          Does that hurt?

                    KATE
                    (defiant)
          No.

                    GEMMA
          Alright. How about this?

She pushes hard.

                    KATE
          Ow! Yep.

                    GEMMA
          It's a little tender. It's
          probably nothing, but to be sure,
          I'm just going to get some blood
          samples.

Gemma turns and grabs two syringes.

                    KATE
          Doesn't the nurse do that?

                    GEMMA
          I don't mind.

Gemma efficiently ties the tie round Kate's arm, as
tight as possible.

                    GEMMA (CONT'D)
          I need to ask you a few standard
          questions.

                    KATE
          Okay.

                    GEMMA
          How much do you drink on average?

                    KATE
          Couple of glasses of wine?

                    GEMMA
          A night?

                    KATE
          A week.

                    GEMMA
          And do you smoke?

She puts the needle in, painfully, and takes three
blood samples over the following.

                    KATE
          No.

                    GEMMA
          Sexual partners?

                    KATE
          Sorry?

                    GEMMA
          I'm just trying to rule a few
          things out. Do you have any
          sexual partners?

                    KATE
          One. I don't tend to sleep
          around.

                         GEMMA
                         (beat)
               Are you having sex regularly?

                    KATE
          Not enough. He's married.

                         GEMMA
               Right.

                    KATE
          But unhappy. It's sad. Actually.

Gemma takes a breath. Stays focused.

                         GEMMA
               Why doesn't he just leave his
               wife?

                    KATE
          Family, I suppose.

                         GEMMA
               But the wife doesn't suspect?

                    KATE
          Not a clue.

                         GEMMA
               Sounds complicated.

This just sinks Gemma. She takes out the needle in
Kate's arm, and puts a cotton wool ball on it.

                    GEMMA (CONT'D)
               You can put your clothes on now.
               You seem fine. I hope you don't
               mind all the questions but it
               helps to get a picture and you
               seem very healthy.

CUT TO -

A moment later, Kate is dressed. Gemma gives her
a pot.

                    GEMMA
          Just in case, could you pop next
          door, pee in that and bring it
          back.

                    KATE
          Yeah. No problem.

Kate takes the pot and goes.

Gemma stops now. What's she doing? This girl is
just a girl.

But she finds herself looking at Kate's handbag
which she's left by the chair. It's right there.

Has she got time? She's not sure. But this might be
the only opportunity.

She could just... she reaches for it - but just as
she does, the door opens - Kate comes back in.

                    KATE (CONT'D)
          Excuse me.

She picks up her bag and leaves again.

Gemma stands. Looks at herself in the mirror. Feels
old. Out of shape.

Gemma looks at the framed photo on her desk.
A picture of her family. The three on them at
a picnic. Is he really as unhappy as all that?

K-KLUNK! - the door opens - as Kate comes back in.
Kate gives the pot of urine to Gemma.

                    GEMMA
          This'll just take a minute.

Gemma efficiently puts a pipette in the sample and
puts a few drops in one test, and then another drop
in the plastic well of a separate rectangular test.
Then she sits and waits.

                    GEMMA (CONT'D)
We'll do the bloods, see what
comes back. It's probably just
a cold. In the meantime, take it
easy and avoid doing anything
strenuous or stressful.

                    KATE
What are the bloods for?

                    GEMMA
Measures all sorts - iron, sugar -

                    KATE
And that one?

                    GEMMA
Oh this is just a -

Gemma glances down at the result. And just stops.
She can't believe what she's looking at.

Close up - the test producing two pink lines.

                    KATE
What? What is it?

                    GEMMA
Kate, are you having unprotected
sex?

                    KATE
I... no.

                    GEMMA
Have you been trying for a child?

                    KATE
What are you talking about?

Gemma looks straight at her.

                    GEMMA
Two lines means it's positive.

They stare at each other for a second. Both
completely shocked.

                         KATE
              Sorry. Are you saying I'm...?

She looks at Gemma, unbelieving.

                         GEMMA
              Yes. You're pregnant.

Kate stares at her. Thoughts racing through her
head.

                    GEMMA (CONT'D)
              I assume the father is... this
              man.

An awkward moment. Them both taking it in -

                    GEMMA (CONT'D)
              It's a lot to take in, I know.
              You'll want to consider the
              stability of this relationship -

                         KATE
              Can I see Doctor Mahendra? She is
              my doctor and this is a... shock.
              So can I see her instead - please?

INT. THE SURGERY. CORRIDOR. DAY

Kate is now sat in Ros's consulting room with the
door open. Ros stands in the corridor outside with
Gemma.

                         ROS
              I'll let you know.

Then she turns, goes into her room and shuts the
door.

Gemma stands, reeling from the shock of all of
this...

Then she turns and walks to the waiting room.

INT. THE SURGERY. RECEPTION. DAY

Gemma walks into the reception area, looking at her
list, distracted –

>   GEMMA
>   Okay –

>   GORDON
>   Excuse me –

>   GEMMA
>   Gordon. Just wait. You're next.
>   (she calls out)
>   Anwar Shamsi.

Nothing.

>   GEMMA (CONT'D)
>   Anwar?

Julie leans out from the reception desk.

>   JULIE
>   He just left.

>   GEMMA
>   (frustrated)
>   Really?

EXT. THE SURGERY CAR PARK. DAY

Gemma comes out looking for Anwar. She sees him
walking towards the car park.

>   GEMMA
>   Mr Shamsi –

>   ANWAR
>   I'm a solicitor with a client
>   that needs me urgently. The
>   receptionist said if I had the
>   first appointment of the day I'd
>   be straight in.

> GEMMA
> I'm so sorry, I hope she
> explained there's no guarantees -
> I'm having quite a morning -

> ANWAR
> Why have you come out here?
> That's not normal.

> GEMMA
> Because men your age don't tend
> to see doctors when you should.
> And you look extremely worried,
> so I'm not going to let you leave
> until you tell me the problem.

> ANWAR
> (beat)
> I'm often sick first thing in the
> mornings.

> GEMMA
> Mmm-hmm. Often?

> ANWAR
> Every few days. We're going to do
> this here?

She reaches in her pocket.

> GEMMA
> Yeah, I am. You drink a lot?

Gemma pulls out an ophthalmoscope. Then opens up
his eyelids, to check them.

> ANWAR
> Not usually.

> GEMMA
> Look forward...

> ANWAR
> Recently I can't sleep, I worry
> about things, so yeah, I have a
> drink.

                    GEMMA
Your eyes are a little bloodshot.
I take it you've googled your
symptoms?

                    ANWAR
Yeah.

                    GEMMA
And?

                    ANWAR
It says being sick like that
first thing in the mornings could
be a warning of a brain tumour.

                    GEMMA
               (sceptical)
Yeah. That's possible but there
are many more likely
explanations. Tummy bug, virus or
your late-night drinking.

                    ANWAR
               (worried, unsure)
So... it doesn't suggest anything
to do with the brain?

                    GEMMA
               (slowing down - careful)
Not unless there's more to say.

A moment. He turns away. Emotional. A strange
moment.

                    GEMMA (CONT'D)
Are you sure you don't want to
come in for a moment?

He checks his watch.

                    ANWAR
No, if you think it's nothing
then I should go. Thank you.

He gets in his car and closes the door. As he
starts the engine, and drives away, Gemma watches
him. Knows there's something else he's not telling
her...

But it's too late. And she's got other things to
worry about.

She walks back inside.

INT. THE SURGERY. RECEPTION. DAY

As she comes back in, Kate is coming towards her
leaving, teary. She doesn't look at Gemma, just
heads to the door. Ros appears, and goes with Gemma
into the corridor.

INT. THE SURGERY. ROS' OFFICE. DAY

Ros and Gemma enter.

>   ROS
>   She's not going to keep it, and
>   she doesn't want anybody to know.

>   GEMMA
>   Not Simon?

>   ROS
>   No. She's going to find
>   somewhere. They'll do it as soon
>   as possible.

>   GEMMA
>   (cautious)
>   Isn't she worried that I might
>   tell him?

>   ROS
>   Well why would you? I mean as far
>   as she's concerned you're
>   oblivious.

A moment. Gemma's unsure - so many thoughts in her
head.

>   GEMMA
>   But... Simon. He should know
>   she's pregnant.

>   ROS
>   (amazed that she's thinking of Simon)
>   What? Gemma -

>   GEMMA
>   He'd want to know.

>   ROS
>   Do you want to make things work
>   with him?

>   GEMMA
>   ...

>   ROS
>   Because if she ends up with his
>   baby, then forget it. Her and
>   this child, are going to be in
>   your life forever. You don't have
>   to tell him, it's better for him
>   if you don't - besides -
>   according to the General Medical
>   Council and every professional
>   standard, you're not allowed to.
>   So be quiet for the next twenty-
>   four hours and let it happen,
>   then talk to your husband and
>   sort out your marriage. This girl
>   is a fling. You're not.
>   (beat)
>   Don't tell him.

CUT TO -

INT. FOSTER HOUSE. DINING ROOM. NIGHT

The three of them sit round the table, eating
dinner. This is an Edward Hopper, *American Beauty*,
Conrad Hall shot – but in a British style.

Single overhead light. Piles of paper around as
normal.

They're eating a pasta dish – easy to cook. Gemma's
looking at Simon, unsure if she's doing the right
thing. Tom's laughing. A lot.

> SIMON
> We had to take penalties, and
> when I took mine I fell over.

> TOM
> He was really serious. He, he did
> this long run up and then he just –

He does an impression of his dad falling over.
Laughs a lot. Gemma smiles, despite herself.

> SIMON
> Yeah, alright. Thanks, mate.

> GEMMA
> How did you do?

> TOM
> Scored.

> GEMMA
> No! Did you?

> TOM
> Yeah, and he was a professional
> keeper.

> SIMON
> Tom was really good actually.
> They said he was the best.

> GEMMA
> Well done. So pleased you had a
> good time!

                    SIMON
          How was work?

                    GEMMA
          A mess.

                    SIMON
          Why?

                    GEMMA
          Just... appointments. You know.

                    SIMON
          You alright though? Feeling
          better?

                    GEMMA
          Yeah.

                    SIMON
               (looks at her, loving)
          Good.

They look at each other. He smiles, kindly.

                    TOM
          You should come next time, Mum.
          Watch him have another turn.
          You'd find it really funny.

Tom laughs again. Simon shares a look with Gemma —
loving their son.

                    SIMON (O.S.)
          Yeah alright! Next weekend we'll
          find a goal, we'll do penalties
          and settle this.

                    TOM
          Er, can you deal with the
          humiliation?

CUT TO —

INT. FOSTER HOUSE. BEDROOM. NIGHT

Simon is asleep on his side - facing away from her.
Both lights are off - the room just lit by the
street light/moonlight coming in through the
curtains.

Gemma is sat in bed again. Not sleeping. The alarm
clock glows 12.12 a.m. She picks up her phone. The
light of the screen on her face. She composes a
text. To Carly. *'You around? Gemma.'* Sends it.

She looks at Simon. Definitely asleep.

Thinks of everything he's done to her.

She gets up and leaves.

CUT TO -

EXT. PARMINSTER. NIGHT

Gemma walks along the road, we see she's now
slightly better dressed than before. A quick
attempt at something you might wear to go out.

Across the square the pub is still open - from the
lights on inside, but in the other direction, Gemma
looks at the bar she's headed towards. A light on
in the doorway. Gemma heads towards it. Never been
in here before...

INT. TOWN SQUARE BAR. NIGHT

The bar's clean, brightly lit, the sort one would
find in a hotel. It might surprise us from the Gemma
we've seen up till now (mother, GP), but she's
actually very at home in a bar - she spent her early
twenties in places like this - and loved it.

She's sat with Carly at a table, both of them with
drinks. They've been there a little while, and are
both a bit tipsy.

                    CARLY
    It's been proven, statistically,
    men all fancy twenty-two-year-old
    women. Doesn't matter how old
    they are themselves, or what
    they say, that's just who they're
    after, sexually. They might
    happen to like their partner as
    well, but biologically twenty-two
    and fertile is what it's all
    about. He's just had a hot
    summer and messed it up. He'll
    come back. I mean you love him,
    don't you?

Gemma shrugs.

                CARLY (CONT'D)
    When it's done, and she's got rid
    of the baby, give him hell, and
    then let him back.

                    GEMMA
    I shouldn't tell him?

                    CARLY
    Tell him? You're sort of innocent
    sometimes, aren't you? I mean
    you're not. Clearly. But you
    think the world's better than it
    is.

Carly produces a packet of cigarettes, offers Gemma
one.

                    GEMMA
    Yes.

Gemma and Carly stand, and walk towards the door.
They pass Anwar at the bar.

                GEMMA (CONT'D)
                (to Carly)
    I'll join you.

                        CARLY
      Okay.

Carly continues. Gemma goes over to Anwar who has
an empty glass.

                        GEMMA
      Hi.

                        ANWAR
            (surprised, confused)
      Hi...

                        GEMMA
      What are you drinking?

                        ANWAR
      (beat. He smiles. Accepts the situation)
      Becks.

Gemma leans over to the barman.

                        GEMMA
      Becks and a rum and Coke.

He makes them.

                        GEMMA (CONT'D)
      I thought when you said you had a
      drink in the middle of the night
      you meant in your kitchen.

                        ANWAR
      Why are you here?

                        GEMMA
      It's Saturday night Anwar and as
      you can see I'm a party girl.
         (beat - alright - the truth)
      I couldn't sleep either.

                        ANWAR
      Why not?

                        GEMMA
      Got a lot going on.

The barman delivers the drinks. Gemma gives him
a tenner.

                    ANWAR
          Like what?

                    GEMMA
          At home. Doesn't matter. Tell me
          about you.
                    (beat)
          You were holding something back
          this morning. Weren't you?
          Something you weren't saying.

Anwar drinks his beer, then turns to her.

                    ANWAR
          I'm married.

                    GEMMA
          Okay.

                    ANWAR
          Alesha's six months pregnant.

                    GEMMA
          Congratulations.

                    ANWAR
          Five years ago, I had this
          dizziness, they eventually did a
          scan and found a tumour, in my
          brain. Couldn't operate - said it
          wasn't doing any harm at that
          point but it was growing, and
          that one day it would kill me.

                    GEMMA
          I'm sorry.

                    ANWAR
          I should've told Alesha at the
          time. I just didn't want to scare
          her away.

                    GEMMA
She doesn't know?

                    ANWAR
If I tell her now she'll ask why
did you make all these promises?
Start a family, all this time...

                    GEMMA
Go for another scan.

                    ANWAR
I came in because it'd be good to
know if the symptoms fit. Is this
it?

                    GEMMA
You didn't tell me your history.

                    ANWAR
What do you think now?

                    GEMMA
I can't be sure.

                    ANWAR
Well, can you guess?

                    GEMMA
                  (beat)
The symptoms fit. Talk to your
wife.

                    ANWAR
Right.

                    GEMMA
There's two things. There's the
mistake and then there's the lie,
to cover it up. And the mistake
is a lot easier to forgive.

                    ANWAR
You reckon?

                    GEMMA
I know.

                    ANWAR
     If I tell her that'll be it.

                    GEMMA
     She'll find out eventually.
     She'll see it in your notes.

                    ANWAR
     Medical records are confidential.

                    GEMMA
     Not the medical records. The post
     mortem.

Anwar's shocked. And offended. Gemma's getting
carried away.

                    GEMMA (CONT'D)
     Sorry but you married her, you've
     made a promise.

Anwar drinks, annoyed with the pressure she's
putting him under.

                    ANWAR
     Trouble at home... something's
     happened with your husband.
     That's what normally sends women
     your age to a bar in the middle
     of the night. Yeah?

                    GEMMA
     Yeah.

                    ANWAR
     See I do a lot of divorce and you
     should know that a woman might
     get the house, the assets, the
     children, but that doesn't mean
     that she's won. Because a few
     years later, he's with someone
     new, making lots of money, no
     real responsibility. But she is
     struggling. Kids, work, no time
     to move on. We've all got
     problems that we can't solve.

                    GEMMA
          Tell your wife the truth.

                    ANWAR
              (he drains the bottle)
          I can't.

He goes to the toilet. Gemma drinks her drink.

Then notices he's left his jacket on the bar, and
has an idea...

CUT TO -

Anwar comes out of the toilet and walks back.
Gemma's gone - but on the bar is her empty glass,
and next to it, his phone - she must have got it
from his jacket.

What's more, it's ringing - he looks at it.
A picture of a woman - the name - Alesha. He's
surprised. It's 2.30 a.m. She never rings at this
time...

EXT. PARMINSTER TOWN SQUARE. NIGHT

Gemma walks out of the club with Carly. They're
both quite drunk.

                    CARLY
          I'm this way.

                    GEMMA
          How much?

                    CARLY
          Doesn't matter.

                    GEMMA
          No, go on.

                    CARLY
          Seven for the cigarettes, two
          fifty for the lighter.

Gemma gives her a £10 note.

>   CARLY (CONT'D)
>   Thank you. You'll be alright
>   getting back?

>   GEMMA
>   Who says I'm going back?

Carly looks at her. A kebab van is standing in the
centre of the square, surrounded by a few very
drunk people.

>   CARLY
>   Be careful yeah?

Gemma turns and, quite drunk, heads towards the
kebab van.

>   GEMMA
>   Night.

CUT TO -

EXT. THE RED LION. NIGHT

A bench, just outside the pub, by the cab rank. On
it is slumped Jack, unconscious. In his hand is a
half-empty plastic glass. He's been there a while.

Someone's walking towards him. Silhouetted by the
light from the lamp post.

She gets closer. Kneels down - and suddenly the
light catches her face. It's Gemma, holding a
kebab, unsteady.

>   GEMMA
>   Want a drink?

CUT TO -

EXT. JACK'S FLAT. NIGHT

We see Jack's flat – the top floor of a town home.
The only light on.

>   GEMMA (V.O.)
>   What's going on in there?

>   JACK (V.O.)
>   Shower's broken.

INT. JACK'S FLAT. NIGHT

Jack is sat in his chair by the window. A side lamp
on. He's beginning to sober up a little, picking at
half of Gemma's kebab, now on a plate. His flat is
a mess – very dirty.

Gemma comes through from the kitchen with two cups
of coffee. She gives him one.

>   GEMMA
>   No milk.

>   JACK
>   Fridge doesn't work.

>   GEMMA
>   Your flat's a shithole Jack.

>   JACK
>   You're very welcome to go home.

>   GEMMA
>   (beat)
>   When we first moved here, you and
>   David had us over for dinner and
>   looked after us. You remember?

>   JACK
>   Yeah. David's missed. As you can
>   see.

Pause.

                    GEMMA
    How long were you together?

                    JACK
    Oh, thirty years.

                    GEMMA
    Did you ever cheat?

                    JACK
    No.

                    GEMMA
    Did he?

                    JACK
         (he looks at her)
    There's something in your head.

                    GEMMA
    Can you keep a secret?

She drinks her coffee.

                    JACK
    Don't be ridiculous Gemma, I'm an
    alcoholic. Of course I can keep a
    secret.

                    GEMMA
    Simon's been sleeping with
    another woman.

                    JACK
    Oh, I'm sorry. Are you two –

                    GEMMA
    I haven't told him that I know.

                    JACK
    Why not?

                    GEMMA
    Because I'm not that woman – that
    gets cheated on and finds out and
    has screaming rows. I'm not
    maintenance and divorce and all

that stuff. I'm better than that.
I'm clever.

JACK
Yeah, and I'm not a pissed
widower who hasn't showered in
three weeks. I'm clever too.
Doesn't mean a thing.

Gemma's overwhelmed. Gets up - turns away. She's in
the shadows of the flat. We just see her back.

GEMMA
(without turning round)
She came into the surgery today,
this other woman, and I did some
tests, turns out she's pregnant.
She's decided to have an abortion
and not tell anyone.

JACK
She went to see you?

GEMMA
I told her I was the only doctor
available.

JACK
Be careful.

GEMMA
Yeah.

A moment. Jack looks at her. Sighs.

JACK
I'm not entirely surprised. In
his twenties Simon used to sleep
around. Always in The Crown.
Different girl every other week.

GEMMA
Simon?

JACK
Then when he came back from
London with you, we all thought
he'd grown up.

> GEMMA
> No one's ever told me that
> before.

> JACK
> Well they wouldn't. His dad
> cheated on his mum, didn't he?
> Left her.

> GEMMA
> Yeah.

> JACK
> (looking at one of his empty
> bottles)
> My dad loved Scotch. Sons are
> their fathers.

> GEMMA
> (beat, thinking of Tom)
> I hope not.

Gemma starts walking around, looking at things,
picking them up, starting to tidy.

> GEMMA (CONT'D)
> Three weeks, you couldn't use the
> sink?

> JACK
> Look, while it's been lovely to
> be dragged home by someone who's
> actually more depressed than
> myself, maybe we should call it
> a night.

He stands, winces.

> JACK (CONT'D)
> OW!

> GEMMA
> What's wrong?

> JACK
> Gout. Diagnosed by me. You don't
> need to see it. I'm going to bed.

                    GEMMA
        You can't live like this.

He looks at her, then walks to his bedroom.

                    JACK
        You should tell him you know.
        Tell him she's pregnant.

                    GEMMA
        I'm not ethically allowed to.

                    JACK
        Tell him all of it, then take
        your son, and leave. Start again.

                    GEMMA
        It's just a fling, it doesn't -

                    JACK
        It doesn't mean he won't do it
        again.
                    (beat)
        Look he, he's lived here all his
        life. You don't need to stay.
        Sometimes it's the place that's
        the problem.

He goes into his bedroom and shuts the door.

Gemma goes over to a table by the side. Lots of
different bottles of spirits.

In front of them, are two bottles of pills with
their lids off. Some of the pills are scattered.
Gemma looks at what they are, then picks them up
and puts them in her pocket.

Then she goes and sits in his chair by the window,
overlooking the town.

As the light comes up, she gets her phone out -
starts typing.

INT. FOSTER HOUSE. KITCHEN. DAY

Morning. Gemma is in the kitchen, habitually putting the cereal out for Tom and putting the coffee in the machine.

She's wearing the same clothes as last night, but with a jumper over the top.

She gets halfway through making the coffee, then gets a text.

It's from Ros - *'She's found a place. They'll do it today at 1 p.m.'*

She reads it, gives up on the coffee. Goes to the table. Sits and puts her head in her hands. Looks at the text again - tired. Uncertain of everything –

A noise - as the door opens and Simon is there.

> SIMON
> I woke up this morning and you weren't there.

Gemma stays at the table, starts to well up a little. She can't stop herself. The mask slipping.

> GEMMA
> I came down to work. I couldn't sleep.

She stares at him. Tense. She's not going to cry but she's so angry that she's in this situation. Meanwhile he goes to the coffee machine and realises it's half-done. Finishes it off.

> SIMON
> I was dead to the world. Weeks are long at the moment, I know that's always true for you but we start the build in a week so it's full-on. You know?
> (beat)
> And all that running around with Tom yesterday -

But she's not listening. She had a whole thing
about not telling him, but -

                    GEMMA
          You're having an affair.

Simon just stops.

                    GEMMA (CONT'D)
          Aren't you?

He turns and looks at her, confused.

                    GEMMA (CONT'D)
          I'm convinced of it.

                    SIMON
          You're... 'convinced'.
                    (beat)
          Okay...

                    GEMMA
          There would be two things, if you
          were. There would be the
          relationship itself. The sex, all
          of that. And then there would be
          the lie.

                    SIMON
          Gem -

                    GEMMA
          I think that I could accept the
          relationship eventually, if you
          put an end to it. We said when we
          got married that there would
          probably be other people that we
          fancied, over a lifetime.

                    SIMON
          Yes, we did say that.

                    GEMMA
          So the lie would be the bigger
          problem. If you'd been with
          someone else, and you didn't just

> come out and tell me, then that
> would be the real betrayal. Don't
> you think?

He just looks at her. Knows well enough when not to interrupt.

> GEMMA (CONT'D)
> And I don't want to prove it, I
> don't want to catch you. I want
> you to be honest. Unprompted. To
> just tell me. To say 'Yes. I'm
> sorry, but yes. I have been
> seeing someone else.'

He stares at her.

> GEMMA (CONT'D)
> You can. And then - all of the
> consequences. We can talk about
> all of it, together. That'll be
> hard but it'll be better. For
> both of us. Because actually...
> even if you have done this.
> I think I still really love you.

A moment. Now it's Gemma that braces herself for his reply.

He looks down. Then up again.

He runs his hand over his hair. Then moves closer and smiles sincerely.

> SIMON
> I'm not.

Thud. That was Gemma's heart just dropping to the floor - after all the energy, that set-up. She gave him every chance.

> SIMON (CONT'D)
> Where has this come from? You
> follow me to Mum's... and now
> this. Why would you suddenly
> think -

> GEMMA
> It's okay. Doesn't matter. You've
> said you're not, you're not.

They look at each other. He takes her hand, then,
calmly:

> SIMON
> You really think I could do that
> to you?

She stares at him. Tears pouring down her face.
He's saying this, but he <u>has</u>. She <u>knows</u> he <u>has</u>.

> SIMON (CONT'D)
> You're working too hard.

> GEMMA
> (pretends to smile)
> Yeah. Work. That's it.

Tom comes in, and Gemma quickly turns away, grabs
her coat, and heads for the door.

> GEMMA (CONT'D)
> Hiya, Tom. Sleep well? Cereal's
> there, love.

> SIMON
> You want toast?

She goes.

CUT TO -

EXT. FOSTER HOUSE. DAY

A sunny morning as Gemma leaves the house and heads towards her car. Neil and Anna come out of their house in beautiful weekend clothes and get into the wonderful sports car. Neil sees Gemma and smiles.

                    NEIL
          Morning!

Gemma looks at them. Bitter.

                    ANNA
          Hi!

                    NEIL
          Fancy a drive?

She doesn't reply.

                    NEIL (CONT'D)
          It's got wing mirrors and
          everything.

                    ANNA
                 (quietly)
          Leave her alone...

Gemma ignores him. Gets in her car. We hear Neil start his car.

Gemma closes her eyes and waits. We hear Neil's car roar away.

EXT. THE STATION. DAY

We start on the station clock - 9 a.m.

Move down to find Gemma, using her card to get tickets from the machine. She looks at the time - then the board.

Then heads for the platform.

CUT TO -

EXT. THE STATION. PLATFORM. DAY

Gemma walks on to the platform, holding the
tickets. She watches as the train arrives.

Deep breath - has she had enough? Is she leaving?

Then she spots a man standing with a rucksack and
coat. He turns, and we see... it's Jack.

CUT TO -

The two of them talking - the train behind them.

                    JACK
          My two alarms go off at seven-
          thirty, then a woman arrives at my
          door, pushes in, starts packing my
          bag, informs me her name is Casey,
          and there's a taxi waiting.

                    GEMMA
          Carly.

                    JACK
          She tells me if I don't get in
          it, Gemma Foster will have me
          arrested.

                    GEMMA
          Practising medicine while under
          the influence. Plenty of evidence
          if I need it. You're going on
          holiday.

She gives him the tickets.

                    JACK
          I can't afford a holiday.

                    GEMMA
          All expenses paid. Out and open
          return, but stay there a while.
          Your train'll be here in a minute.

                    JACK
          I'm not going anywhere.

Gemma reaches into her doctor's bag and produces
the two bottles of pills.

                    GEMMA
          I found these in your flat.
          Sleeping pills.

                    JACK
          Yes.

                    GEMMA
          And these to stop the vomiting...

                    JACK
               (sad and serious)
          But I didn't go through with it.

                    GEMMA
          But you kept the pills in case
          you changed your mind. This is an
          intervention Jack so trust me.
               (beat)
          Sometimes it's the place that's
          the problem.
               (beat)
          You'll be met when you get there.

                    JACK
               (considering)
          By whom?

                    GEMMA
          Mary.

                    JACK
          Mary who?

                    GEMMA
          She's a friend.

He looks at her. Accepts he's in her hands now.
Nods.

                    JACK
          What happened with the girl? What
          are they going to do?

Gemma shrugs.

                    JACK (CONT'D)
          You told him?

                    GEMMA
          He doesn't deserve to know.

He looks at her. Doesn't approve but he's said all
he can. The train engine starts. Jack looks round.

                    JACK
          A 'friend'?

                    GEMMA
          I think you'll like her.

                    JACK
          You're mad.

Gemma smiles.

He turns to get on the train - and we CUT TO -

EXT. BRIDEWELL. DAY

Simon and Tom play with a football on the grass.
We see that he's a fantastic father - encouraging
to Tom, and huge amounts of fun.

Watching them, at a distance, is Gemma, who's
pushing Helen in a wheelchair, on a path around the
grounds. Helen is, as in Episode One, in a lot of
pain, but enjoying seeing her son, and grandson.

They come to a stop. Gemma sits on a bench, next to
Helen.

She's about to tell her more about the tour when -

                    HELEN
          You didn't sleep last night.

                    GEMMA
          Do I look that bad?

HELEN
When you came in last week, there
was a change. You kept a distance
from him.

They look at Simon and Tom playing for a moment.
Then -

HELEN (CONT'D)
You know, don't you? About this
other woman.

Gemma looks at Helen - an understanding. She
doesn't need to say anything.

HELEN (CONT'D)
Simon swore me to secrecy, but he
told me about it. He's acting
exactly like his father. I'm
sorry.

GEMMA
She's pregnant. Kate. Her doctor
told me. She's having an abortion
today.

HELEN
(looks at Simon playing football with Tom)
He doesn't know?

GEMMA
No.

HELEN
When's it happening?

GEMMA
Soon... one o'clock.

HELEN
Tell him.

GEMMA
(sharp)
Why should I?

                    HELEN
         He's got a right to know.

CUT TO -

BRIDEWELL. HELEN'S BEDROOM. DAY

Helen is in bed now. They have a tray with tea on
it. Simon is pouring. He gives a cup to his mum,
then pours another.

                    SIMON
         We're really close. All the
         preparation's done so literally
         a couple of weeks - that's what
         we're looking at to start.

                    HELEN
                (looking at Gemma)
         How, how long then until it's
         finished?

                    SIMON
         Eight months.

                    HELEN
         Right.

                    SIMON
                (to Tom)
         Tea?

                    TOM
         No thanks.

                    SIMON
         Biscuit then?

                    TOM
         Okay.

Helen and Gemma both glance at the clock.

                         SIMON
              I'll bring the model in one day.
              You can see it.

Simon sits on the windowsill.

                         SIMON (CONT'D)
              Tom mate, you gonna tell Gran
              about what we did yesterday?

                         TOM
              Well we went on a tour of Villa
              Park, it's a football ground, and
              it was really, really good. We
              saw everything, the pitch, the
              changing rooms, the museum bit at
              the back of the club with the
              history.

                         SIMON
              Can you remember when it was
              built?

Gemma looks back from the clock to Helen. An
unspoken desperation. Then Gemma looks to Simon
and Tom.

Makes a decision. Gets out her phone. Texts.

                         TOM
              Yeah. What...?

                         SIMON
              Go on then, what year?

                         TOM
              1897 it was built originally but
              they've replaced most of it now.

                         HELEN
              Is it big?

                         TOM
              Massive, yeah.

As we hear the following, we see Gemma's text.
'Call him now. Tell him she's pregnant. For me. x'

She presses 'Send'.

                    TOM (CONT'D)
          We got a tour. Only like
          celebrities or whatever get it
          normally. That was really cool
          actually. And then we went and -

Then Simon's phone rings.

                    SIMON
          Sorry.

He sees who it is. (It's Ros - but we don't see
this.) He answers.

                    SIMON (CONT'D)
          Hi.
                    (beat)
          Yeah, just give me a minute.

Simon mimes an apology and leaves the room. As Tom
carries on talking, Helen takes Gemma's hand and
holds it tight.

                    TOM
          We went and met the players and
          had a go on one of the goals. Dad
          missed. It was really funny.

                    HELEN
          And you won this day out?

                    TOM
          In a raffle, yeah. It was second
          prize.

                    HELEN
          Second prize? That's a good
          raffle. Very lucky.

Through the window, we see Simon walk away from the
building a little, looking very concerned. He
checks his watch. Seems a little angry. Then hangs
up, and makes another call.

His call's connected and he tells Kate he knows.

                    TOM
          Dad's always on his phone.

                    GEMMA
          He's very busy.

CUT TO -

A few minutes later.

Simon re-enters the bedroom.

                    SIMON
          I'm really sorry. An investor's
          pulled out. I need to get on the
          phone to see if he'll reconsider.
          The paperwork's in the office. I
          need to take the car. Can I?

                    GEMMA
          No problem. We'll get a taxi
          home.

                    SIMON
          Sorry, Mum.

                    HELEN
          It's okay.

                    SIMON
               (to Tom)
          See you later, mate.

                    TOM
          See ya.

He goes. A moment. Helen looks at Gemma who's
nearly crying, and turns to Tom.

                    HELEN
          Will you take the cups out to the
          kitchen?

                    TOM
          Yeah, sure.

>   HELEN
>   You know where it is, don't you?
>   Down the corridor on the right.

>   TOM
>   Yep, I know.

>   HELEN
>   If you put them in the
>   dishwasher...

>   TOM
>   I know.

He lifts the tray and leaves the room.

>   GEMMA
>   Do you think it's serious?

>   HELEN
>   Well, when they make a decision
>   on this child you'll know.
>   (beat)
>   But two years... it says
>   something.

>   GEMMA
>   Two years? Ros said it was three
>   months.

Helen looks at her - her eyes widen, and we see
more expression than at any other point. Real
compassion as she realises Gemma doesn't know.

>   HELEN
>   Oh Gemma. No.

Gemma hits the back of the chair. Hard.

>   GEMMA
>   For two years...?!

>   HELEN (O.S.)
>   I thought you knew? You said
>   you'd found out about it. Oh, I'm
>   sorry, Gemma... Why don't you
>   come and sit down.

INT. FOSTER HOUSE. GEMMA'S BEDROOM. NIGHT

It's late. Gemma is in bed, going over some paperwork. Simon appears at the door. He looks shattered.

> GEMMA
> All sorted?

> SIMON
> For now.

He starts taking off his clothes. Gemma watches him.

A long moment. Him undressing. Both of them not speaking.

Thinking it through. Him concerned she might know something. Her trying to work out what decision he made with Kate.

There's something about the intimacy of this routine - sharing a bedroom.

He gets into bed. Looks at her.

> SIMON (CONT'D)
> Love you.

He kisses her, then turns over to go to sleep.

INT. THE SURGERY. OFFICE. DAY

Gemma's lurking in the office, seemingly doing some paperwork. She notices, through the window into reception, Kate leaving. Still sad, unsure, arms folded.

Ros comes in to join Gemma.

They're the only ones in the office -

> ROS
> She wasn't happy I told him, but she's clearly pleased he knows.

> GEMMA
> They're gonna keep it?

> ROS
> I think so.

A moment.

> GEMMA
> Two years.

> ROS
> Yeah. He lied. Seems that's what
> he does.

> GEMMA
> Jack said when Simon was young he
> had a different girl every week.
> You never told me.
>
> You were at school with him.

> ROS
> It didn't matter. I thought he
> was committed.

> GEMMA
> But when you found out that he
> was cheating, were you surprised?

A moment. Ros sighs, she can't hold any more of
this back.

> ROS
> To be honest, I'm surprised it
> took him so long.

Gemma looks at her, then opens the door.

> ROS (CONT'D)
> Where are you going?

> GEMMA
> Work. I've got work to do.

And she goes.

INT. THE SURGERY. RECEPTION. DAY

Gemma comes out through from the office - and sees
Anwar standing waiting - he sees her and comes over -

> GEMMA
>
> Morning -

> ANWAR
>
> You told my wife everything.
> Absolutely against the code of
> ethics and the law.

> GEMMA
>
> Do you want to talk in private?

> ANWAR
>
> Not acceptable.

Gemma continues down the corridor to her room.
Anwar following.

> GEMMA
>
> What did she say? When she called
> you back?

> ANWAR
> (beat)
>
> She was upset. Some madwoman
> calling her in the middle of the
> night. She thought I'd been up to
> something at first.

They go into Gemma's office.

INT. THE SURGERY. GEMMA'S OFFICE. DAY

Gemma closes the door.

>   ANWAR (CONT'D)
>   But she asked me if what you'd
>   said was true. And I said yeah.

>   GEMMA
>   What did you decide?

A moment. Anwar sheepish.

>   ANWAR
>   She's... she's going to come with
>   me. To the scan.

>   GEMMA
>   Good.

>   ANWAR
>   (beat)
>   Still worried what they're going
>   to find though.

>   GEMMA
>   Of course.

>   ANWAR
>   But the point is, you calling her
>   like that was illegal.

>   GEMMA
>   I know.

>   ANWAR
>   You shouldn't do it.

>   GEMMA
>   Understood. Would you like to
>   make a formal complaint then?

She just looks at him. He's awkward...

>   ANWAR
>   No.

                    GEMMA
        Boy or girl?

                    ANWAR
        Little girl.

Gemma opens the door of her room.

                    GEMMA
        Oh, you said you did a lot of
        divorce work.

                    ANWAR
        Yeah I do. Why?

Gemma looks at him.

                    GEMMA
        I'd like to book an appointment.

CUT TO BLACK.

EPISODE THREE

EXT. STREET OUTSIDE GEMMA'S HOUSE. DAY

Reflected in her new wing mirror, we see Gemma
emerge and head towards her car. She looks good,
professional, but somehow, not herself.

Neil arrives back after a morning run. He's clearly
very fit and very sweaty. He sees her, stops outside
her house and takes his white in-ear headphones out.

>   NEIL
>   Hey. Early start for you.

She walks towards him. He is out of breath.

>   GEMMA
>   Hi.

>   NEIL
>   Looking good.

>   GEMMA
>   Meeting.

>   NEIL
>   Right.

A moment. They look at each other. Is there, almost
for the first time, and despite Gemma's animosity
towards him, a raw <u>mutual</u> attraction?

Gemma smiles, and gets in her car. He looks at her
for a moment, then turns and jogs across the street
to his house.

CUT TO -

EXT. PARMINSTER BORDER. DAY

Gemma's car zooms past the sign: 'Welcome to Parminster'.

INT. GEMMA'S CAR. COUNTRY ROAD. DAY

Gemma drives along a country lane, music on. Up ahead she can see a stationary mini.

> GEMMA
>
> No...

As she gets closer she sees on the road - the motorbike's on its side. In front, on the tarmac, the biker is sprawled, his arm twisted round.

The driver of the mini, Belinda (seventeen, asymmetrical pigtail, dressed in bright colours) staggers from the car, mouthing 'Oh my God' –

The biker is moaning in pain. Gemma parks to block the road, grabs her phone and bag, gets out and hurries across, already dialling 999.

> GEMMA (CONT'D)
> (on phone)
> I've got a motorcycle accident
> just beyond Junction 6 of the
> A4220 out of Parminster –

> BELINDA
> Is he going to die?

> GEMMA
> (to Belinda)
> No.

Gemma, bag in hand, runs to the side of the biker and kneels.

                    GEMMA (CONT'D)
                     (on phone)
          ...the rider's male, conscious,
          possible fractured arm -
                    (to the biker)
          Can you try and stay still for
          me. I'm just lifting up your
          visor, okay?

She lifts it up.

                    GEMMA (CONT'D)
                     (on phone)
          I'm a doctor, I just happened to
          be passing. He's breathing. Thank
          you.

She ends the call.

                    GEMMA (CONT'D)
                    (to the biker)
          You seem fine, but I need you to
          stay absolutely still. Partly
          because of the risk of nerve
          damage but also I don't want
          blood on my shirt because I've
          got a really important meeting,
          is that alright?

The biker makes a muffled noise.

                    GEMMA (CONT'D)
                (getting closer to hear)
          Sorry?

Biker - louder muffled noise.

                    GEMMA (CONT'D)
                (getting even closer)
          What?

The biker suddenly vomits. It sprays out of the
helmet, all over Gemma's jacket. Belinda screams.

CUT TO -

INT. G56 SOLICITORS. RECEPTION. DAY

A quiet reception. A sofa, water cooler. A prim
receptionist waters a house plant. Classical music
plays.

With a bang, the door opens and in walks Gemma -
blood and vomit stains on her shirt, laddered
tights, dishevelled hair. She's clutching a
crumpled pile of papers.

Out of a door appears Anwar, in a suit. He sees
Gemma -

                    ANWAR
          Jesus. What happened to you?

                    GEMMA
          Traffic.

TITLE SEQUENCE

INT. G56 SOLICITORS. ANWAR'S OFFICE. DAY

Close on Anwar. He's had a stressful last couple of
weeks and we can tell. He looks tired, perhaps
unshaven. In front of him is a small pile of bank
statements from Gemma's current account.

Anwar's office has legal books on the shelves.
Certificates of qualification. On his desk, a recent
picture of himself with his heavily pregnant wife,
Alesha.

Gemma is sat across a desk from Anwar. She's
changed into a man's large white shirt. She's
halfway through talking about what's happened -
passionate and emotional.

                    GEMMA
          My thoughts keep running over the
          last two years. Birthdays,

holidays. When we've had sex and
I've told him that I love him.
Walking around in the bedroom
without any clothes on, thinking
he likes what he sees. He was
lying the whole time. Sorry
you're a lawyer you don't need to
hear this.

                ANWAR
It's fine. I asked you to bring in
details of your finances...

                GEMMA
There.

                ANWAR
These are just your current
account. Presumably there other
savings, investments -

                GEMMA
He handles the money, always has
done -

                ANWAR
Why?

                GEMMA
He said he was better at it.

                ANWAR
So you don't know your financial
situation at all?

                GEMMA
No, I suppose -

                ANWAR
This project - what's it called?

                GEMMA
Academy Green.

                    ANWAR
          And will it pay off?

                    GEMMA
          He says it's doing well.

                    ANWAR
          He 'says'.

She stands up, and walks away.

                    GEMMA
          Sorry. This is - no offence - but
          I'm not interested. This is
          really dull. This is not what my
          life is about. I just want to
          skip to the bit where I move on.

                    ANWAR
          In a divorce he'll officially take
          fifty per cent of everything. Your
          salary, your savings, your
          pension.

                    GEMMA
          He cheated. Not me.

                    ANWAR
          Doesn't matter. Fifty per cent is
          the default. But if you're telling
          me he has complete control of your
          finances, he might already have
          hidden money away in preparation.
          Meaning you could get even less.
          Are you happy with that?

                    GEMMA
          Of course not.

                    ANWAR
          By not telling him that you know,
          you've got an unusual advantage.
          You can look into this without
          him suspecting anything.

> GEMMA
> So what do I do?

> ANWAR
> Depends what you want.

A moment. They look at each other. He is resolute
and confident in a way that steadies her.

She sits back down, thinks for a moment.

> GEMMA
> I want my son to stay living
> in the town where he was born.
> I want to keep the life that
> I chose, the job that I love.
> My dignity. My money. My house.

> ANWAR
> Good. Then in the meantime find
> out what he's planning, how much
> money he's got, and while you do
> that, play the dutiful wife so he
> doesn't suspect a thing.

EXT. BUILDING SITE. DAY

We see we're in a roughly cordoned-off area for
parking at the back of the old school building we
saw in Episode One. Gemma starts to walk towards
the building, past the hoarding, with 'Simon Foster
Property Development' and 'Academy Green' on it.

Gemma, dressed excellently, listens to Simon with
Ros and Tom. Relaxed with the right amount of
glamour – Gemma's playing the First Lady to Simon
today, and she's going to look the part.

A group of about forty people are gathered in an
old playground. Behind them, a derelict school.
Builders wait, to start the work.

Simon's in the middle of the group. He looks
excited, confident as he gives a speech to start the
work. This is the fulfilment of his dream. In the
crowd are supporters of the project, local
individuals from the community and council, maybe a
reporter from the local paper.

Behind him is a huge poster advertising Academy
Green. In front of him is a model of the completed
development.

> SIMON
> Good morning ladies and
> gentlemen, thank you for coming.
> Highbrook has a proud history.
> Generations of children have been
> educated here, including myself.
> Then three years ago the building
> was deemed unsuitable.

In the crowd, listening, we also see Neil and Anna.

Neil turns and notices Gemma looking at him. He
smiles.

> SIMON (CONT'D)
> The school relocated to a
> purpose-built facility, and now
> I'm proud that the Academy Green
> development will give a new lease
> of life to this historic site.
> Twenty luxury flats, right in the
> heart of town. This isn't just a
> business opportunity for me, but
> a way of protecting the legacy of
> a building I love. So I hope
> you'll all join me for a glass of
> champagne. Let's move forward.
> Let's build!

He smiles, proud, and slightly moved. This is
really a big moment for him.

                         SIMON (CONT'D)
                          (to Gemma)
            Was it alright?

                              GEMMA
            Yes.

INT. BUILDING SITE. PRESENTATION ROOM. DAY

In a room next to the playground, the crowd are now
gathered, clutching plastic cups of champagne.
Through the windows, the building work continues on
the school.

Tom's watching, fascinated –

                              ANNA
            That'll be you one day, Tom.

                              SIMON
            Tom!

Tom turns to Simon.

                         SIMON (CONT'D)
            Come and have a look at the
            model! Anna, Neil, come on.

Simon leads Tom and Anna across to a model of the
development. Neil's about to follow when he catches
Gemma's eye.

                              NEIL
            He's not bad at this is he?
            Public speaking.

                              GEMMA
            He's worried about his suit.

                              NEIL
            Why?

                    GEMMA
He says he looks like he's
selling cars.

                    NEIL
        (he looks at him again)
Right, yes I see what you mean.

                    GEMMA
Neil, I wanted to ask, could we
find a moment to go over my
accounts? I've always left it to
Simon but I've realised perhaps
maybe I should pay more
attention. I thought you could
talk me through it.

                    NEIL
Sure.

                    GEMMA
Over dinner maybe.

Neil looks at her. Surprised by the proposition.
Smiles.

                    NEIL
Absolutely.

                    GEMMA
And maybe don't mention it to
Simon. I wouldn't want him
thinking that I don't trust him.

                    NEIL
Of course. Just let me know when.

Neil goes across to join the others at the model.
As he does, Ros comes over -

                    ROS
Simon's right, this is historic.
I gave Karl Lucas a handjob
against that wall in 1993. And
now they're knocking it down.

Gemma looks at Simon, playing with the model. Tom's
loving it. Simon's being distracted by Becky, who's
stressed, asking him a lot of questions...

                    ROS (CONT'D)
          There was no internet or mobiles
          in the early nineties. So, in a
          town like this, nothing to do
          except each other.
                    (beat)
          Kate's changed surgery. We got
          the paperwork through today.

                    GEMMA
          Makes sense.

                    ROS
                    (beat)
          Still need me tomorrow?

                    GEMMA
          Yes.

                    ROS
          Never been undercover before.
          It's exciting.

                    GEMMA
          Thanks.

                    ROS
          Okay.

                    TOM
          Mum? If you haven't seen the
          model, you should.

They stop talking and turn, as Simon and Tom come
over.

                    GEMMA
          Impressed?

                    TOM
              (playing it cool)
     I suppose...

                  GEMMA
     Proud of your dad?

                    TOM
                 (smiling)
     A bit.

Simon looks at Tom - that means a lot to him.
He goes to Gemma and hugs her - kisses her.

                  SIMON
     Thank you.

Gemma smiles - surprised and slightly embarrassed.

                  GEMMA
     What for?

                  SIMON
              (sincere, warm)
     Everything.

                  GEMMA
           (as warm, as sincere)
     It's my pleasure.

CUT TO -

EXT. SANDBRIDGE HOUSES. DAY

Close on Carly as she nervously makes her way across
the road, towards Kate's front door. She's very
unsure about this, and after taking a few steps,
chickens out - turns round and walks in the opposite
direction, back down the road, and over to Gemma's
car, which is hidden in a line of other cars.

Gemma is sat inside. She's close to Kate's house
here - she knows she's taking a risk.

                         CARLY
          She's gonna think I'm selling
          something, or mental.

                         GEMMA
          You've moved round the corner,
          just thought you'd say hello.

                         CARLY
          People don't do that any more.

                         GEMMA
          They might if they're pregnant and
          want a sense of the community.

                         CARLY
                    (sarcastic)
          Right, I'll just drop all that
          into the conversation...

                         GEMMA
          Say you're tired, put your hand
          on your tummy, and she'll work it
          out.

Carly looks over at the house, unsure.

                    GEMMA (CONT'D)
          Just get her to like you. And
          then tomorrow, come back, get her
          talking about Simon, divorce,
          plans, anything. Worst that can
          happen, she shuts the door in
          your face. And if she does, I'll
          still give you the money.

                         CARLY
          Okay, okay.

Carly goes back across the street, and goes up to
Kate's door. Gemma watches from a distance, as Kate
opens the door. She looks unhappy, in jeans and a
hooded top. Carly talks with her, points,
explains... Kate smiles politely. Starts to talk.

Gemma watches - gets a text message. From Ros -
'*What time tomorrow? Ros*'

They talk some more. Gemma watches.

Gemma's replying to the text - '*After 8 o'clock.
I'll be gone.*'

As she sends it, Carly and Kate say goodbye. Kate
shuts the door. Carly walks back over to Gemma.

> CARLY (CONT'D)
> How did you know?

> GEMMA
> We moved here when I was
> pregnant. First thing I did? Made
> friends. At least... that's what
> I thought they were.

CUT TO -

INT. BRIDEWELL. HELEN'S BEDROOM. DAY

From the corridor we see into the bedroom. A group
of people is stood round the bed - almost like a
vigil. Helen is in bed. Around her are gathered, for
a case conference, Simon and Gemma (Gemma's holding
his hand for support), Luke, the home manager,
Lilly, and the consultant anaesthetist, Doctor
Stevens. Helen is frustrated by the whole thing.

> DOCTOR STEVENS
> We can stop the current
> medication, but in terms of a
> replacement it's difficult. Your
> pain has proven very resistant to
> treatment. From a medical
> perspective I would advise we go
> on as we are. But that's not to
> say there aren't any practical

>   steps to make you more
>   comfortable that you could
>   discuss with the staff here.

>   LILLY
>   We're having those conversations.

>   DOCTOR STEVENS
>   Good. Good.

A moment.

>   LUKE
>   Alright. Thank you for coming.

>   SIMON
>   Thank you.

A moment. It's clearly the end of the meeting.
Everything's been said.

>   HELEN
>   That's it then. We just give up.

>   SIMON
>   Mum, no.

>   HELEN
>   If you have a pain in your head
>   like a drill all day, and all
>   night, how long do you wait?

>   SIMON
>   Wait...? What do you mean?
>   (beat)
>   Mum, it'll be okay.

He goes to her and she kisses him. They're close,
despite everything that's been going on. But he
clearly can't cope with this.

>   HELEN
>   It went well today?

>   SIMON
>   Yeah. Really well.

                    HELEN
          Proud. You better get going.

                    SIMON
          Call us if you need anything.
          Love you, Mum.

He turns, still upset, but hiding it, and moves off
to the corridor, to allow Gemma to say goodbye.
Gemma goes in close to kiss Helen - she speaks
quietly to her.

                    HELEN
          You understand don't you?

                    GEMMA
          Yes.

                    HELEN
          I can't do this forever. I just
          can't...

                    GEMMA
          I can't have this conversation.
          We're not giving up. I promise.
          I'll look into options.

She squeezes Helen's hand.

                    GEMMA (CONT'D)
          See you very soon.

INT. FOSTER HOUSE. EN-SUITE BATHROOM. EVENING

Gemma is getting ready to go out, putting on her
make-up. Her hair now done. She looks great, sexy,
ready.

If only she could _feel_ those things too.

INT. FOSTER HOUSE. KITCHEN. EVENING

Gemma enters, now wearing heels for the evening,
ready to go. All she needs is Simon to come back –
and he's late. Tom is on his tablet.

>   TOM
>   You don't look normal.

>   GEMMA
>   You could just say I look nice.

>   TOM
>   Well yeah, that's what I mean.
>   It's unusual.

>   GEMMA
>   Thanks, Tom.

Simon comes in, exhausted, his tie already off.

>   SIMON
>   Long day. Taxi's outside.

>   GEMMA
>   (puts on her coat)
>   Right.

>   SIMON
>   Where are you going again?

>   GEMMA
>   Local Medical Committee dinner.

>   TOM
>   Sounds boring.

>   SIMON
>   Right. Okay. And that's a...

>   GEMMA
>   What?

>   SIMON
>   And you wear heels for that do
>   you?

> GEMMA

I'm a woman on a night out, so
it's heels or flats, and flats
don't go. What do you want me to
wear? Trainers?

> SIMON

No. Just. You look really...

> GEMMA

What?

> SIMON
> (beat)

Doesn't matter.

> GEMMA

No, don't stop there, on the way
out the house. I look really what?

> SIMON
> (looking in a cupboard)

I'm knackered. Have we got any
crisps?

> GEMMA

I've had a tough day too.

> SIMON

What time are you home?

> GEMMA

Late.

> SIMON

I might have gone to bed. Does
Tom know what he's having for
dinner?

> TOM

Yes.

> SIMON
> (still not looking at her)

And is there anything for...

                    GEMMA
        Left-overs in the fridge. Crisps
        are in the bottom-left cupboard.
        Tom can show you if you get
        stuck.

                    SIMON
                (barely listening)
        Right...

He continues to root around. Gemma watches him for
a moment - he's a shit sometimes.

CUT TO -

EXT. DRIVEWAY. FOSTER HOUSE. EVENING

A scraping sound - like fingernails down a
blackboard. As Gemma walks down the drive past
Simon's immaculate car, she's holding her key out
and leaving a long scratch down the side.

She gets to the cab, where the astonished driver
has watched the whole thing.

CUT TO -

EXT. KATE'S HOUSE. FRONT DOOR. EVENING

Carly knocks on the door, and stands waiting. She
has two identical books under her arm.

After a moment the door opens. It's Kate. She's in
pyjamas, and her eyes are a bit red. She's clearly
just been crying.

                    CARLY
        Hi!

                    KATE
        Hi.

                    CARLY
        I know this is weird, I ordered
        a copy of this book...

Carly holds up the book, *I Love Being Pregnant* by
Dr Sandra Clacy.

                    CARLY (CONT'D)
        ...but I must've ordered it twice
        cos I got two copies through. I
        thought, well, you're just down
        the road, you might want it.

Carly almost winces at how bad and unconvincing all
this sounds to her. Kate looks a little confused.

INT. FOSTER HOUSE. FRONT DOOR. NIGHT

Simon opens the front door. It's Ros - smiling too
much, a little nervous. Not a natural liar.

                    ROS
        Is Gemma about?

                    SIMON
        She's at a dinner.

                    ROS
        Oh. Annoying. You alright?

                    SIMON
        Yeah.

                    ROS
        Told her yet?

                    SIMON
                    (beat)
        No.

                    ROS
        Who's Kate changed doctors to?

>   SIMON
>   We shouldn't talk about all this
>   now.

>   ROS
>   Is Tom...

>   SIMON
>   Upstairs.

EXT. KATE'S HOUSE. FRONT DOOR. NIGHT

Kate and Carly at the front door.

>   KATE
>   Are you sure you don't wanna send
>   it back?

>   CARLY
>   Nah. Hassle.

>   KATE
>   I can give you the money for it?

>   CARLY
>   (offering it)
>   No. Go on.

Kate smiles a little, and takes the book.

>   KATE
>   Thanks.

INT. FOSTER HOUSE. FRONT DOOR. NIGHT

Ros and Simon at the front door.

>   ROS
>   I've come all the way over, it
>   turns out, for no good reason,

and I know you're going through
a lot, but the normal thing, the
polite thing would be to ask me
in for a cup of tea -

EXT. KATE'S HOUSE. FRONT DOOR. NIGHT

Carly turns to go, pleased with herself, next step
done! Now she can leave and do something else -

> KATE
> Do you want to come in?

Carly stops. Her smile falls. What? This was not
part of the plan. She turns back round. Kate's so
obviously been crying, and she wants someone to
talk to.

> KATE (CONT'D)
> Cup of tea?

INT. FOSTER HOUSE. FRONT DOOR. NIGHT

Ros and Simon at the front door.

> ROS
> - or a gin and tonic?

A pause. Simon looks at her, a little charmed - old
friends. He opens the door.

INT. KATE'S HOUSE. EVENING

Carly goes in nervously.

> CARLY
> Sure.

EXT. FOSTER HOUSE. FRONT DOOR. NIGHT

Ros enters and closes the front door behind her.

INT. BEDFORD ARMS. NIGHT

Gemma enters The Bedford Arms - a high-end
gastropub. Lit well at night. She feels great.
Tonight, for the first time in a long time, she is
free, glamorous, unpredictable.

The tables are mostly in secluded corners, divided
booths. This place is all about the food.

In an area in the corner - at a table with a candle
on it - is Neil. He looks great. Attractive, not
sleazy, just very assured. He sees Gemma and
smiles, impressed. She sits down opposite him.

                    NEIL
          Drink?

She smiles.

INT. KATE'S HOUSE. LIVING ROOM. NIGHT

Over the beginning of the following conversation,
we see Kate's house. It's small, new-build. One big
room downstairs, with a small kitchen off it.

Kate's decorated it precisely, and very neatly.
Everything has its place. Occasional nods to her
age - a poster or an ironic soft toy. Photos on the
mantelpiece. A photo of Kate with her parents -
Chris and Susie.

Kate and Carly are sat drinking cups of tea.

                    KATE
          Can I be honest with you? I keep
          forgetting I'm pregnant?

                         CARLY
You forget?

                         KATE
Yeah, yeah... it, it wasn't
planned.
                    (beat)
So how's the dad? Sorry, are you
with the dad?

                         CARLY
Huh. No. He was drinking eight
pints a night and grabbing me
when I got home - I had enough.
Got rid of him.

                         KATE
Good.

                         CARLY
Better without. You?

                         KATE
Yeah, we're together.

                         CARLY
He doesn't live here though, does
he? You can tell. It's spotless.

                         KATE
Yeah, well... long story.

                         CARLY
                    (sips her tea)
Go on.

INT. FOSTER HOUSE. LIVING ROOM. NIGHT

Ros is sat on the sofa with a gin and tonic. Simon
is by the television, anxiously fiddling with the
remote control, changing the batteries.

                    SIMON
People say that the perfect story
is that you meet this one person
and fall completely in love, and
then from that moment you don't
need anyone else. Despite the
fact that the world keeps
changing, people change as well,
your work, your house and
everything alters, you're
expected to stick with just this
one person. And despite that
sounding unlikely, when I met
Gemma, I thought I could. I
thought actually, yes, I'll never
need anyone else. What I didn't
realise, is that it's possible to
feel that about two different
people at the same time.

                    ROS
You're still in love with...

                    SIMON
With Gemma. Of course. Yes! And
Kate. Both of them.
                    (beat)
The moment I tell Gemma I lose
her. And I lose my son. Weekends,
evenings, and he'll know the
truth and he'll hate me.

                    ROS
And that's the only reason you
haven't told her?

                    SIMON
                    (pause)
She asked you to come tonight,
didn't she?

                    ROS
No.

                    SIMON
She suspects.

                    ROS
              (beat - nervous)
Alright, yes. Well she, she
doesn't think that you're with
someone else. She's worried that
you may be hiding something with
the business, the money. She
thought you might open up.

                    SIMON
Why would she think anything's
wrong with the money?

                    ROS
She's probably noticed how
stressed you look.

                    SIMON
I don't look stressed.

                    ROS
Stressed is an understatement.
Actually you're right, you don't
look stressed you look <u>ill</u>.

Simon stands. Gives up on the remote. Looks away.
Emotional.

                 ROS (CONT'D)
<u>Is</u> there something wrong? With
the money?

                    SIMON
Well, if there was I wouldn't
tell you now, would I? You'd just
go straight back to Gemma.

                    ROS
I'm not on her side, I'm stuck in
the middle. I just want what's
best. Tell me the truth.

He looks at her. Smiles a little, almost
hysterical.

                    SIMON
          The truth... about the money?
             (he holds up his fingers)
          Is that everything's about this
          far from fucked.

INT. BEDFORD ARMS. NIGHT

Neil and Gemma are sat, having just finished the
starter. On the table is an already mostly finished
bottle of wine. As the waiters clear away the
plates, Neil tops up Gemma's glass.

                    NEIL
          Financial matters?

                    GEMMA
          Yeah. As our accountant, I hoped
          you could talk me through things.

                    NEIL
          Over dinner.

                    GEMMA
          Yeah.

                    NEIL
          Earnings, tax, that sort of
          thing?

                    GEMMA
          That sort of thing exactly.

                    NEIL
          Right.
             (playing)
          Well, I'm afraid I didn't bring
          any files with me.

>   GEMMA
>   (playing along)
>   That's a shame.

>   NEIL
>   I forgot.

>   GEMMA
>   I always had you down as
>   organised.

>   NEIL
>   Me too.

>   GEMMA
>   We'll just have to enjoy the
>   food.

A pause. Neil watches her. Enjoying this. He leans forward.

>   NEIL
>   The way Simon describes you when
>   you first met. Very different to
>   now.

>   GEMMA
>   How does he describe me?

>   NEIL
>   He makes you sound like an
>   animal.

>   GEMMA
>   Really?

>   NEIL
>   Feral.

>   GEMMA
>   (smiles)
>   You don't see that?

Gemma looks at him. He doesn't answer.

                    GEMMA (CONT'D)
How is Simon? You see him more
than I do some weeks. Tell me how
he's getting on, at work.

                    NEIL
Simon's ambitious. As you know.
This project's a big step for
him.

                    GEMMA
Will it make money?

                    NEIL
I expect so.

                    GEMMA
So it's going well?
          (beat)
He won't tell me. Thinks I'll
worry.

                    NEIL
     (watching what she's doing)
Right...

                    GEMMA
As you know from our accounts,
I've supported him over the last
few years as he's started out. So
I'm keen it doesn't all go wrong
now.

                    NEIL
You're spying.

                    GEMMA
What?

                    NEIL
Like a doctor I can't disclose
anything that happens with my
clients -

                    GEMMA
I'm not.

                    NEIL
Even if the person asking is
extremely persuasive.

                    GEMMA
I'm just making conversation.

                    NEIL
Well, I don't want to talk about
his work. Actually, I don't
really want to talk about Simon
at all so if that's why you're
here -

                    GEMMA
                    (smiles)
I'm here because I think that
life is passing me by and I'm
missing out.
                    (beat)
I don't care what we talk about.

She pours more wine into both their glasses.
He takes his and drinks.

                    NEIL
                    (beat)
Let me give you a test. I'm going
to tell you why I'm here, and if
it offends you, you can get up,
go home, we never have to speak
of it again. But if it doesn't,
you can stay sat right there.

                    GEMMA
Go on then. Why are you here
Neil?

                    NEIL
Because in the last five years
I've thought a lot about your

body and it's got to the point
that I desperately want to know
what's going on underneath that
dress. Basically Gemma I'm here
because I think we'd have a
really good time fucking.

He sits back. Said it. Gemma looks at him. She
could go now.

She still looks at him. Strong.

The waiter comes over.

> WAITER
> Are you ready for the main
> course?

> GEMMA
> Yes I think we are.

He nods and goes. She smiles at Neil.

He smiles and drinks his wine.

INT. KATE'S HOUSE. NIGHT

Kate and Carly talk.

> CARLY
> You've met her?

> KATE
> Couple of times. She's arrogant.
> Looks down at people. Sorry,
> I sound like a bitch but -

> CARLY
> Is that why he wanted someone
> else?

> KATE
> What?

                    CARLY
That she's arrogant.

                    KATE
He didn't.

                    CARLY
No, I mean –

                    KATE
He didn't want 'someone else', it
was about us, we got on. He
wasn't looking to cheat. Actually
that was always the problem. I
said to him you need to tell her
straight away or it's over. That
was two years ago.

                    CARLY
And now you've got a baby.

                    KATE
I was going to get rid of it.
                    (beat)
Sorry, you, you probably don't
want hear that –

                    CARLY
It's fine.

                    KATE
I wasn't ready but he knows
I want kids eventually, so he
said why not? Promised me that
if I kept the baby he'd tell her
straight away. But nearly two
weeks later...

Kate looks very upset.

                    KATE (CONT'D)
He'd said we'd get a proper house
together, that he'd move her out
to London with their son.

                    CARLY
        Has he got a divorce lawyer, all
        of that?

                    KATE
        I doubt it.
                    (beat)
        He's showing no signs of breaking
        up with her at all. I've thought
        recently maybe I should -

                    CARLY
        Should? What, leave him?

                    KATE
        How did you feel when you split
        up with yours?

                    CARLY
        Terrible.

                    KATE
        Right.

                    CARLY
        For two days. And then I felt
        better.

                    KATE
        So you didn't regret it?

                    CARLY
        Not at all.

    Kate looks at her. A determination growing.

INT. FOSTER HOUSE. LIVING ROOM. NIGHT

Simon moves to the sofa where Ros is sitting.

                    ROS
        The only way out is to tell her
        the truth and deal with what
        happens.

                    SIMON
    I can do it. The money's there,
    it'll all be fine once we start
    selling the flats. It, it's close
    but I need <u>time</u>... six months
    maybe.

                    ROS
    You want to keep all of this
    going for another six months?

                    SIMON
    I have to.

                    ROS
    What about the baby?

Simon turns away, upset.

                    SIMON
    Yeah. Well.

A noise on the stairs. Simon breaks away from Ros,
wipes his eyes quickly.

The door opens. Tom comes in, in his pyjamas. He
sees Ros, looks upset.

                    TOM
    Oh... hi, Ros.

                    ROS
    Hiya.

                    TOM
              (to Simon)
    When's Mum home?

                    SIMON
    She might be late. You okay?

                    TOM
              (looking at them both)
    Yeah, I'm fine.

                    SIMON
            (sees something's wrong)
        Sure?

                    TOM
            (a glance at Ros)
        Yeah. I was going to ask her
        something, but it doesn't matter.

                    SIMON
        Okay.

                    TOM
        Yeah, bye.

He goes.

                    SIMON
        Night, mate. I'll come and see
        you in a minute.

Simon suddenly turns away. Moved.

                SIMON (CONT'D)
            (slightly desperate)
        Please don't tell her anything's
        wrong. Say the money's good.
        It'll all work out best for
        everyone in the end. I promise.

INT. BEDFORD ARMS. NIGHT

Gemma and Neil have finished dessert, and another
bottle and a half of wine. They've both loosened up.

                    NEIL
        I booked a room. Upstairs. They
        have good rooms. And I booked one.
        So there it is. Now you know.

                    GEMMA
        I already knew.

                    NEIL
                (disappointed)
Oh.

                    GEMMA
When I went to the bathroom
I checked with reception.

                    NEIL
You went to the bathroom when you
first arrived.

                    GEMMA
That's right.

                    NEIL
So you've known my intentions all
evening.

                    GEMMA
Neil, I've known your intentions
for five years.

                    NEIL
Oh God. You make me sound
desperate.

                    GEMMA
It would only be desperate if you
were trapped in this marriage
with Anna, and completely in love
with the woman across the street,
but I don't think that's the
case. Is it?
                (beat)
I'm not unique, am I? I'm not the
first other woman.

                    NEIL
There have been other women, yes.

                    GEMMA
What are you into?

                         NEIL
        What you mean...

                         GEMMA
        Why do you do it, these women?

                         NEIL
        Honestly... Pleasure.

                         GEMMA
        Right. So, let me be specific.
        What are you into?

                         NEIL
        Don't ask questions like that
        lightly, cos they have an effect
        coming from you.

                         GEMMA
        I know.

    She waits for an answer.

                         NEIL
        Nothing weird.

                         GEMMA
                    (playing)
        Shame.

                         NEIL
        Physical.

                         GEMMA
        Sort of has to be physical.

                         NEIL
        Anna's great. I love her. But
        she's into it being loving, calm,
        gentle. So... sometimes I like
        to... go for it.

    Gemma laughs.

                    NEIL (CONT'D)
     Right, I'm better at doing than
     describing. I don't fucking know.
     I improvise. What about you?

A moment. She thinks. Then looks at him.

INT. BEDFORD ARMS. ROOM. NIGHT

A luxury room. Minibar, big bed. Everything's
comfortable and designed. As Gemma enters, Neil
takes a bottle of champagne that's in an ice
bucket, and opens it. He pours it into two glasses.
Gives one to her. They drink, without saying
anything.

Then Neil puts the glass down and unbuttons his
shirt.

Gemma stands and looks at him.

                    NEIL
     I think we start by taking off
     our clothes...

                    GEMMA
     I'm married. I made a promise.

He looks at her.

                    NEIL
     I'll let you into a secret. There
     are only two types of married men.
     Those you know who cheat on their
     wives, and those who are better at
     hiding it. Every man I've met
     who's in a long-term relationship,
     they've all been unfaithful at one
     point or another.

                    GEMMA
     Really?

                         NEIL
It's biological. Men like sex.
They can hang around with one
woman, but only if now and then,
they're allowed to fulfil their
function. I don't feel guilty.

                         GEMMA
What about women?

                         NEIL
Well I think women probably like
sex too.
                    (beat)
The point is. It's, it's all very
common.
                    (beat)
Up to you.

Gemma drinks her champagne, then walks across to
him, and kisses him. Tentatively at first.

They kiss again, but now it's passionate. Taking
off each other's clothes, taking off their own.

They fall onto the bed - a blur of close-ups -
breathing - kissing - clothes taken off - her on
top -

But we're not shooting this like Hollywood - this
is real.

Really good, equal, vigorous sex.

There's a moment, where we see Gemma think of
Simon... think of what she's doing, but she puts it
out of her mind and carries on, more into it than
ever -

More and more - until we -

SNAP TO BLACK.

INT. BEDFORD ARMS. ROOM. DAY

Slow fade-up of light as Neil wakes. The morning
light is coming through a crack in the curtains.
There's a light on in the bathroom. He smiles, then
opens the curtains a little more, to let light into
the room.

He gets out of bed, puts on a towelled robe. Pours
himself some water. Happy, content.

The bathroom door opens and Gemma comes out wearing
last night's dress. He makes a slight move to kiss
her but she changes direction to put a few things
in her bag.

> GEMMA
> I've got work.

Neil looks at the time - it's 4.30 a.m.

> NEIL
> Already?

> GEMMA
> I have to go home first.

> NEIL
> I thought we might have another
> go.

> GEMMA
> When do we tell Anna?

Neil smiles.

> NEIL
> Yeah. Or Simon for that matter.
> Wait! What if we don't?

> GEMMA
> I'm serious. She's my friend.

Neil smiles again. Drinks the water.

> NEIL
> Well you didn't think about Anna
> too much last night.

> GEMMA
> I know. She's going to be really
> upset, but she'd be far more
> upset if she finds out that we
> tried to hide it from her.

> NEIL
> What are you doing?

> GEMMA
> I'm saying we should be honest.

> NEIL
> No, no, no you're not, you're
> playing a game and I don't get it
> so it's making me nervous.

> GEMMA
> I don't like deceit.

> NEIL
> I'm not going to tell Anna about
> this and neither are you. If you
> did, I could tell Simon.

> GEMMA
> Go ahead. I'll tell him myself.

> NEIL
> What do you want?

Beat. She waits.

> NEIL (CONT'D)
> Was last night to blackmail me?

> GEMMA
> In reverse order: no, last night
> was because I fancy you and
> I wanted to have a good night.

I enjoyed the sex, the company,
last night was fantastic -
everything I'd hoped for.
>   (beat)
But this morning? What do I want?
Well if you're asking me to lie,
I want something to make up for
it.

>   NEIL

Like what?

>   GEMMA

Simon's accounts. His personal
and business. Copies of
everything stretching back the
last three years, every detail,
not just the official stuff. I'm
going to have them looked at so
don't try and hide anything.

>   NEIL

That's a lot of work.

>   GEMMA

I want them this afternoon.

>   NEIL

It's not possible to get all that
together.

>   GEMMA

How long have you been married?
Fifteen years? I've seen you and
Anna together a lot. You look
after her, you take her on
holiday, you genuinely love her,
don't you? She's what really
matters.

>   NEIL

Yes.

                    GEMMA
     What we just did, it's just
     a bonus.

                    NEIL
     Why do you want his accounts?

                    GEMMA
     Because I think there are things
     going on in our finances that
     I don't know about.
                    (beat)
     Am I right?

                    NEIL
     Now I see it.

                    GEMMA
     See what?

                    NEIL
     Feral.

                    GEMMA
                    (beat)
     This afternoon. Your office, or at
     home?

Pause.

                    NEIL
     Home. Anna's out.

She goes to him and kisses him on the cheek.

                    GEMMA
     Honestly, it was really good.

She leaves.

Neil sits on the bed, confused, exhausted.

INT. FOSTER HOUSE. KITCHEN. DAY

Gemma comes in. She's exhausted and hungover.
The clock says 5.10 a.m. She pours herself a pint
of water. Drinks it.

Then goes through into the hall.

INT. FOSTER HOUSE. UPSTAIRS HALL. DAY

Gemma is about to go up the stairs - but doesn't
want to explain herself. She thinks again, turns
and goes into the living room.

INT. FOSTER HOUSE. LIVING ROOM. DAY

Gemma goes to the armchair, sits on it, pulls a
throw over herself -

SUDDEN CUT TO -

INT. FOSTER HOUSE. LIVING ROOM. DAY

The same, but bright light. It's the morning.

                TOM
     Mum...

Gemma snaps awake to find Tom and Simon both looking
at her. Both serious. Tom's sat on the armchair.
Simon's stood. He hands her a mug of coffee, which
she takes.

                SIMON
     Late night?

                TOM
     You don't look well.

                    GEMMA
                  (standing)
     I'm fine. I just need a shower.
     What's the time?

                    TOM
          Eight o'clock.

                    GEMMA
     Oh...

Gemma drinks from the cup of coffee. Sheepish.

                    SIMON
          You had a good time?

                    GEMMA
                  (guilty)
          Yeah.

She looks at them both.

                    GEMMA (CONT'D)
          What?

Simon picks up the tablet.

                    SIMON
          Last night Tom was looking at
          CheckmyGP, it's a ratings site
          for -

                    GEMMA
                  (sharp)
          What are you looking at that for?

                    TOM
          Harry told me about it.

                    SIMON
          Because normally they say good
          things. And he's proud of you.

                    GEMMA
          Right. Right. So what d'you
          mean... normally?

Simon gives her the tablet.

> TOM
> They started last night.

Gemma reads the comments.

A moment, while she takes it in.

> GEMMA
> Have you read all of these?

> TOM
> Most of them.

> GEMMA
> They're not true.

> SIMON
> We'll get them taken down, won't
> we? Sometimes people write things
> like this on the internet.

> TOM
> Why?

> SIMON
> Someone wants to get at Mum.

> TOM
> Who?

> SIMON
> (looks at Gemma)
> We don't know.

> GEMMA
> (quietly)
> I'll deal with this. I should
> have a shower.

She turns and goes and we CUT TO -

INT. SURGERY. RECEPTION AREA. DAY

Gemma enters the reception and bumps into Luke,
arriving back from visiting Helen.

                    GEMMA
          You've just seen Helen?

                    LUKE
          Yes, and I agree with the
          specialist. There's not much to
          be done in terms of medication.
          So we talked through changes to
          the home, management - coping
          strategies.

                    GEMMA
          I don't know that that's enough.

                    LUKE
                    (he agrees)
          Yeah.
                    (beat)
          And she asked me to tell you that
          she wanted to see you. Today if
          possible.

                    GEMMA
          Okay, thanks.

Ros enters.

                    ROS
                    (to Luke)
          Busy morning!

She beams at Luke, who goes.

                    ROS (CONT'D)
          I give up.

Luke comes back.

                    LUKE
Ros. Sorry, can I just say that
I'm not really comfortable with
flirting. Not at work.

                    ROS
Okay.

                    LUKE
Is that alright?

                    ROS
              (defensive)
Yeah. Fine.

                    LUKE
Thanks.

He goes. Ros turns to Gemma.

                    ROS
I've gone off him.

They walk down the corridor - we follow them -

                    ROS (CONT'D)
Last night...

Ros struggles to maintain her honesty, but also her
commitment to Simon not to tell Gemma.

                    ROS (CONT'D)
The bad news is I had to tell him
you'd sent me.

                    GEMMA
Why?

                    ROS
Because he guessed, so I said
alright, yes, you asked me to
come round but it was only
because you were worried about
the money.

                    GEMMA
    And?

                    ROS
    He said there's enough to keep
    the project going and in time
    it'll, it'll be okay.

                    GEMMA
    So no problems then?

                    ROS
                 (careful)
    He... seemed sure that it would
    all work out.

                    GEMMA
    But if that's true, now that
    she's pregnant, why doesn't he
    just come out and tell me? What's
    he waiting for? I'm told Kate has
    exactly the same question.

                    ROS
    How do you know?

Gemma doesn't reply.

                ROS (CONT'D)
                 (beat)
    I know it's weird, but from what
    he said last night... he still
    loves you. Maybe that's the
    reason.
                 (beat)
    And it's good to be loved, Gemma.
    It really is.

Ros disappears into her room.

Gemma just stands for a moment. That last comment
caught her unawares. He <u>loves</u> her?

INT. NEIL'S HOUSE. KITCHEN. DAY

Gemma sits opposite Neil at the table. In front of him are piles of paper. He shows her various documents, efficiently and quickly. Gemma's disorientated by it all. She's struggling to keep up. We're jumping in halfway through -

> NEIL
> So as you can see he's raided everything.

> GEMMA
> My friend said he had it under control.

> NEIL
> Well, your friend was wrong.
> ISA, savings, Tom's fund for university -

> GEMMA
> That money came from my parents when they died.

> NEIL
> Remortgaged the house...

> GEMMA
> I'm sorry?

> NEIL
> Presumably you know about that.
> You signed it.

Neil hands over another piece of paper - a mortgage agreement with a forged signature.

Gemma looks at it.

> GEMMA
> No, I didn't.

Neil looks at it, and her.

                    NEIL
Okay, well... look, I don't give
advice, I just do the accounts.
                   (beat)
But you really shouldn't have
just left it up to him. He can
barely add up. Let alone run a
business.
                   (beat)
Anyway, as you can imagine, all
that wasn't nearly enough. He got
halfway into it, secured the
building but had no funds for the
development itself. Then this new
investor arrives. 'White Stone',
starts ploughing in cash. So far,
just over a million, in a number
of instalments. That's how he's
managed to start the work.

                   GEMMA
Who's 'White Stone'?

                    NEIL
No idea. They're registered
offshore so I can't find out.
Simon won't tell me. If that
money keeps coming in, what
you've heard from your friend is
right, he might get to the end of
the project, sell the flats, make
it all back, and a lot more.
                   (beat)
But if for any reason it stops,
he'll be bankrupt within a week.

                   GEMMA
My savings, mortgage, everything.

                    NEIL
Gone.

She gathers up the papers, and puts them in the cardboard box they came in.

                    NEIL (CONT'D)
          If Simon asks how you got this
          information -

                    GEMMA
               (gathering up her things)
          I'll make something up.

                    NEIL
               (with an implication...)
          And if you need any more
          information or advice, we could
          meet again.

                    GEMMA
               (laughs disbelievingly)
          I'm sorry? Neil, I'm blackmailing
          you.

                    NEIL
               (shrugs)
          Yeah.
               (beat)
          The truth is I don't really like
          Simon. He's a mate, he's a
          client, but he's patronising.
          Thinks he knows it all. It's
          annoying.
               (beat)
          I keep thinking about last night.
               (beat)
          We could meet again. If you want.

                    GEMMA
          White Stone?

                    NEIL
          Yeah.

                    GEMMA
          Will you keep trying? To find out
          who it is?

The sound of the front door opening. It's Anna.

> ANNA (O.S.)
> Hello! Not a bad day out there
> now. Got bread and wipes for the
> kitchen but there was some...

Anna comes through into the kitchen and sees Gemma
stood. Neil sat at the table.

> ANNA (CONT'D)
> Oh! Hi! I didn't know you were
> here.

> GEMMA
> Neil was helping with my
> accounts. I think we've got
> everything sorted, so I should
> probably head off. Sorry, I'm in
> a hurry -

Gemma goes. Anna looks at Neil intensely.

INT. BRIDEWELL. DAY

Gemma stands at the foot of Helen's bed. Helen is
a little upset. Worried.

> HELEN
> He'll get nothing once the
> divorce starts, it'll all come
> out, him taking your money,
> forging your signature -

> GEMMA
> Yes, and the project will
> collapse probably. We'll lose it
> all. But I earn enough. And what
> he's done only strengthens my
> case. Tom and me, we'll be okay.

Helen looks away. She's crying.

                    GEMMA (CONT'D)
And I promise we'll always look
after you.

                    HELEN
What about him? You probably
don't care, I understand that.
But you'll look after him? You
won't leave him with nothing?

They look at each other. Helen looks worried. Gemma
takes her hand. Holds it tight.

                    GEMMA
It'll be fair. I promise.

A look between them, of understanding.

EXT. COUNTRY LANE. DAY

The sound of a phone's dialling tone and it being
answered. Gemma's car drives along the lane.

                    GEMMA (O.S.)
Anwar, hi, I think I've got
everything. I want to proceed.
Can you call me back?

EXT. PARMINSTER. DAY

We see Parminster in the bright morning sun – going
to work. Traffic, shoppers, school run...

INT. ROSE AND CROWN. DAY

It's late afternoon. Carly is behind the bar, in
the pub, taking glasses out of the dishwasher.
She's humming to herself. (Adele? Sam Smith?) In
the pub are a few people at the tables (no one at
the bar). Not a busy day, but a bit of custom..
There's an almost tranquil atmosphere. Cutlery.
People talking. Which is broken by -

Kate who storms in and goes straight to Carly at
the bar. Kate is furious. Upset.

>   CARLY
>   Hey. What's the matter?

Carly crosses to Kate.

>   CARLY (CONT'D)
>   Are you okay?

>   KATE
>   I did it.

>   CARLY
>   What? Your boyfriend...

Simon enters.

>   KATE
>   Oh shit, he followed me...

He's furious, but also very concerned they're doing
this in public. As he comes straight over to Kate,
Carly instinctively turns away and cleans the
surfaces, overhearing the following:

>   SIMON
>   We can't do this in here -

>   KATE
>   I told you I'm only keeping it if
>   you finish it with her. You said
>   you would.

                    SIMON
          I want to.

                    KATE
          It's not good enough that.
          Anyway, it's gone now. It's
          better. It's my body. It's up
          to me.

                    SIMON
          You know why I couldn't tell her.

                    KATE
          Either go and tell her now, or
          that is it.

                    SIMON
          It was my child too.

                    KATE
          Are you going to go and tell her?

                    SIMON
                (beat. Hard now)
          No.

A moment. They look at each other. She's almost
expecting him to keep arguing now. To keep trying.
But Simon makes a decision. He's very upset, but
almost more sure, more calm now.

                    SIMON (CONT'D)
          You're right. You shouldn't wait
          any more.

He stares at her a second, then goes, really upset.

EXT. PARK OVERLOOKING PARMINSTER. DAY

Gemma and Carly sit on a bench overlooking the
town. Gemma's taking in what Carly's told her
happened in the pub.

>   GEMMA
>   And do you think it's really over?

>   CARLY
>   She had it done without telling
>   him. He looked like he'd never
>   forget that. Maybe it doesn't
>   matter, but in the end, he was
>   the one that finished it. He told
>   her not to wait.

>   GEMMA
>   (beat)
>   That doesn't change anything.

INT. FOSTER HOUSE. LIVING ROOM. EVENING

Close on Simon, sat in an armchair in front of the
TV.

We're close enough to see, from the light of the
TV, that his eyes are full of tears.

Tom is on the sofa watching the same thing,
laughing. He hasn't noticed anything wrong with
his dad.

Gemma appears at the door, watches them for
a moment. They don't see her.

INT. FOSTER HOUSE. KITCHEN. EVENING

Gemma begins to unwrap a frozen pizza.

Simon enters. He looks utterly drained.

>   SIMON
>   Everything alright?

>   GEMMA
>   Just about.

Gemma looks at him. Wishes she could talk to him
about everything - but he's the problem...

>   SIMON
>   Hard at the moment, isn't it?

Gemma smiles bitterly, then turns away and carries
on with the pizzas.

>   SIMON (CONT'D)
>   We were watching a thing. It's,
>   it's funny.

Simon wants to go near her, be with her, but can't.

>   GEMMA
>   I'll be over in a minute.

He looks at her, then goes. Gemma puts the pizzas
in the oven. Sad, but determined.

CUT TO -

INT. FOSTER HOUSE. LIVING ROOM. EVENING

Gemma, Simon and Tom are sat together on the sofa
watching TV and eating the pizza.

Simon's sat in a chair on his own - grim-faced.
Devastated. Things couldn't get any worse than they
are right now...

INT. FOSTER HOUSE. GEMMA'S BEDROOM. DAY

It's early. The red neon alarm clock says 5.18 a.m.

The phone's ringing.

Gemma wakes. Simon's already walking round to her
side of the bed. He picks up the phone and answers
it - bleary.

                    SIMON
                 (on phone)
          Hello? Yes?

The blood drains out of his face - he's utterly
shocked.

                 SIMON (CONT'D)
                 (on phone)
          Yeah, yeah. I'll be there as soon
          as I can.

EXT. BRIDEWELL. HELEN'S BEDROOM. DAY

Helen's body is sprawled on her bed. On the table
next to her is a written note.

A police officer makes notes.

INT. BRIDEWELL. RECEPTION. DAY

Gemma and Simon wait, having just arrived. Luke
comes towards them, having been with the police.
Simon and Gemma go with him.

                    LUKE
          I'm so sorry.
                 (beat)
          Have the police spoken to you?

                    GEMMA
          No.

                    SIMON
          They just said to wait.

Luke looks around - this is against procedure but
he can't just leave them hanging. He talks quietly.

                         LUKE
          She took an overdose of sleeping
          pills. Left a short note. It says
          that the pain had got too much,
          and she couldn't carry on.

                         SIMON
          But... then why didn't she tell
          us.

                         GEMMA
          She did.

                         SIMON
          Yes but -

                         GEMMA
          We knew she was suffering, there
          just wasn't anything that we
          could do to help.

A moment. Simon takes it in. Gemma watches him,
goes to him.

                         SIMON
          How did she get the pills?

                         LUKE
          In the note she talks about
          storing them up for a long time,
          pretending to take them and
          saving them. This sort of thing.
          It does happen.
                  (quietly, to Gemma)
          You never gave her -

                         GEMMA
          I'm sorry?

                         LUKE
          Something they asked me. Whether
          you might.

                         GEMMA
          I wouldn't.

EXT. FOSTER HOUSE. KITCHEN. DAY

Gemma comes into the kitchen. Puts a wrapped present down on the table. Simon comes in. They look at each other, apprehensive of what they're about to do...

INT. FOSTER HOUSE. LIVING ROOM. DAY

Tom appears in the doorway of the room, having been called.

> TOM
> What's happened?

He finds Simon and Gemma waiting for him. Gemma's holding the present.

> GEMMA
> Come and sit down.

He picks up on the tone, and does.

Gemma looks at Simon.

> SIMON
> Mate, you know Granny was very
> ill. She was hurting all the
> time.

> TOM
> Yeah.

> SIMON
> Well I'm afraid last night, she
> passed away. She died in her
> sleep.

Tom just looks at his dad. Eyes wide, about to cry.

> TOM
> She's...

> SIMON
> It was peaceful, she's not in
> pain any more.

Tom's trying really hard not to cry. This makes his
dad go too.

> SIMON (CONT'D)
> It's really sad. I'm sorry.

They hug tightly. Simon reaches for Gemma and the
three of them hug together.

EXT. FOSTER HOUSE. BACK GARDEN. NIGHT

An hour later. Through the glass doors at the back
of the house, in the kitchen, we see Tom at the
table. He's unwrapped the present and Gemma is
talking to him.

> GEMMA
> I thought it might help. Maybe
> you could give it a try? You
> think it's silly?

She looks outside to where Simon is standing.

> GEMMA (CONT'D)
> I'm just gonna go and see your
> dad.

She walks out to where Simon is standing in the
garden. The outside light is on, and they both seem
shattered. Simon just needs some air.

> GEMMA (CONT'D)
> When my mum and dad died, the
> woman who looked after me, Mary,
> she gave me a notebook to write
> down how I felt. Stupid.

                         SIMON
          Not at all.

Simon looks away, devastated, but holding it in.
So much in his head right now. Gemma looks at him -
despite everything, she wants to help.

She moves closer to him. Unsure what to do, driven
almost by instinct. He's also unsure. Both of them
desperate not to be dishonest right now.

They look at each other.

She takes his hand.

This compassion is enough to make him go. He cries.
They don't hug but he appreciates just this. Just
the hand.

Her phone rings.

                         GEMMA
          Sorry...

She moves away. It's Anwar.

She looks at it. Then back to her husband. After
everything she's set up, she still <u>loves</u> Simon.
Still <u>wants him</u>. And maybe the affair is really
over, and they can still save what they have.

She looks at Tom in the kitchen.

Then we're close on her as she walks round the side
of the house - away from them both, and answers the
phone, discreetly.

                    GEMMA (CONT'D)
                     (on phone)
          Hi. Anwar. Yeah... No.
                     (beat)
          I've changed my mind. We're
          alright.
                     (beat)
          We're going to try again.

CUT TO -

A moment later. Simon sits on the step. Gemma comes back to him. She touches his shoulder to let him know she's there, and he almost immediately collapses into her, hugging her, <u>crying</u>. She hugs him back. We get the sense it's not just Helen that's making him cry like this. Making him cling on to his <u>wife</u> now.

Tom comes out from the kitchen - very upset. He goes to his mum and dad, they hug him together, as he cries.

CUT TO BLACK.

EPISODE FOUR

INT. FOSTER HOUSE. HALLWAY. DAY

Gemma watches Tom and Simon in the kitchen as she stands in the hall.

>   TOM
>   Do we have any butter?!

>   SIMON
>   Mate I used it this morning, let
>   me have a look - Did you try the
>   fridge?
>   (shows Tom the butter)
>   Hey presto... the butter!

Gemma watches as Simon helps Tom make a sandwich. It should be a lovely family scene, but...

>   SIMON (CONT'D)
>   What did your last servant die
>   of? Cholera?

>   TOM
>   What's cholera?

>   SIMON
>   Cholera is like typhoid. 'What's
>   typhoid?'

Gemma looks on the wall. There's a framed black-and-white photo of the two of them. In love. As they should be.

>   SIMON (CONT'D)
>   Typhoid is what?

>   TOM
>   Typhoid...

>   SIMON
>   Typhoid, yeah, it's very serious.

>   TOM
>   Thai food?

                         SIMON
          Do you want lemon curd?

                          TOM
          I thought you said Typhoo.

                         SIMON
          Typhoo is a brand of tea. Thai
          food is quite nice.

Gemma enters the kitchen to see Simon eating toast
with lemon curd.

                         GEMMA
                        (laughs)
               Lemon curd!

INT. SURGERY. OFFICE. DAY

Close on Gemma - surrounded by sudden noise and
bustle. Harsh light. The surgery feels different.
Sharper. The waiting room packed. Ros sorts papers
next to Gemma. They talk quietly.

                          ROS
          He still hasn't admitted it?

                         GEMMA
          I doubt he ever will.

                          ROS
          And you haven't told him that you
          know.

                         GEMMA
          We're just moving on.

                          ROS
          With this massive secret sat
          underneath the relationship?!

Nick comes past, on the way to his office.

                    NICK
          Can I speak with you?

                    GEMMA
          Sure. Two minutes.

Nick goes off for a moment. Ros carries on, quietly -

                    ROS
          You're sure you're okay? It's
          just very sudden. After
          everything how can you simply
          take him back -

                    GEMMA
               (turns to her sharply)
          Because we have a child together,
          a life together, fourteen years
          under our belt so if there's any
          way of keeping all of that, I
          have to try.

A moment.

                    ROS
          And you honestly think that he's
          never going to see her again?

                    GEMMA
          I'm told when they broke up, it
          was very final. Nick...

                    NICK
          There's been a complaint -

Gemma turns and leaves the room, out of reception,
towards the corridor. Nick follows her, as do we.
As they go, Ros watches Gemma, concerned...

INT. SURGERY - CORRIDOR. DAY

- following Nick and Gemma walking towards Gemma's
room.

                    GEMMA
        Fantastic. Another one. The power
        of the internet. The latest
        yesterday was that I don't dress
        appropriately for a senior
        doctor. He was annoyed I wore
        a skirt.

                    NICK
        This one's not online. He came in
        and asked to speak to me
        personally.

                    GEMMA
        Who is it?

                    NICK
        He's requested anonymity for the
        time being. I'm speaking to the
        GMC -

                    GEMMA
        Why the GMC? Doctors get
        complaints all the time.

                    NICK
        Yes, but as you say there's also
        the comments on the website, and
        what happened with your mother-
        in-law -

                    GEMMA
        My mother-in-law took her own
        life, I don't know why everyone -

                    NICK
        It's as much about protecting you
        as anything. This new complaint.
        He talked about your personal
        life - your marriage.

Nick makes to leave.

> GEMMA
>
> Wait!

Gemma stops and looks right at him. This scares him slightly.

> GEMMA (CONT'D)
>
> You really can't tell me who this is?

> NICK
>
> Sorry.

> GEMMA
>
> Fine.

Nick goes off, Gemma goes into her room.

TITLE SEQUENCE

INT. SURGERY. GEMMA'S OFFICE. DAY

Gemma comes in, dumps her bag by the desk. Wakes up the computer, about to start work as she usually does, but then goes to the web browser - finding a website.

She glances at the clock - nearly 8.45 a.m., time for the first appointment. We come back to the computer, and see she's on CHECKMYGP.COM.

Under her name Doctor Gemma Foster, Parminster, are a list of mostly negative comments.

Rude attitude, poor behaviour / DON'T VISIT THIS GP! / just found this and so pleased other people are saying the same thing / she's really rude.

As Gemma reads them, she gets increasingly upset, then there's a knock on the door.

                    GEMMA
        Come in.

Gemma shuts the page down and turns to find Gordon.

                    GEMMA (CONT'D)
        Gordon! Long time no see!

                    GORDON
        You're not normally sarcastic.

                    GEMMA
        Sorry?

                    GORDON
             (upset)
        'Long time no see.' That's what
        I expect from the others.

                    GEMMA
        Sorry. Come on. Come in, sit
        down.
             (she takes a breath)
        Let's start again. What's wrong?

                    GORDON
        My shoes don't fit any more.

                    GEMMA
        Your shoes?

                    GORDON
        Yes.
             (beat)
        There must be something wrong
        with my feet.

Gemma stares at him for a moment.

INT. FOSTER HOUSE. KITCHEN. NIGHT

Gemma is cooking - but it's going wrong. There's curry in a saucepan, but the heat's on too high, and it's burning. Rice is in another pan, which is also on too high, and the water's spilling out on to the hobs.

Gemma's failing at this because her hands are shaking. The stress of it all. This should be simple!

She can't contain it much more...

Meanwhile Simon and Tom are sat at the island in the kitchen; talking, waiting for dinner.

>   TOM
>   Were you sick?

>   SIMON
>   I don't think you're picking up
>   on the right bit of the story.

>   TOM
>   Yeah Mum just said, when you and
>   her met you had a few too many.

>   SIMON
>   Me? No. Only one of us was tipsy
>   that night.

Gemma accidentally tips the sieve and the rice goes in the sink, as well as the water.

>   GEMMA
>   Shit.

>   SIMON
>   You okay?

>   GEMMA
>   Yeah, yeah.

                    SIMON
                (back to Tom)
You wanna be careful of alcohol.
Makes you say things you
shouldn't and stand on chairs.

Gemma fishes the rice out of the sink and puts it on
the plates. She's trying to stay breezy, casual...

                    TOM
        What do you mean?

                    SIMON
I think we need to tell him the
whole thing.

                    GEMMA
        Fine.

                    SIMON
It was your mum who'd drunk too
much that night. She stood on
this chair, looked around, and
then saw me, pointed, and said
I was the best-looking man in
the room.

                    TOM
                (laughs)
        You?

                    GEMMA
        (plating up the food)
Your dad was younger then, and
the room was not in a very nice
pub -

                    SIMON
It's true there wasn't much
competition.

                    TOM
        Then what?

> GEMMA
> They started to play ABBA, I
> tried to dance on the chair, but
> fell off. Your dad helped me up
> and said that maybe I should have
> some food. We got a curry. And
> that's how we met.

They move to the table and she hands them plates of
curry.

He looks at the food. Realises.

> SIMON
> Oh god! It's today. That's why
> you were talking about it. I'm an
> idiot.

> GEMMA
> Don't worry.

> SIMON
> I'm so sorry.

> TOM
> What have you done?

> SIMON
> Every year, since then, on the
> 26th of May, your mum makes a
> curry. And I get her a card.

> TOM
> But you forgot?
> (cheeky)
> Dad! You are rubbish sometimes.

> SIMON
> Yeah...

Simon looks a little forlorn.

> GEMMA
> Honestly. It's okay. You've been
> busy.

Simon slides his plate and table mat to one side.

Underneath is a card addressed to 'Dr Foster'. He takes it and gives it to her.

>   TOM
>   You liar!

She smiles, and takes it. She opens it. On the front of the card it says 'I REALLY FUCKING FANCY YOU.' Gemma's surprised.

>   TOM (CONT'D)
>   Can I see?

>   GEMMA
>   No.

She opens it. Inside he's written '*Seriously. All my love Simon xx*'

Simon and Gemma stare at each other.

>   GEMMA (CONT'D)
>   Thank you.

A spark flickering again between them... it's been a while.

Simon drinks from his glass of wine.

SHARP CUT TO -

INT. FOSTER HOUSE. BEDROOM. NIGHT

Simon and Gemma having great sex. Passionate, very loving - as if they haven't seen each other for a long time.

Kissing, intense, looking at each other, deeply, in the eyes.

CUT TO -

INT. FOSTER HOUSE. BEDROOM. NIGHT

Simon and Gemma curled up together. Content.

> GEMMA
> Everything's going wrong at work.

> SIMON
> Can I do anything?

> GEMMA
> Will you beat them up?

> SIMON
> Tuesday?

> GEMMA
> Perfect.

She smiles, cosy. Content. A buzz. Simon's phone is on the side table - a text. A moment.

Then he reaches across to read it. As he does we see Gemma trying to ignore it. Trying not to be suspicious.

> GEMMA (CONT'D)
> Everything alright?

> SIMON
> Yeah... just a problem.

He turns it off, comes back and cuddles her.

> GEMMA
> At work?

> SIMON
> Yeah. Yeah, it's fine.

She wants to be comforted, wants this to work. But there's so much doubt now... getting in the way...

CUT TO -

INT. SURGERY. RECEPTION/CORRIDOR. DAY

Gemma walks in. The usual horde of waiting patients.
She smiles to Julie, who smiles back, but a little
nervously, and glances behind her, looking for Nick.
As Gemma's about to go past the reception desk, Nick
appears from the back office, and stops her.

>   NICK
>   Can I have a word?

>   GEMMA
>   Sure.

CUT TO -

INT. SURGERY. MEETING ROOM. DAY

Gemma is in the room with Ros and Nick. Gemma goes
to sit in one of the three chairs.

>   NICK
>   Ah. Sorry... can you sit on this
>   side?

>   GEMMA
>   There's only three of us Nick,
>   I'm not sure it matters.

>   ROS
>   We should take it seriously.

Gemma looks at Ros. What's she doing...?

>   GEMMA
>   (beat)
>   Here?

>   NICK
>   Thank you.

Ros sits down next to Nick. A moment, when they all
face each other. Gemma's watching them, bemused,
impatient.

                    NICK (CONT'D)
You've got the outline details of
the complaint there that you
threatened to burn this man with
a lit cigarette. I'm assuming you
deny it?

                    GEMMA
Of course.

                    NICK
As you know, normally there are
internal procedures -

                    GEMMA
There are.

                    NICK
But I spoke to the GMC this
morning and they indicated we
that should consider the wider
context -

                    GEMMA
What's going on?

                    ROS
              (slightly sharp)
Gemma, if you let Nick finish
he'll explain.

Gemma's surprised. Waits for Nick to continue.

                    NICK
Obviously the online comments are
anonymous but we can't ignore
them entirely.

                    ROS
To an outside eye, they might
appear to have a pattern of
behaviour.

Gemma looks at Ros - surprised at this
interruption.

                    NICK
Also we've had the police here,
asking questions about the death
of your mother-in-law.

                    GEMMA
Who talked to them?

                    NICK
Luke, mostly, he was -

                    GEMMA
Mostly?

                    ROS
They asked about some things to
do with procedure as well.

                    GEMMA
Do you think that I've done
anything wrong?

                    NICK
There needs to be a process.

                    GEMMA
But you, personally, Nick. What
do you think?

                    NICK
Well...

                    ROS
You have been going through
a lot, lately. In your life.

                    GEMMA
How is that relevant?

                    ROS
You said we were talking
personally.

Ros and Gemma look at each other.

                    NICK
          The GMC have suggested we
          mutually agree you take a leave
          of absence, informally, while the
          complaint is investigated, and we
          look at the website.

                    ROS
          It would help as well, wouldn't
          it, to have some time off?

                    GEMMA
          No.
                    (to Nick)
          What if I don't agree?

                    NICK
          Then we'd have to look at a
          temporary suspension.

                    ROS
          And Gemma that would be so much
          worse -

                    GEMMA
                    (finally)
          When? When do you want me to stop
          then?

A glance between Ros and Nick.

                    NICK
          Immediately.

Gemma looks at them, disbelieving.

CUT TO -

INT. SURGERY. GEMMA'S ROOM. DAY

Gemma has a plastic bag, and is packing up personal
items from her desk. The family photo, a few pens,
other pictures, and items. She's furious, and very
upset. We're moving fast now. Dialogue and camera,
as we try to keep up with Gemma.

There's a knock on the door, then Ros enters.
As she does, Gemma finishes packing the bag, grabs
another plastic bag that's already full, as well
as her doctor's bag. It's all slightly too much
to carry.

>   ROS
>   You don't have to pack up. It's
>   only a couple of weeks.

>   GEMMA
>   Presumably while I'm away, you'll
>   become senior partner?

>   ROS
>   You think I _want_ you to go? We're
>   following professional advice.
>   It's not my fault. I helped you!
>   I told you everything about Kate
>   and the baby, I spoke to Simon,
>   did everything you asked.

Gemma exits her room and Ros follows.

INT. SURGERY. CORRIDOR/RECEPTION/BACK OFFICE. DAY

>   ROS (CONT'D)
>   Then suddenly you're giving him
>   another chance which is up to
>   you, but forgive me if I stop
>   trying to keep up and take a step
>   back, and act professionally.
>   Gemma -

They get to the end of the corridor and into reception - Ros stops talking.

Gemma heads through into the back office. Ros follows.

INT. SURGERY. BACK OFFICE. DAY

Gemma picks up a mug of hers, and her coat.

            ROS (CONT'D)
Whatever's going on, some time off would be a good idea wouldn't it?

            GEMMA
What did you tell the police?

            ROS
What?

            GEMMA
You said they asked about procedure?

            ROS
Yes.

            GEMMA
Something was said to them here to make them suspect me.

            ROS
Alright, well, they asked about our access to pills. And I told them what I found in your bag.

            GEMMA
Why were you looking in my bag?

            ROS
I wasn't looking, I needed some hand gel and your bag was there on the side and open, and when

                    I found it I saw that there was
                    a bottle of sleeping pills. With
                    some anti-sickness medication.
                    And then the next day your
                    mother-in-law did what she did -

                              GEMMA
                    They were Jack's.

                              ROS
                    So... Jack's?

                              GEMMA
                    He wanted to kill himself. I took
                    them off him.

A moment. Ros unsure whether to believe Gemma.

                              ROS
                         (beat)
                    You still have them then? In your
                    bag?

                              GEMMA
                    Yeah. Yes I have.

She puts her plastic bags down on the floor, opens
the doctor's bag, and goes to get them out... she
looks... but...

                         GEMMA (CONT'D)
                    I don't know where they've gone.
                    They were...

                              ROS
                         (pitying)
                    Gemma...

                              GEMMA
                         (still looking)
                    Don't!

She stops. Her stuff on the floor now - feeling
ridiculous.

> GEMMA (CONT'D)
> Don't make me feel stupid. They
> were there.

Ros kneels down and notices the two bottles on the
floor. She picks them up.

> ROS
> I'll tell the police I made
> a mistake. But take this time...

Gemma gathers up her bits and pieces, turns and
walks away down the corridor.

INT. SURGERY. RECEPTION DESK. DAY

Gemma, in her coat, and holding the bags, walks
through the waiting room to the exit. She keeps her
head up - going for the door, but then -

> GORDON
> They said I have to see someone
> else -

She keeps walking. Gordon follows.

> GEMMA
> Yes.

> GORDON
> The other doctors laugh at me.

> GEMMA
> They don't.

> GORDON
> They do. You know they do. What's
> happened?

> GEMMA
> Google me and you'll find out.

She leaves.

CUT TO -

EXT. CARLY'S HOUSE. FRONT DOOR. DAY

Close on Gemma knocking on the door, three times.
Hard. It opens and we see Daniel, much more clean-
cut than before.

> GEMMA
> Hi. That's what I thought -
> you're back with Carly?

> DANIEL
> Yeah - not drinking any more.

> GEMMA
> I was suspended today. Because of
> your complaint. You know why I
> came round that day. She needed
> help.

> DANIEL
> No, you found out what your
> husband was doing. You were
> angry, you took it out on me.

> GEMMA
> Look, I'm pleased if you've
> sorted yourself out.

> DANIEL
> Not if.

> GEMMA
> Carly's given you a second chance.

> DANIEL
> Yeah.

> GEMMA
> Give me a second chance too.

He looks at her.

> DANIEL
> Carly showed me the website.
> You're out of control.

                         GEMMA
            No. I've been through a lot in
            the last few weeks, but things
            are better now. Please. I can't
            stop working. I need it.

But in that moment, she, and we, know she looks
dishevelled, rushed, and quite mad. Carly appears.

                    GEMMA (CONT'D)
            Carly -

                        DANIEL
                     (to Carly)
            They've suspended her.

                         CARLY
                      (awkward)
            Okay, Dan, maybe you should tell
            them not to go forward with this.

                        DANIEL
                     (to Gemma)
            Have you admitted it? Said what
            happened?

                         GEMMA
            They'd start a disciplinary
            procedure and I can't -

Gemma stops, thinks, then gets out her wallet.

                    GEMMA (CONT'D)
            How much? How much to withdraw
            the complaint.

Gemma standing there, her wallet open. Carly's sort
of disgusted.

                         CARLY
            You really need to stop offering
            me money.

                         GEMMA
                  (caught. Guilty)
            Yeah. Yeah okay.

Carly stares at Gemma. That's the end of it.

Gemma turns and walks away. As she does, they close the door.

Gemma goes back to the car.

Gets in.

Sits in the seat. Feels very alone.

CUT TO -

EXT. HIGHBROOK SCHOOL FOOTBALL PITCH. DAY

A cloudy afternoon. Gemma walks from the car park to the edge of the football pitch. There are two games going on - various parents and teachers standing round, watching, cheering.

She doesn't know if she can do this - but then she sees Tom... playing football for his school under-twelves. He's a forward, and he's good - dribbles round the defender, shoots...the goalkeeper saves it. An 'oooh' both from the players, and the parents, stood at the side. Tom looking over to his dad, who's standing at the side of the pitch, but... Simon is talking intensely to Chris Parks - he missed it. Chris, however, spots it, points and they both turn and applaud.

This moment means they finish the conversation. Simon goes to watch Tom's game. Chris returns to a separate game, on the pitch next door, where Andrew is playing. Susie's there, and Kate. This afternoon her choice of a short skirt stands out.

Gemma walks round the edge of the field. To get to Simon she has to go past the Parks. As she approaches, Chris is now talking to the well-dressed senior teachers.

                    CHRIS
        Leave it with me.
            (he turns and sees Gemma)
        Hey! My favourite doctor!

                    SUSIE
        Hi!

They kiss. Chris looks over at Simon, who's
shouting encouragement to Tom.

                    CHRIS
        Your husband's taking this very
        seriously.

                    GEMMA
        Well he was never very good at
        sports himself, so it matters.

                    SUSIE
                (about Chris)
        He's just the same!

                    GEMMA
                (to Kate)
        How are you?

                    KATE
        Good thanks.

                    GEMMA
        You going out?

                    KATE
        What?

                    CHRIS
        She's talking about the skirt.
        I had the same question but she's
        twenty-something -

                    KATE
        Twenty-three.

                    CHRIS
    Yeah, well, apparently I don't
    get a vote.

                    KATE
    I like it.

                    CHRIS
    I'm sure the boys do as well.

                    KATE
    Shut up Dad!

                    CHRIS
            (to Andrew on the pitch)
    Get up! Least I could run in a
    straight line! Get up! That's
    better!

Chris applauds as Andrew gets to his feet. Kate
turns to watch the game with her dad, leaving Gemma
talking to Susie, more quietly now, confidentially.

                    SUSIE
    I've been meaning to say, it is
    ridiculous that we haven't all
    got together, the four of us.
    It's what happens when you leave
    it to the men.

                    GEMMA
    Sounds fun.

                    SUSIE
            (winks)
    I'll email you.

                    GEMMA
    Bye.

Gemma makes her way over to Simon, who's
encouraging Tom.

She reaches him. He can't believe she's here.

                    SIMON
         I thought you were at work?

                    GEMMA
         I wanted to see our son.

He takes her hand, seemingly pleased she's here.
Tom looks over. Sees his mum. Is embarrassed to
wave, but smiles slightly, really pleased she's
here.

Then he gets on with the game.

Simon and Gemma watch together.

                    SIMON
         Come on Tom!

CUT TO -

EXT. HIGHBROOK SCHOOL. CAR PARK. DAY

Simon and Gemma walk back to their cars.

                    GEMMA
         Simon the... the partners at work
         have asked me to take some time
         off. Pending an investigation.

                    SIMON
         You mean -

                    GEMMA
         Suspended me, effectively-

                    SIMON
         Why?

                    GEMMA
         There's been a formal complaint
         that I went to the home of a
         patient and assaulted him.

Gemma glances as the Parks' car drives past.

> SIMON
> Assaulted him? You? Ros – she's a
> partner. Can't she –

> GEMMA
> ...there's been the stuff on the
> internet, and the police have
> been round asking questions about
> your mum. Apparently that 'paints
> a picture'.
> (she's upset)
> Sorry...

Simon suddenly hugs her. She's surprised at first,
but this is what he was good at. Knowing what she
needs, steadying her, and for the first time in the
series, she fully responds.

> SIMON
> (quietly)
> It's alright.

She hugs him back, invests in him, and releases how
she's feeling. Enjoying the comfort, the security.
this is what she missed.

> GEMMA
> (quietly)
> Thank you. Thank you.

The man she married - knowing it's him. Simon, the
father of her child, the man she saw at the end of
the aisle on her wedding day - then suddenly -

Two buzzes - which make him jump slightly - she
notices, as do we, in close up, his hands on her
tense. But he keeps hugging. It's a really strange
way to react.

She pulls back slightly.

> GEMMA (CONT'D)
> That was you.

                    SIMON
          Yeah.

He lets go.

                SIMON (CONT'D)
          Right sorry. I didn't want to...

He gets out his phone and looks at it.

                    GEMMA
          Who is it?

                    SIMON
          Work.

                    GEMMA
          Okay.

She looks at him. He puts the phone away.

                GEMMA (CONT'D)
          Are you not going to reply?

Another moment. She looks at him. An implication
now.

                GEMMA (CONT'D)
          I don't mind if you want to.

                    SIMON
          What?
                    (beat)
          What's going on?

                    GEMMA
          When you got the text, your...
          your body went tense.

                    SIMON
          I was surprised. That's what
          people do when they're surprised.

                    GEMMA
          Okay. Honestly. You can reply.

He rolls his eyes, a distinctive, frustrated,
gesture.

                    SIMON
        You still... you think I'm lying?
        You still don't trust me?
            (beat)
        Look do you want to see the text?
           (he gets his phone out)
        Time, date, details of the
        supplies for the foundations.
   (he holds out the phone, slightly aggressive)
        Here. Look.

She wants to take it and check. But wants to trust
him too.

He holds it out - serious. Offering it. She could
just have a look... but...

                    GEMMA
        No. It's fine.

Tom comes running out from the sports centre, over
to them.

              GEMMA (CONT'D)
        Well done!

                    TOM
        We lost.

                    SIMON
        Only just and not because of you.

They turn to their cars, to leave.

              SIMON (CONT'D)
        Right. Two cars. Who are you
        going to go with?

                    TOM
           (beat)
        No offence Mum but you don't know
        much about football and me and
        Dad have to talk.

Simon gets another text. Reads it. Gemma tries to
ignore it, continue to enjoy the moment instead.

> GEMMA
> Where to? Somewhere to celebrate?

> TOM
> Celebrate what?

> GEMMA
> You of course! Pizza?

> TOM
> (smiles)
> Yeah, actually that would be
> really good.

Tom and Gemma both look over to Simon, who's now
staring down at his phone - reading the text
properly.

> GEMMA
> (to Simon)
> Simon? Pizza?

> SIMON
> Argh - really sorry. Crisis.

> TOM
> What?

> SIMON
> The thing with the supplies. We
> need to talk about options, today
> - sorry. Boring. Be a couple of
> hours. I'll join you later.
> (to Tom)
> Pizza is a great idea. You can
> teach Mum about the offside rule!

> TOM
> Well why can't you come now, and
> sort out your problem later?

>   SIMON
>   Sorry mate. It just doesn't work.
>   I'll be around tonight and we can
>   catch up then, yeah?

Gemma nods. Uncertain.

Simon gets in his car, starts the engine, waves,
and drives off.

Tom looks over at his mum. She's just standing
there. Staring at Simon's car.

>   TOM
>   You already know the offside
>   rule, don't you?

>   GEMMA
>   Yeah.

She's being weird, distracted. Tom's worried, but
tries not to show it.

>   TOM
>   Is there anything you don't know?

She watches Simon's car drive away.

>   GEMMA
>   Quite a lot.

CUT TO -

INT. GEMMA'S CAR. DAY

Gemma's driving. Tom's in the passenger seat.
They're waiting at some lights. Tom looks ahead at
Simon's car.

He waves. Trying to get his dad's attention. Simon
eventually notices, and waves back.

Simon eventually pulls away.

                        TOM
         He works really hard doesn't he?

The lights change. Simon's car turns left. Gemma's right, and she drives away from him.

Close on Gemma. She doesn't want to do this. But she has no choice. She doesn't trust him at all. She suddenly swings the car round - a U-turn in the road.

                  TOM (CONT'D)
    Mum!

She speeds up, dodging in and out of traffic to keep up with Simon's car. Following it, at a distance.

                  TOM (CONT'D)
       You're going the wrong way!

CUT TO -

EXT. SIMON'S OFFICES. DAY

We see Simon's car parked outside his office. We then pan across to find, round the corner, where Simon couldn't see it, Gemma's car.

INT. GEMMA'S CAR. DAY

                GEMMA
     I need five minutes with your dad.

                TOM
    You said we were having pizza!

                GEMMA
    Do your homework.

                TOM
    I want to come in!

                        GEMMA
        You can't.

She gets out and slams the door, leaving Tom
inside, fuming.

CUT TO -

INT. SIMON'S OFFICES. RECEPTION. DAY

Becky stands, silhouetted against the large window
in her office. She's thinking, anxious. She turns.
To see Gemma.

                        GEMMA
        Shit...

                        BECKY
        What?

                        GEMMA
        Your face.

                        BECKY
        I didn't know you were coming
        over. They normally buzz up -

                        GEMMA
        I told them that I wanted to
        surprise my husband. I'm not
        having a good day.

        Is he in there?

                        BECKY
        He's... on the phone. Gemma are
        you -

                        GEMMA
        You're holding something back.
        I mean you've been doing that for
        a long time, but something's
        changed.

>   (beat)
>   You've suddenly become really bad
>   at lying.

                              BECKY
               I... don't know what you're
               talking about.

                              GEMMA
               Does my husband bully you? Not
               physically but he patronises you.
               I suppose that's why men want
               female assistants. So they can
               push at least one woman around.
                         (beat)
               You've been covering for him for
               years.

                              BECKY
                    (trying to hold the line)
               I don't cover.

                              GEMMA
               I'd like to believe that.

                              BECKY
               You should.

                              GEMMA
               But your face.

                              BECKY
               If you take a seat, when he's off
               the phone, I'll let him know that
               you're here.

                              GEMMA
               I wanted his support. I've
               basically just lost my job, but
               from the expression on your face,
               I think he's off having sex with
               Kate Parks again.

Becky looks at her.

                    GEMMA (CONT'D)
        You split with your husband. So
        you can imagine something of what
        I'm feeling.
                    (beat)
        I've known for a while.

A moment. Becky's compassionate for Gemma. She
hates this.

                    BECKY
        They have no idea.

                    GEMMA
        They will now. I assume it's not
        locked.

Gemma heads straight to the office door - opens it -

INT. SIMON'S OFFICES. PRIVATE OFFICE. DAY

- bursts into the room, and there's no one there.

She walks in. The office is a mess. Worse than when
she was last here. She looks round. Then walks back
out to Becky's office - angry.

INT. SIMON'S OFFICES. BECKY'S OFFICE. DAY

Becky's staring at her, from her desk.

                    GEMMA (CONT'D)
        Where is he? His car's outside.

Becky stares at her.

                    GEMMA (CONT'D)
        Well?

Still staring.

                        GEMMA (CONT'D)
          What?

                        BECKY
          He was always worried that
          someone might follow him, or see
          him. They had a system. You can
          get out from the back of the
          building...

Becky goes to the window again. Looks out.

Gemma understands she's supposed to go too.

They look down.

Outside, is a park. It's secluded, but from above
you can see in. On a bench are Simon and Kate
holding hands, talking intensely.

Simon leans over and kisses her, has her face in
his hands. They're really in love. Gemma steps back
from the window.

                        BECKY (CONT'D)
          They're back together. He'll
          never leave her.
                        (beat)
          I kept telling him to stop.
          I hate what he's doing.

Gemma looks at them again. Now Kate's laughing at
his joke - he's flirting, no sign of the betrayal
he's currently making.

A moment, Gemma almost losing it - then sucks it
up, turns -

                        GEMMA
          You went on holiday with them.

                        BECKY
          He said he needed me, that they'd
          be working...

                    GEMMA
          Where did you go?

                    BECKY
          Kate's dad has a house in France.
          Said she could use it for
          friends.

                    GEMMA
          Her dad wasn't there?

                    BECKY
          No. They don't know about Simon.
          They'd kill him if he did.

                    GEMMA
                    (beat)
          Show me pictures.

                    BECKY
          What...?

                    GEMMA
          Of the holiday. On your phone.
          You, him, her. Neil, Anna. I want
          to see.

                    BECKY
          Why would you want to see?

                    GEMMA
          I thought that I had a chance to
          sort this out, but clearly I'm
          delusional.

Gemma stares at her. Becky reaches to her phone.
Looks through then gives it to Gemma.

Gemma flicks through photos. More than she saw
before. The six of them on holiday. Many of Simon
and Kate together.

One of Becky posing outside the front door - a
little sign of the name of the house 'La Pierre
Blanche'.

Gemma looks out the window again, at the two of
them, together. In love. Kate laughing, Simon
flirting. She wonders if they're laughing about her.
Laughing at her?

>   BECKY
> Not that it matters but you're
> right. He can be horrible.
> Especially when he's stressed.

Gemma gives her back the phone.

>   GEMMA
> Can you email these to me?

>   BECKY
> I... If you want.

>   GEMMA
> And don't tell him I know.

>   BECKY
> Why not?

>   GEMMA
> I want to do it myself. But not
> now.

>   TOM
> Do what?

Tom is standing in the doorway. Gemma looks at him.

>   GEMMA
>   (quietly)
> I told you to stay in the car.

>   TOM
> Where's Dad?

Gemma walks to the window. Looks out. Becky's not
sure what to do.

>   TOM (CONT'D)
> Mum what's wrong with you? You're
> so weird at the moment.

                    (beat)
          Mum! Why are you such a mad
          bitch? It's scary.

Gemma turns and looks at her son - who for the first
time seems more like a teenager. More like a small
version of Simon. Something in her changes - and
she's made a decision.

                    GEMMA
          Your dad's gone out for a couple
          of minutes. You know Becky, don't
          you? Becky could you text Simon,
          tell him that his son's waiting
          in his office and needs some pizza
          before going home? And then when
          he gets back could you explain
          that I've forgotten that I need
          to go to a conference tonight.
          I need to leave immediately. Be
          gone a few days.

                    TOM
          What?

                    GEMMA
          Your dad'll look after you. You
          can talk about football.

                    TOM
          A conference? It's always work!

                    GEMMA
                    (to Becky)
          Yes?

                    BECKY
          Okay.

                    GEMMA
                    (leaving)
          Good. Bye then. Bye.

                              TOM
                            (upset)
                  Mum!

Gemma can't ignore him. She swings back round -
she's all over the place now. Edgy, smiling, almost
manic, talking fast -

                          GEMMA
                You're too clever! Alright. There
                is no conference. That's a lie
                Becky and I are gonna tell your
                dad, because I can't deal with
                everything at the moment so I
                need to go away for a couple of
                days. And I don't want him to
                worry so I'm making an excuse.
                          (beat)
                Now you have a choice. You can
                tell Dad the truth, or you can
                join me and Becky and tell him
                it's a conference.
                          (beat)
                It's up to you.

He looks at them both, then rolls his eyes.

                     GEMMA (CONT'D)
                Don't do that. Your dad does
                that.

                          TOM
                What d'you mean, you can't deal
                with everything?

                          GEMMA
                Life's hard sometimes.

He looks at her. Doesn't know what to say...

                          TOM
                How long are you gone for?

                         GEMMA
          Couple of days.

                          TOM
                (a moment. Then:)
          Okay.

                         GEMMA
                (she kisses him)
          Good boy. See you soon.

She turns and quickly leaves.

Tom's left standing in the middle of the room.
Becky by her desk, awkward.

CUT TO -

EXT. PARMINSTER STREET. DAY

Gemma drives, fast, through the town.

EXT. GEMMA'S CAR. MOTORWAY. DAY

She's driving far, far away. Her phone on the
passenger seat is flashing -

Simon's calling.

She looks at it - his face appearing as he calls.
Ignores it. Keeps driving.

EXT. SEAFRONT. JETTY. DAY

Close on rippling sea water, reflecting a fresh,
clear, afternoon sky. Reflected in the water we can
see a moon - out too early in the day. Under the
surface we can occasionally make out fish, swimming
around.

Suddenly with a splash the surface of the water is broken, by a knife, stabbing - the fish scatter.

                              JACK
          Shit.

Now we see it's Jack, who's attempting to stab the fish with a knife, strapped to the end of a broom handle. He's quite different to how we last saw him. A little thinner, more tanned, maybe healthier. And has swapped his old suit for jeans and a jumper. His jeans rolled up, he's sitting on an old wooden jetty, the water lapping at his feet. It's a beautiful British, empty beach. It's a crisp sunny day - and yes - weirdly - there's the moon.

Then Jack hears a sound. An engine roars down the path. He turns, recognising the car, gets up and heads towards it.

Gemma gets out of the car. Hassled, drained. She takes her bag from the back seat, locks the car, then turns and sees Jack, as he walks up to her -

                    JACK (CONT'D)
                 (re: his spear)
          I'm fishing.
                 (beat)
          Saw it in a film. Doesn't work.
                 (beat)
          You okay?

INT. MARY'S HOUSE. LIVING AREA. DAY

An old wooden door - sunlight pouring in through the cracks.

Jack enters the house, followed by Gemma.

The room they're coming in to is an old kitchen. Large flagstones on the floor. Old range. Wood and

stone, rather than plastic. On one wall, a huge
open fireplace. A doorway leads to the living room.
Stairs in one corner.

                    JACK
                  (shouts)
          Mary! Visitor!

As Gemma puts her bag on a chair, down the stairs
comes Mary, a woman in her sixties. Tough,
Methodist, slightly stern, with a shock of black
hair.

                    MARY
          My husband used to shout at me.
          Now he's dead. Those two things
          might not be connected Jack, but
          are you sure you wanna take the
          risk?
                  (she sees Gemma)
          Oh.

                    GEMMA
          Hi.

She goes and hugs Gemma. Gemma doesn't really
respond.

                    MARY
          Jack make some tea.
                  (to Gemma)
          What's happened? You look upset.
          Where's Tom?

                    GEMMA
          With Simon.
                  (to Jack)
          Did you tell her?

                    JACK
          No.

                    MARY
          What? What's going on?

                    GEMMA
          Can I stay?

                    MARY
          I've got no clean towels.
                    (beat)
          I'll find some. Course. You can
          stay as long as you like. Sit
          down.

Gemma's phone rings. 'Simon.' She looks at it for
a moment, worried, anxious.

                    GEMMA
          I thought you didn't have mobile
          reception.

                    MARY
          Oh, they put a mast up. I wrote
          a letter, it made no difference.

                    GEMMA
          He cheated on me.

Gemma stares at the phone, anxious. Mary hears
this. Then -

                    MARY
          Alright.
                    (she turns to Jack)
          Where's that tea?

Mary gently takes the phone off Gemma, hangs up,
then switches it off.

                    MARY (CONT'D)
          Problem solved.

CUT TO -

INT. MARY'S HOUSE. KITCHEN. EVENING

It's still light, but turning into the evening.
Mary's cooking - efficiently and brusquely. Gemma
looks out the window at the sea.

>   GEMMA
>   Thanks for taking Jack in.

>   MARY
>   He's a pain in the neck but like
>   you said, he's useful round the
>   house.

>   GEMMA
>   Sorry he's so rude.

>   MARY
>   It's the right thing to do. So it
>   must be done.
>   (beat)
>   Stuck in the past, that's been
>   his problem.

>   GEMMA
>   He was with David a long time.

>   MARY
>   I know. But when you lose someone
>   like that, when you're going
>   through hell, you've got to keep
>   going.

She continues to cook.

>   GEMMA
>   Can I help?

>   MARY
>   No thank you.

>   GEMMA
>   (beat)
>   Don't suppose you have any wine?

                           MARY

What do you think? And Jack
shouldn't so don't you dare buy
it. You can have another cup of
tea or there's some squash.

Gemma looks out the window again, at the sea. She's
thinking. Still upset.

                       MARY (CONT'D)

Was it advice you wanted? Is that
why you're here?

                       GEMMA

No.

                       MARY

You'd never be told before.

                       GEMMA

I just needed to get away.

                       MARY

I see.

A moment. Mary's keen to say something.

                       MARY (CONT'D)

You'll want to get back for Tom
soon, though, of course.
                  (beat)
You'll wanna get back for him.

Gemma looks out the window once more, and thinks.
But doesn't answer.

Mary glances over at her for a second. A little
concerned but she's not going to make a big thing
over it.

                       GEMMA

I might just... get some air.

                       MARY

Dinner's twenty minutes.

Gemma goes outside.

EXT. MARY'S HOUSE. EVENING

Gemma comes out and looks at the sea. The light just starting to fade. She sits on a low wall, near the house. She puts a shawl around her shoulders.

The sea looks windswept - lonely, as the light fades. Threatening and inviting at the same time.

Gemma takes out her switched-off phone. Looks at it. Looks out at the sea. Then switches the phone back on.

She looks at Becky's email, and opens the photos.

Simon and Kate together. Neil and Anna. All having fun. Seemingly care-free.

That photo again of Becky next to the sign for the house 'La Pierre Blanche'. We notice the name here now, as Gemma does. She zooms in on it - as she realises. Now it makes sense...

Jack appears, with a fabric bag-for-life, having walked to get supplies. He approaches her.

>   JACK
>   You're addicted to those things.
>   Same as David, he was never off
>   his iPad.

Gemma shows him the phone. He puts his bag down and takes it, looks at the pictures.

>   JACK (CONT'D)
>   How did you get these?

>   GEMMA
>   His assistant.

Jack sits down on the wall next to Gemma, notices her looking at the sea.

>   JACK
>   You grew up around here.

GEMMA

Yeah. Mary helped us out. Picked
me up from school. When my mum
and dad died, she was all I had.

JACK

What happened to your parents?
She wouldn't say.

GEMMA

Car accident. When I was sixteen.
I stayed with Mary for a year,
but she... I was bored of people
feeling sorry for me, so I went
to London. A levels, medical
school, met Simon, moved, started
a new life, had a child, then we
got the house...
                (beat)
I love that house.

A moment.

GEMMA (CONT'D)

How's this working out for you?

JACK

Off the booze, health's improved,
and she's got someone to do the
gardening.

GEMMA

So you'll stay a bit longer then?

JACK

Forever.
                (beat)
But not with her. Moving on
Gemma. I can recommend it. Get
Tom on a train up here. You don't
need to stay in that place.

                    GEMMA
Why should Simon win?

                    JACK
Who cares about winning?
  (he gives her back the phone)
Be happy.

INT. MARY'S HOUSE. NIGHT

Gemma, Jack, and Mary are sat around the table
having had dinner. We start in the middle of their
conversation -

                    MARY
I understand all that but you
made a commitment.

                    JACK
She can't stay there. Come on!

                    MARY
Better or worse.

                    JACK
Rubbish!
                (to Gemma)
You need to leave.

                    GEMMA
But it's my town. I've got
friends.

                    JACK
It's Simon's town, and if you're
talking about friends, you could
do a lot better.

                    GEMMA
It's not fair.

                    MARY
     'Fair'! Gemma not to be mean but
     that's the sort of thing you were
     saying when you were a little
     girl. Life isn't fair. It's how
     you deal with it.

A moment.

                    GEMMA
     I was thinking in the car, what if
     I never came back? Women do that
     sometimes. Tom'd be upset but he'd
     have his dad, friends. Maybe it'd
     all work out. Who would actually
     miss me if I... vanished?

                    MARY
     You shouldn't say things like
     that. You know what it's like to
     lose a parent.

                    GEMMA
     I coped. And he would too.

                    JACK
     What do you mean 'vanish'?

A look between them. The implication of what that
means.

                    GEMMA
     You thought about it. Those
     pills.

                    JACK
                  (beat)
     The one person in my life that
     ever loved me, had gone forever.
     It's completely different.

                    GEMMA
     I agree.

                    JACK
Right.

                    GEMMA
What's happened to me is worse.

                    MARY
Now you're being / ridiculous -

                    JACK
David died in pain, coughing up
liquid, desperate. There was
nothing I could do -

                    GEMMA
At least the time you had
together was real.

                    MARY
You can't compare the two -

                    GEMMA
It isn't like Simon's just gone.
He never existed. I mean every
moment that we spent together was
false, because he was never / the
person that I thought he was.

                    MARY
Gemma, he's made a mistake, that
doesn't mean he's a / completely
different person.

                    GEMMA
        (ignoring Mary, to Jack)
And my parents died, also in
pain, and I don't know exactly
what happened in the crash but
I bet it wasn't instant like
everyone said - so I know what
it's like to be left behind.
But I'm really sorry Jack,
I loved David too, but what's

happened to me is so much harder
to deal with, I promise you.

Jack stands. Angry. Upset.

                    JACK
                 (quietly)
        I'm going to bed.

He leaves.

                    MARY
        You need to be careful when
        you're upset.

Mary gets up from the table and collects the plates
together.

                MARY (CONT'D)
        You've always known.

                    GEMMA
        What?

                    MARY
             (clearing the plates)
        Exactly how to hurt people.

She takes the plates through to the kitchen.
Gemma's left at the table, alone. Upset.

                    GEMMA
                 (quietly)
        Yeah.

The sound of the sea, very faintly.

CUT TO -

INT. MARY'S HOUSE. SPARE ROOM. NIGHT

Gemma can't sleep. Yet again. She gets out of bed and looks out the window at the boats. She puts on her trousers.

CUT TO -

INT. MARY'S HOUSE. LIVING ROOM. NIGHT

Gemma comes down the stairs. She goes to the mantelpiece where, amongst other photos of Mary's life, and relatives, there's a photo of Gemma as a girl - with her parents.

Then she finds that Mary's also got a small version of the black-and-white picture of her and Simon, that we saw earlier. Close-up. Smiling.

The sound of the sea.

She's suffering. Doesn't know what to do. Nowhere to turn.

EXT. MARY'S HOUSE. NIGHT

Gemma walks out of the house and towards the sea. The moon is full - lighting the beach.

She's barefoot.

EXT. BEACH. NIGHT

Gemma walking along the beach. Looks out to the sea.

Her phone rings again. Even now, at 2 a.m. She looks at it. It's Simon. She answers it.

                    GEMMA
          Hi.

                    SIMON (V.O.)
              (surprised she's answered)
          ...Hi! Where are you?

                    GEMMA
          In a hotel. The conference.
          Didn't Becky say?

                    SIMON (V.O.)
          But you just... left. I've been
          trying to call.

                    GEMMA
          I'll be back in a couple of days.

                    SIMON (V.O.)
          You just forgot about it?

                    GEMMA
          Things've been difficult...
          recently, so -
                    (beat)
          Yeah I forgot.

Gemma's walking now. Her conversation with Simon
continuing...

                    SIMON (V.O.)
          You asked about that text. I
          thought you might've...

                    GEMMA
          What?

                    SIMON (V.O.)
          ...been upset.

                    GEMMA
                    (beat)
          How are you?

                    SIMON (V.O.)
          I couldn't sleep. I was worried.

A moment. Tears pouring down Gemma's face, but she
pretends on the phone that she's fine.

                         GEMMA
          Any news?

                    SIMON (V.O.)
          What? News?

                         GEMMA
          Anything you want to tell me?

                    SIMON (V.O.)
          No.

Gemma's crying now, really sobbing, but manages to
make what Simon's hearing sound normal.

                    SIMON (CONT'D)(V.O.)
          Okay. Well... look... I'll call
          you tomorrow.

                         GEMMA
          Bye then.

                    SIMON (V.O.)
          Bye.

She then really <u>screams</u>! Really <u>cries</u> - unlike
anything we've seen before. She <u>hates</u> herself. This
is her fault, and yes, the world's unfair!

So why should she keep struggling. She drops the
phone on the beach, and then, still wearing her
clothes, she walks into the water.

She lets it hit her, cold at night, and she gulps,
loses her breath. But she keeps going, starts to
swim out...

EXT. THE SEA. NIGHT

We're close on Gemma. Swimming out. Swimming fast.
Too fast.

Close on her face, gulping in some water with the
air. Frantic.

She's getting further away from the coast and out
into the open sea.

Further and further. She's not turning round, or
stopping. Just swimming. Determined.

Eventually, a long way from the beach, she stops
and looks up. She's distraught. At a loss.
Exhausted.

She's crying. Sobbing.

But why keep fighting?

She lets herself sink, the water covering her
face...

Sinking...

Under the water now...

Sinking down... deeper and deeper.

TO BLACK.

EXT. MARY'S HOUSE. NIGHT

The moon in the night sky.

Jack emerges from the front door and puts his coat
on. He looks around, worried.

Jack walks past Gemma's car. Looks inside for her.

>   JACK
>   (calls)
>   Gemma! Gemma!

EXT. BEACH. NIGHT

Jack walks along the beach.

Then he notices something on the sand. It's Gemma's phone. He reaches down. Picks it up.

>   JACK
>   Shit...

He looks around. But she's nowhere to be seen.

>   JACK (CONT'D)
>   (calls)
>   Gemma!

He puts the phone to his ear but then sees a figure, further up the beach, at the edge of the water – it's Gemma. Her hair is soaked, plastered across her face. Her clothes soaked as well, dark. She is walking slowly back on to the beach - but somehow now she's different. The image is slightly disturbing.

She's been transformed in some way. She's darker, elemental. There's a clarity in her look - hard, behind the eyes.

>   JACK (CONT'D)
>   What are you doing? It's
>   freezing!

>   GEMMA
>   (clear, factual)
>   I wanted to drown.

Jack looks at her for a moment, slightly stunned.

>   JACK
>   I told you, that's not -

>   GEMMA
>   But then I thought... no.

He looks at her. For the first time he can't work out what she's thinking.

                          JACK
           What do you mean?

A moment.

                    JACK (CONT'D)
          (takes off his coat to give to her)
           Best put this on.

But Gemma starts to walk up the beach, fast, away
from him.

                    JACK (CONT'D)
           Gemma, stop. Wait! Where are you
           going?

                          GEMMA
                      (determined)
           Home.

Gemma starts to walk back towards the house,
determined. Jack follows.

CUT TO -

EXT. MARY'S HOUSE. DAY

Very early morning. Gemma comes out of the house,
now showered and re-dressed, and gets in her car.
She's still the steely, hard-eyed person that came
out of the sea. No softness left. No smiling. Mary
follows her out, with Jack.

They watch as she starts the engine and drives away
at speed.

EXT. HIGHBROOK SCHOOL. DAY

Tom comes out of school, playing with his mates, to find Gemma standing waiting for him.

She stands out amongst the other parents - tough, iconic now. Not smiling. As he comes across the playground towards her, Becky approaches Gemma.

> BECKY
> I thought you were away? Simon asked me to pick up Tom.

> GEMMA
> I need your help.

> BECKY
> What do you mean?

She looks at Gemma, unsure of her.

> GEMMA
> (hard, firm)
> You owe it to me.

Tom arrives, smiling a little. Nervous.

> TOM
> You're back.

Gemma looks at Becky.

INT. FOSTER HOUSE. KITCHEN. DAY

Gemma is dressed up to go out. Looking in the mirror, putting her make-up on. It's all considered now. Cold.

Simon enters. As soon as he does, she's pretending normality again, but now it seems slightly... fraught... unhinged...

                    SIMON
          Hey! I saw your car... You said
          two days...

                    GEMMA
          I changed my mind. I didn't want
          to be away. I'm all over the
          place at the moment. Can you
          tell?

                    SIMON
          That's why I was worried.

                    GEMMA
          Are you ready?

                    SIMON
          What for?

                    GEMMA
          Dinner, we're due at half seven.

                    SIMON
          What? Who with?

                    GEMMA
          (rolls her eyes, playing humorous)
          Go and get a shirt on.

Simon hesitates.

                    SIMON
          It's mad living with you
          sometimes.

As soon as he's out of the room, Gemma's smile
disappears.

CUT TO -

INT. FOSTER HOUSE. HALLWAY. DAY

Three minutes later, Simon rushes down the stairs, and into the hall, doing up his sleeve buttons. He heads into the kitchen.

> SIMON
> What about Tom, who's -

He gets into the kitchen, and Becky is there with her daughter Isobel, and Tom. Gemma's made her a cup of tea.

> GEMMA
> Becky's looking after Tom
> tonight.

Simon's looking at both of them. Very much thrown. Worried. This is not an alliance he wants. What does Gemma know?

> BECKY
> Gemma called, said she was coming
> back, and wanted to keep this
> dinner, but the short notice
> meant she didn't have childcare
> so I offered.

A moment. Simon slightly bewildered.

CUT TO -

INT. GEMMA'S CAR. DAY

Gemma's driving. Simon's in the passenger seat.

> SIMON
> You really won't tell me where
> we're going?

> GEMMA
> (smiling)
> You used to be into surprises.

A moment.

                    SIMON
     Fine.
                 (beat)
     Do I like these people?

Close on Gemma.

                    GEMMA
     You love them.

CUT TO -

EXT. PARKS HOUSE. DRIVEWAY. DAY

Gemma pulls into the driveway.

INT. GEMMA'S CAR. DAY

                GEMMA (CONT'D)
                 (to Simon)
     It's the Parks. They invited us
     yesterday, at the football.

                    SIMON
     Gemma... I can't.

                    GEMMA
     What?
                 (beat)
     Why not?

She gets out and walks towards the house.

Simon looks at her go, and has no choice but to
follow.

CUT TO -

EXT. PARKS HOUSE. FRONT DOOR. DAY

Gemma rings the bell. Simon arrives behind her, noticing Kate's car in the drive.

Susie comes to the door and opens it. When she does, she looks surprised.

> SUSIE
> Oh... Hi!

> GEMMA
> Hi!

Gemma's smile fades as she sees the look on Susie's face.

> GEMMA (CONT'D)
> What?

> SUSIE
> Gemma -

> GEMMA
> Oh god. What's going on?
> (beat)
> You're not expecting us...

Chris appears behind Susie.

> CHRIS
> Hello Fosters! What's this?
> You're...

> SUSIE
> I think you're a week early.

> GEMMA
> Really? But this is the...
> I thought - you said Thursday in
> your email...

> SUSIE
> I meant next week. Oh, I'm so
> sorry... it's my mistake!

>   GEMMA
>   (playing awkward)
>   Oh!

>   CHRIS
>   Come in anyway!

>   SIMON
>   No, it's fine, we'll head back,
>   we're tired actually -

>   CHRIS
>   No! Nonsense! We can rustle up
>   something, you're here now.
>   That'll be alright won't it,
>   Susie?

>   SUSIE
>   Absolutely, for these two we will
>   make it work, come on! Come in!

>   GEMMA
>   (entering)
>   Are you sure?

>   SUSIE
>   Positive.

>   SIMON
>   Honestly I think we should go.

>   CHRIS
>   We've got the kids in tonight so
>   there'll be plenty of food, it'll
>   be fun!

>   SIMON
>   I'm really not -

>   CHRIS
>   Come on!

Gemma makes her way in. Simon hangs back - Chris
looks at him. Beams, warmly and they go inside.

CUT TO -

INT. PARKS HOUSE. DINING ROOM. NIGHT

A lengthy one-shot moving round the table. They are all talking, but we can't hear. Instead we hear music, the raw tension of the subtext of this dinner.

The camera moves around the table and we see, in order - Andrew, who's bored, sat next to Chris, holding court, oblivious, and passing the salad to Simon, who is having the worst evening of his life -

Opposite Simon is Kate, shooting daggers at him, then Susie talking to Gemma, who's smiling, listening politely, taking all of this in...

Closer on Gemma.

We can see she's got a plan. She's going to detonate it all.

CUT TO BLACK.

EPISODE FIVE

INT. PARKS HOUSE. HALLWAY. EVENING

Gemma and Simon enter the house. Susie takes
Gemma's coat – Chris now in full flow –

>   CHRIS
> Yes! Finished this six months
> ago, I'll give you the grand
> tour. Susie finds it embarrassing
> but I can't help it! I'm so
> proud!

>   SUSIE
> Do tell him to shut up if you
> need to.

>   CHRIS
> You'll find this really
> interesting.

>   SUSIE
> I'm just gonna nip in the
> kitchen. Give me a shout if you
> lose the will to live.

>   SIMON
> We can easily come back in a week.

>   SUSIE
>   (leaving)
> No, it's fine!

>   CHRIS
> Come on, let's go upstairs, you
> get a better view.

Gemma strides after him. Simon reluctantly follows.

INT. PARKS HOUSE. UPSTAIRS HALLWAY. EVENING

Chris reaches the top of the stairs. Gemma behind.

>   CHRIS (CONT'D)
>   We used a new type of glass on
>   the back of the house, I don't
>   understand the technology but
>   essentially it's double height,
>   thin, and stays hot. Like Naomi
>   Campbell.
>
>   A little joke.

>   GEMMA
>   It's beautiful.

>   CHRIS
>   Hope you don't mind me showing
>   off?
>   (he turns to look out
>   at the garden)
>   If you look out, there's a pool
>   at the end, we loved the one in
>   our house in France. Copied the
>   dimensions -

>   GEMMA
>   You have a place in France?

>   CHRIS
>   Yeah. If you guys ever want to
>   get away?

>   GEMMA
>   Really?

>   CHRIS
>   We have a wonderful maid,
>   Angelique, she sorts everything
>   out.

>   GEMMA
>   What's it called?

>   CHRIS
>   The house?

                    GEMMA
          Does it have a name?

                    CHRIS
          'Pierre Blanche.'

                    GEMMA
          What does it mean?

                    CHRIS
          WAIT!

Simon looks a bit concerned.

                    CHRIS (CONT'D)
          You haven't got any drinks!
          I'm chatting away like an idiot.
          Would you like some wine?

                    GEMMA
          White if you have it?

                    CHRIS
          Of course.
                    (to Simon)
          Beer I assume, beer?

                    SIMON
          Yeah. Cheers.

Kate appears from her bedroom having heard voices.
She sees them, and is stopped in her tracks.

                    CHRIS
          Kate - yeah, you know the
          Fosters. Gemma and Simon.

Gemma smiles.

                    KATE
          ...Hi.

                    CHRIS
          They're staying for dinner.

                    KATE
          I thought... next week?

                    CHRIS
          There's been a bit of a mix-up so
          it's happening now which is nice.
          Just going to get some drinks, do
          you want one?

                    KATE
          I'll... come with you.

                    CHRIS
          Okay.

Kate goes downstairs with her father, who's
slightly bemused at this. Simon turns to Gemma,
a completely different tone now their host has
moved away. They move back towards the window,
so they're not overheard.

                    SIMON
          How could you get it wrong?

                    GEMMA
          She said 'next Thursday'.

                    SIMON
          Yeah, that means the Thursday of
          the following week.

                    GEMMA
          Oh, okay.

He looks at her for a second, full of contempt.
Then turns away.

                    SIMON
          It's just he's more of a
          colleague, than friend. An
          important... adviser for me.
          A contact.

Simon goes to the window and continues to talk with
his back turned. Gemma picks up an expensive-
looking ornament from the mantelpiece.

                    SIMON (CONT'D)
          I only see him a couple of times
          a year. So if you're going to

             organise something like this,
             then it would be nice to have
             a bit more notice and...

SMASH! Gemma deliberately drops the ornament. Simon
turns and stares at the floor in disbelief.

                 SIMON (CONT'D)
             You, what did you -

Chris comes back up the stairs with the drinks.
He's also got a beer for himself.

                 CHRIS
             Wine for the - oh -

                 GEMMA
       (not making much effort to cover it up)
             Sorry. I knocked it with my...
             hand.

                 CHRIS
             Not to worry, we'll just... this
             is for you.
              (he gives Gemma the wine)
                 (calls)
             Kate!

                 GEMMA
             So sorry.

                 CHRIS
           (giving Simon the beer)
             It's not a problem.

                 GEMMA
             Was it expensive?

                 CHRIS
             It doesn't matter.

He opens the sliding glass doors.

               CHRIS (CONT'D)
          Come on, let's step outside.

                 GEMMA
         We can pay for it. Simon...

Simon glares at her. Kate enters, reluctantly.

                    CHRIS
                (to Kate)
        Could you get the dustpan and
        brush please?

                    KATE
                (looking at it)
        That was Mum's.

                    CHRIS
        Accident. Will you help me deal
        with this please? It's not a
        problem.

Kate glances at Gemma, then turns and goes. They
step just outside.

                    CHRIS (CONT'D)
        Alright! Cheers!

They 'cheers' with their drinks. Simon glares at
Gemma, who ignores him, smiling at Chris.

                    GEMMA
        So you two have known each other
        a while?

                    CHRIS
        Yeah, we meet occasionally, I
        give him a few pearls of wisdom.

                    GEMMA
        But you've never been tempted to
        go into business together?

                    CHRIS
        No.

                    SIMON
        I wish.

                    CHRIS
        He's on his way up, so he's
        working all the hours I expect,

that's in the past for me now,
I'm living off the fat. A lot of
my time is spent at the council
and you know, we open the odd new
restaurant -

Kate appears inside with a dustpan and brush.

> KATE
> (interrupting)
> How did it happen?

> CHRIS
> You're interrupting darling -

> KATE
> How did it break?

> GEMMA
> I knocked it.

> KATE
> (to Chris)
> Mum's upset.

A moment. Awkward.

> CHRIS
> Could happen to anyone.

Kate noisily carries on tidying, looking
disbelievingly at Simon. Simon avoids looking in
her direction. Chris is awkward. Gemma smiles
politely at everyone.

CUT TO -

TITLE SEQUENCE

INT. PARKS HOUSE. DINING ROOM. NIGHT

As Chris comes back into the room, we find an
expensive-looking oval dining table. He makes his
way back to the head of the table, between Simon
and Gemma. Kate and Susie have just brought in the
food - a casserole dish. And some plates.

Throughout the next section we're on the move,
Susie coming and going, plates being exchanged,
Chris getting up for the wine, etc....

      CHRIS
   I assume we can start?

      SUSIE
  Please.

Andrew enters. Sees them. Surprised.

      CHRIS
   Ah! At last! You remember Gemma
   and Simon, from the party.

      ANDREW
  Hi.

Andrew sits, embarrassed.

      SUSIE
   Shall we have music?

      ANDREW
   Please God / no.

      CHRIS
   We'll talk. Gemma - help
   yourself.

As Chris, Simon and Andrew discuss the football, we
move to Gemma, who's turned to Kate. They're both
playing at small talk, very good at hiding their
real feelings.

      GEMMA
   How's the restaurant?

> KATE

Good.

> GEMMA

You're a waitress, that must be -

> KATE

It's for the money mostly. Dad
wants me to take over as manager
but I'm more interested in going
into events. I'm doing an
internship at a local company at
the moment.

> GEMMA

'Events'. So that's -

> KATE

Weddings.

> GEMMA

Right.

> KATE

Divorce parties.

> GEMMA
> (beat)

Okay.

> KATE

Funerals.

> GEMMA

Is that really something people
do?

> KATE

What? Die?

> GEMMA

Divorce parties.

> KATE

Yeah! You see all the ex-wives
having a great time, and you

                    realise some people are just so
                    much better off out of marriage.
                    There's no point staying in
                    something if it's bad. If you're
                    trapped.

                              GEMMA
                    Right...

Gemma looks at her. They're both playing games.

                              GEMMA (CONT'D)
                    How's your love life?

                              KATE
                    Personal question.

                              GEMMA
                    You talked before about a man you
                    were seeing?

                              KATE
                    Sorry, isn't there a
                    confidentiality thing between
                    doctors and patients?

                              GEMMA
                    Yes.

                              KATE
                    Well can we activate that thing
                    then please?

                              GEMMA
                    Your mum and dad don't know?

                              SUSIE
                         (sitting down)
                    Don't know what?

                              GEMMA
                    Oops.

                              KATE
                    Nothing Mum.

                    SUSIE
Don't tell me you've got secrets?

                    KATE
Course I have. You said you
prefer it that way.

                    SUSIE
Well while you're under my roof
I don't want any big surprises.
I'm still your mum!

                    GEMMA
You live here?

                    CHRIS
Yeah, we can't get rid of her!

                    KATE
I lived on my own and I didn't
like it.

                    GEMMA
Why? What changed?

                    SIMON
                 (to Kate)
Wine?

                    KATE
No thanks.

                    SIMON
Susie?

                    SUSIE
Ooh, yes please. Gemma, actually
I wanted to say - I had an
appointment but then a letter came
through saying that you weren't
available and I had a new doctor.
And then Chris heard something -

                    CHRIS
Yeah, a chap at the council knows
your administrator -

                         GEMMA
          There's been a formal complaint
          made against me, a number of
          negative comments online so -

                         SUSIE
          'Online'. Well there's always
          trouble when you hear that word!

                         GEMMA
          The GMC felt it wasn't
          appropriate for me to stay
          working, so they've asked me to
          take some time off pending an
          investigation.

                         SUSIE
          But you're the senior doctor!

                         CHRIS
          Well what's the complaint?

                         SUSIE
          Chris! You can't ask that.

                         GEMMA
          A man says I threatened to burn
          him with a lit cigarette unless
          he left his girlfriend alone.

                         SUSIE
                    (beat)
          He said you threatened him?

     Susie looks at Simon for sympathy. He shrugs but is
     working Gemma out - what's she doing...?

                      SUSIE (CONT'D)
          Well, you've just got to pity
          some people, haven't you?

                         CHRIS
          Fantasist.

                         KATE
          But why would he make that up?

                         GEMMA
          He didn't.
                         (beat)
          He was beating up his girlfriend
          and I thought she needed help.

                         SUSIE
          Oh... so... you -

                         GEMMA
          Yeah. I've been under a lot of
          stress recently -

                         SUSIE
          Right...

                         GEMMA
          - in my personal life, it's
          clearly affected my work.

                         KATE
          It's not an excuse -

                         GEMMA
                         (to Kate)
          No, it's a reason.

                         SUSIE
          Come on Kate, if the girl was
          gonna be beaten up...

                         KATE
          If the girl was being beaten up
          you call the police?

A moment.

                         SUSIE
                         (sympathetic)
          Things have been tough lately,
          have they?

                         GEMMA
          Yes... yes I'd say so.

                    CHRIS
                (to Andrew)
You listening? Stress.
                (to the table)
Andrew said he wants to be
a doctor.

                    ANDREW
No I don't.

                    GEMMA
The stress is more at home
actually.

                    SIMON
(to Chris, changing the subject)
You must work all hours Chris to
stay on top of everything, I know
you said you take it easy –

                    GEMMA
Simon?

                    SIMON
– but there must be times –

                    GEMMA
You don't mind me saying about
the problems we've had?

                    SIMON
I... What?

                    GEMMA
You don't mind me opening up
about the difficulties we've
experienced?

                    SIMON
            (plays bemused)
Difficulties?

                    GEMMA
Alright. Not difficulties that's
a euphemism I suppose, as we're

in company. But okay good, let's
be precise. Not difficulties.
Betrayals.

Simon looks at her. It's sinking in. This is it.
She knows, and she's going for it. Now. Tonight.

> GEMMA (CONT'D)
> Okay. I know we haven't talked
> about it with each other, but we
> both know what's been going on.
> Don't we?

Gemma carries on eating, but she's the only one
that is. It's suddenly got really tense. Simon is
petrified, but can't be sure yet -

> SIMON
> (quietly, to her)
> Gemma, are you...

> GEMMA
> Do you want me to spell it out?

> SIMON
> (playing confused now)
> If there's really something we
> need talk through then I don't
> think this is the -

> GEMMA
> (still eating casually)
> For the last two years, Simon's
> been secretly having sex with
> another woman.
> (beat)
> Well...
> (beat)
> More of a girl really.

A hush descends on the table. Kate is pretty good
at keeping her expression blank. Simon is staring
at Gemma. His whole world collapsing now.

                    GEMMA (CONT'D)
I know we haven't spoken about
it but these are our friends and
I want to be honest.

                    CHRIS
You haven't talked about this
until now?

                    SIMON
(still trying to make light of it)
I think this is a joke -

                    GEMMA
That's a lie.

                    SIMON
- sometimes she says these things
to get a reaction! But I have no
idea what she's talking about -

                    GEMMA
He's lying right now. You see?

                    CHRIS
Maybe we should call it a night?

                    SIMON
Is that okay?

                    GEMMA
Pierre Blanche.

                    CHRIS
What?

                    GEMMA
Pierre Blanche means White Stone.
Simon, isn't that the name of
your main investor? I thought
that you said that you two didn't
do business together?

Chris looks across to Simon. Gemma's not meant to
know.

> SIMON
> It's confidential.

> GEMMA
> (to Susie)
> Simon has this big project called
> Academy Green, he couldn't raise
> any money so it ended up being
> entirely bankrolled by this
> single mystery company with an
> enigmatic title. 'White Stone'.
> And now it makes sense.

> KATE
> What do you mean bankrolled?

> GEMMA
> Dad has put in nearly all the
> money. Oh. Wait. You don't know?
> That's interesting.

Kate stares at Simon.

> CHRIS
> You two are obviously in the
> middle of something, let's just -

> GEMMA
> (to Susie)
> Simon said ages ago that he had
> a friend on the local council who
> helped him secure the site.
> Pulled some strings, so that
> must've been you?

> CHRIS
> I didn't -

> SUSIE
> Chris, yes, you boasted about it.

> GEMMA
> It's illegal. If you're investing
> in the project yourself. It's a
> conflict of interest.

                    KATE
             (upset. To Simon)
        You're in business with Dad? Why
        didn't you tell me?

A moment as they all look at Kate.

                    SIMON
        Gemma...

                    SUSIE
        Is there something I don't know?

                    GEMMA
             (to Simon)
        Tell them.

Simon looks at Gemma. He has no choice.

                    SIMON
        Chris, Susie...

                    GEMMA
        Actually no, you've had two years.
        I'll do it. Susie, you'll notice
        that Kate looks quite unhappy.

                    SIMON
             (low - steadying Kate)
        It's okay.

                    KATE
             (looking down, upset, dark)
        You're a fucking bitch -

                    GEMMA
        Bitch is right, I'm a wolf
        tonight.

                    SUSIE
             (to Kate)
        You mean you've been...

                    GEMMA
        Sorry, Susie, but your daughter's
        not a little girl any more. You

                    can ask my husband. He likes
                    blowjobs apparently and I'm told
                    she really knows what she's doing.
                              CHRIS
                    Get out. GET OUT NOW.

Kate is really <u>crying</u> now.

                              GEMMA
                    No, there's more...

                              KATE
                    No, no!

                              SIMON
                    Don't.

                              GEMMA
                            (to Simon)
                    Do you want to do it or...

                              KATE
                    Go on then, you'll break all your
                    rules of confidentiality, and tell
                    my parents the most personal
                    thing in my life...

                              GEMMA
                    Kate got pregnant. With Simon's
                    child. And because he messed her
                    around so much, she had it
                    aborted.

Kate didn't really expect her to do it - and she's
furious. Nodding now. Smiling almost, working
herself up -

                              KATE
                    Okay... okay...

She stands up and suddenly <u>slaps</u> Gemma round the
back of her head. Now everyone's on their feet -

                    KATE (CONT'D)
            (unintelligible but she's saying something like)
                YOU ANCIENT FUCKING CUNT.

                         SUSIE
        No!

                         KATE
        Get her out!

Now in slow motion we see Gemma wipe her mouth, get
up, walk away from the table. The others watch her
as she takes her coat and heads to the door.

As Susie half-hugs, and half-manhandles Kate to the
other side of the room, we now see the room from
Gemma's perspective.

This is going be a motif through the episode. The
naturalistic sound fades, and the score takes over.
Gemma is slightly removed - the action around her
at a distance.

As the screaming and arguments continue, Gemma
stands. Looks to Simon, as she puts her hair back
in place. He's talking to Chris.

                         SIMON
                      (to Chris)
             Chris, I'm sorry, you can tell
             she's in a state...

EXT. PARKS HOUSE. FRONT DRIVEWAY. NIGHT

Gemma comes out of the house, wearing her coat. She
goes up to her car, unlocking it before she gets
there.

She opens the door. Stops for a moment. That was an
effort, but she's in the middle of the battle -

The sound of the front door of the house opening.
Simon emerges. He's still in his shirt -

He walks over to her, distraught, breathing,
furious, but she strikes first -

                         SIMON
        What the fuck was that?

                    GEMMA
        I wasn't ill at your party.

                    SIMON
        (defiant, but working this out)
        What?

                    GEMMA
        I found your other phone in the
        boot of your car.

                    SIMON
        Oh Jesus, okay. So you've known
        since...

Behind them, Chris slams the front door shut.

                    GEMMA
        Are you coming back with me? We
        need to talk.

                    SIMON
        (looking at the house, unsure)
        Of course not. I've got to sort
        this out.

                    GEMMA
        It's just that's where our son
        lives.

Simon looks at her, torn. Knows he should go with
her, but can't just walk away...

                    GEMMA (CONT'D)
        Simon they have literally closed
        the door on you. They hate you.
                    (beat)
        I'm assuming that you didn't tell
        them in case Chris withdrew the
        funding -

                    SIMON
        Yeah, and if I had we'd be
        bankrupt. You want the truth?
        Everything we have...

                    GEMMA
- is invested in Academy Green,
yeah, I know. Neil said.

                    SIMON
He wouldn't.

                    GEMMA
Just after we slept together.

Simon is astounded.

                GEMMA (CONT'D)
He was alright actually. I
wouldn't sell tickets but we had
a good time.

                    SIMON
You wanted to get back at me?

                    GEMMA
Is it sinking in? Have you felt
it yet?
    (she looks at him closely)
No. But you will. How was Kate?
I mean the things she must be
able to do with that tongue.

                    SIMON
How was Neil?

                    GEMMA
I came. Hard. Once. He's slightly
bigger than you but not as good.

Simon looks down, trying to take all this in -

                    SIMON
Gemma, I made a mistake but it
wasn't about sex. I didn't want
this to happen. I know you won't
believe me but when I met Kate we
just sparked. I had to find out
what it was.

                    GEMMA
          So helpless.

He turns back, stares at her. She's firm, eloquent,
rooted.

                    SIMON
          And yes I didn't want Chris to
          find out because of the money, but
          that wasn't the main reason
          I didn't tell you.

                    GEMMA
          Selfish. Nasty.

                    SIMON
          It's because I still love you.
          Despite all this, I do.

                    GEMMA
          Shut up and listen - we will never
          have a relationship again. Now
          here's what I want. Leave me and
          Tom living in our house, and go
          away somewhere else, start again.

                    SIMON
                  (beat)
          No. No I'm not moving.

The front door opens and Kate has come out in her
coat with car keys. She walks through the middle of
Gemma and Simon to her car.

                    KATE
               (to Simon as she passes)
          We can't stay here.

She gets to her car and opens the door.

                    KATE (CONT'D)
          We can go to the house. Most of
          my stuff's still there.

                    SIMON
          Please, Kate. Please.

                    GEMMA
                 (to Simon)
        Tom will want to know what's
        happening.

Kate turns to Gemma.

                    KATE
        You know I used to feel sorry for
        you. I've always said he should
        tell you the truth.
                 (beat)
        Now I get why he didn't.
                 (to Simon)
        Why is it women go mad when they
        get old?

Gemma looks at Kate.

                    GEMMA
        You're still pregnant.

Simon looks at Kate - her reaction is giving it
away.

                    GEMMA (CONT'D)
        You didn't drink wine at the
        table.

Gemma nods to Kate's hand - it's on her tummy.

                    GEMMA (CONT'D)
        You didn't have the abortion.
                 (to Simon)
        She was testing you to see if you
        wanted her or just the baby. And
        you passed. Went back. Well done.

                    SIMON
                 (to Kate)
        Really?

                    KATE
                 (beat)
        Yeah.

Kate turns and goes back to her car, gets in,
starts the engine. Gemma looks at Simon, who's
dazed.

> SIMON
> Please don't tell Tom. Not yet.

Gemma shrugs. This is his choice now. To go with
Kate, or come back and speak to his son. He's
unsure...

Kate reverses back in her car. Simon opens the
passenger door, and gets in. The car speeds off.

A moment of stillness. Quiet.

Gemma continues looking for a moment. Then puts her
head down, accepts it, gets in her car and drives
away.

Her perspective as she turns onto the road, the
headlights picking out the houses –

CUT TO –

EXT. FOSTER HOUSE. DRIVEWAY. NIGHT

Gemma drives down the road and into her drive.
She's staring.

Still... staring...

Then she gets out, and looks at her house.

The thing is... it's not that late.

She's about to go inside but then... she turns the
other way - looks across the street. Neil and
Anna's house. The lights are on.

Gemma realises something, and heads towards their
door.

CUT TO –

EXT. FRONT DOOR. NEIL AND ANNA'S HOUSE. NIGHT

Anna opens the door. She smiles.

>   ANNA
>   Hello!

A moment.

>   ANNA (CONT'D)
>   Everything alright?

Anna stares at her, trying to work it out. Not sure what's going on...

>   GEMMA
>   Are you going to invite me in?

Anna hesitates. As she does Neil bounds over.

>   NEIL
>   I recognise that voice! Hello!
>   Are you coming in?

>   GEMMA
>   Thanks.

Neil lets Gemma inside the house. She keeps walking, through to the back of the house - not waiting to be led.

INT. NEIL AND ANNA'S HOUSE. KITCHEN. NIGHT

Gemma glides into the room. Anna comes after her, then Neil. Throughout the scene Gemma is detached, unknowable.

>   ANNA
>   Can I get you anything?

>   GEMMA
>   No.

>   NEIL
>   So to what do we owe this
>   pleasure?

> GEMMA
> (to Anna)
> How did you know about it?

> ANNA
> I'm sorry?

> GEMMA
> What we did? Did you check his
> text messages? He can't have been
> stupid enough to have left them
> on his phone.

Anna looks at her. Works it all out, very quickly.
She's clever, and she's not going be the idiot in
this conversation. She looks at Neil.

> ANNA
> He strays. Which I accept. As
> long as I have knowledge of where -

> NEIL
> You know?

> ANNA
> And who. Sometimes I follow him
> to check who he's meeting.
> Normally it's women I've never
> met. Don't care about. Until you.
> Never one of our friends before.

> NEIL
> Anna, I'm really... I'm sorry -

> ANNA
> (sharp)
> Not in front of her.

A moment. A look between them. Neil gets it.

> GEMMA
> How did you find out about Simon.
> Did he tell you?

> ANNA
> No. We ran into him with Kate, in
> London. It was awkward at first

but actually we got on, ended up
having a drink. And we were very
clear, from the beginning. His
marriage is not our business. We
stay out.
>   (beat)
Was it that hair of hers you
found? Yeah. I thought that might
start things off.

>   NEIL
>   (to Gemma)
So you knew when we were -

>   ANNA
Yeah. That's why she felt able to.

>   GEMMA
You're really clever aren't you?

>   ANNA
I'm not a doctor but I do alright.

>   GEMMA
Why didn't we ever get on?

>   ANNA
>   (laughs)
You're joking?

Anna stares at her, and Gemma starts to understand.
Anna loathes her. Anna picks up her wine.

>   ANNA (CONT'D)
Neil and I might not be perfect,
but we know what the other one
needs. We function. We don't talk
about what he does. Until now -
thanks to you.
>   (beat)
But you and Simon? You don't know
each other at all. Never have.

Gemma sits down. Neil is stood by the wall, staying
out of it, up till now. He relies on Anna hugely,
and is cautious of upsetting her.

                    GEMMA
And why the comments?

                    NEIL
What comments?

                    GEMMA
The night that we met up, someone
started to put negative comments
about me online. It took me till
just now, standing out there, to
work out who it was. Who would
have the time? The reason to do
it?

                    ANNA
You have no idea how you come
across. What people say about you
when you leave the room. They
breathe a sigh of relief. Because
I don't know if you mean to but
you make them feel inadequate,
and even though you say you like
them, it's clear you think you're
very slightly better. Better than
all of us.
                    (beat)
Those stories I put online, they
may be made up, but what they're
saying is all true.

                    NEIL
Delete them.

                    ANNA
Sure.
                    (beat)
But that's not why she came round.
                    (to Gemma)
Is it? So I'd remove the
messages. You came here tonight
to reveal your secret. Break us
up maybe. But look. We're still
together. Aren't we?

They look at each other.

> NEIL
> (quietly)
>
> Yeah.

They both look at Gemma. She stands up.

> GEMMA
>
> Thanks.

She walks towards the front door. Still holding it
together - tense - coiled -

INT. FOSTER HOUSE. HALLWAY. NIGHT

Gemma closes her front door and pauses.

The TV is on as Gemma walks towards the kitchen.
Becky appears.

> BECKY
>
> Hey. How was it?

> GEMMA
>
> Has anyone called?

> BECKY
>
> Here? Tonight? No.

> GEMMA
>
> Okay.
> (beat)
> Well. He's not here. That's how
> it went.

> BECKY
>
> Where did you go?

> GEMMA
>
> For dinner.

> BECKY
>
> So is he staying with her?

Gemma doesn't reply. The answer's obvious from
Simon's absence.

                    GEMMA
          How's Tom been?

                    BECKY
          We watched TV and then he went to
          bed. He's asleep now I think.

She calls Isobel who is asleep on the sofa.

                    BECKY (CONT'D)
          Isobel? Come on love, it's time
          to go home, grab my stuff will
          you?

Gemma seems distracted. She hasn't even taken off
her coat yet...

Isobel comes through with Becky's coat and bag.

                    BECKY (CONT'D)
          I'll... just... leave you to it.
                    (to Isobel)
          Come on.

Becky and Isobel leave. Gemma closes the front door
behind them... and just stands in the hall.

Close on her hand - the pressing of her finger into
her thumb is harder now - her nail into the skin.

It's starting to bleed.

EXT. FOSTER HOUSE. NIGHT

We see from outside. Gemma walks slowly towards the
flickering light from the TV in the front room,
where Becky had been previously.

Framed by the window and the curtains we see Gemma
lit by a lamp and a flickering TV.

She is contemplating havoc. Then she turns, walks
towards the curtains, and suddenly closes them.

CUT TO BLACK.

INT. KATE'S HOUSE. BEDROOM. DAY

BLACK.

Simon opens his eyes to see photos of him and Kate
on the bedside table.

It's early in the morning. From above, in a
parallel shot to many of those we've seen of Simon
and Gemma, we find Simon, waking up, in bed with
Kate. If it wasn't for the events of last night,
and the previous two years, this would be a
beautiful scene. Sunlight pouring in on two people
in love.

But they're not close in bed. Simon hasn't slept
too well, and his head is very full. But he reaches
over and cuddles Kate. Very different to how he is
with Gemma.

We come round and realise her eyes are open. She's
awake.

                    SIMON
          I'm sorry.

                    KATE
          You like secrets, don't you?

                    SIMON
          I'm not the only one.

He lifts up her pyjama top to reveal her belly. He
touches it.

                    KATE
          I want to keep it.

                    SIMON
          Okay.

                    KATE
          Do you?

                    SIMON
          Yeah.

A moment, then she turns to him.

                    KATE
        I could talk to Dad this morning.
        Explain. Get him to keep the
        funding going. Right? That's what
        we need.

                    SIMON
        If you think you can.

He kisses her. She kisses him back. We get the
sense they're going to have sex when -

There's a knock on the front door.

They look at each other. The knock again, and Kate
gets up.

CUT TO -

INT. KATE'S HOUSE. DOWNSTAIRS HALLWAY. DAY

Kate, half-dressed and bleary-eyed, comes down the
stairs and opens the front door.

Standing on the doorstep, in his uniform, is Tom.

                    TOM
        Who are you?

                    KATE
        I'm... Oh... you're...

                    TOM
        Is my dad here?

                    KATE
        He... Yeah, come in.

Tom comes into the room. Looks around.

                    KATE (CONT'D)
                    (calls)
        Simon!

        It's your son.

A moment. Tom stares at Kate. Kate tries to smile, but is <u>very</u> uncomfortable.

Simon comes down the stairs. He looks very confused.

>   SIMON
>   Hey mate, what are you -

>   TOM
>   Mum said that she had some stuff
>   to do, but that you'd be here and
>   you'd take me to school. What's
>   going on?

>   SIMON
>   Yeah okay... I can take you.

>   TOM
>   Who's she?

>   SIMON
>   This is my friend, Kate.

>   TOM
>   Your friend?

>   SIMON
>   Mum and me had a row, Kate let me
>   stay in the spare room.

Tom looks at her, suspiciously.

>   TOM
>   How old are you?

>   KATE
>   Twenty-three.

>   TOM
>   Are you having sex with each
>   other?

>   KATE
>   What?!

>   SIMON
>   Tom -

                         TOM
              Don't lie to me.

                        SIMON
              Mate listen. Kate's just a
              friend. Promise. Yeah?

      Tom looks at her, sceptical.

                       SIMON (CONT'D)
              Now you stay here, I'll get my
              stuff, take you in. Okay? Two
              minutes.
                         (to Kate)
              We'll have to take your car.

      He goes upstairs. Kate and Tom look at each other.

                         TOM
              You're Andrew Parks' sister.

                        KATE
              Yeah.

                         TOM
              At the football some of them
              fancied you.

                        KATE
              Okay.

                         TOM
              But then your brother said they
              shouldn't because you're a slut
              and have sex with loads of people
              all the time.

                        KATE
              Andrew doesn't like me very much.
              He makes things up.

                         TOM
              Is it true though?

                        KATE
              It...

Kate stops herself. Then takes a step towards him.

> KATE (CONT'D)
> Women can have as much sex as
> they like Tom. Just like men.

A moment. Tom suddenly feels out of his depth,
scared.

> TOM
> Not with Dad though?

> KATE
> He just told you. We're... good
> friends. Okay?

She escapes upstairs. Tom sits down.

CUT TO -

EXT. ROAD AWAY FROM THE SCHOOL. DAY

Kate's car has pulled up round the corner from the
school. Simon and Kate are in the car. Tom gets
out.

> SIMON
> We can drop you by the gate.

> TOM
> (looking at Kate)
> No thanks.

He walks off. Kate looks at Simon, frustrated.

> KATE
> Sort this out.

CUT TO -

INT. FOSTER HOUSE. HALLWAY. DAY

Simon enters the house. There's no one here.

He walks through to the kitchen. This house that is about to be split apart. All the things. The coats hanging up.

INT. FOSTER HOUSE. KITCHEN. DAY

In the kitchen, the dirty bowls by the dishwasher ready to be loaded. The stuff on the fridge. He stops. Stares.

He's never going to have a domestic, family life here again. It hits him. It's all gone.

CUT TO -

INT. PARKS HOUSE. HALLWAY/RECEPTION AREA. DAY

Chris opens the door. Kate's there. He sees her, then turns and walks away, leaving it open.

> CHRIS
> You don't have to ring the bell.

Kate enters.

Chris walks into the room and stands looking out at his garden. Kate follows.

> KATE
> Where's Mum?

> CHRIS
> Migraine. What did he do first?
> Get my money or sleep with my
> daughter?

                    KATE
We met at that networking event,
when I was doing the drinks. We
talked, we got on.

                    CHRIS
He was using you to get to me.

                    KATE
Dad -

                    CHRIS
He didn't tell you we were
working together.

                    KATE
He was protecting me.

                    CHRIS
Right.

A moment.

                    CHRIS (CONT'D)
Well whatever he said to you,
he's very bad at business. At
first I thought he was on to
something, but then the further
we got I started smelling
bullshit.

                    KATE
He's been unlucky.

                    CHRIS
Sweetheart that is naive, he's
been incredibly lucky but he's
messed it up every step of the
way.

                    KATE
Well you have to keep going.

                    CHRIS
With him? Giving him money?
I don't think so.

>   KATE
>   Dad, the only reason he took so
>   long to tell you -
>
>   CHRIS
>   He didn't tell me. His wife did!
>
>   KATE
>   Let me finish! He didn't want to
>   leave her and Tom with nothing.
>
>   CHRIS
>   You think I haven't looked at
>   another women since I married?
>   Course I have. But I work hard to
>   fulfil my promise to your mum.
>
>   KATE
>   Yeah, well you're amazing as
>   always!
>   (beat)
>   Fine, don't help him then. Do it
>   for me.
>
>   CHRIS
>   You made a mistake. You're an
>   adult and there are consequences.

Kate's crying a little, she turns away. Really
upset.

A moment. She turns back.

>   KATE
>   You're not even going to hug me.
>
>   CHRIS
>   Course I am. Come here.

He hugs her.

>   KATE
>   Dad? I'm still pregnant.
>   (beat)
>   You can't just walk away from
>   him.

Chris looks at her. Compassionate but resolute.

>   CHRIS
>   Alright. We'll look after you and
>   the child. You have a room here
>   if you need it. You can always
>   come back. Always.
>   (beat)
>   But he's getting no more money
>   from me. Ever.

She pulls away, hurt. She turns and leaves.

The front door slams shut.

Once it has, Chris looks up to see Gemma, who's
been watching all this from upstairs. She was there
the whole time.

>   CHRIS (CONT'D)
>   That do it for you?

Gemma comes down the stairs and walks toward the
door.

>   CHRIS (CONT'D)
>   How do I know you won't say
>   anything?

>   GEMMA
>   (stops, turns to him)
>   We actually want the same thing.

She opens the door.

>   CHRIS
>   What are you going to do now?

She looks at him, shrugs, then goes.

CUT TO -

INT. SURGERY. RECEPTION. DAY

Gemma stands in the doorway to the surgery. Looks around. Patients are waiting. Some of them glance up at her, recognise her, then look away.

She heads for the corridor but Luke has spotted her. He walks up to her.

                    LUKE
          Hey.

A moment. She just looks at him.

               LUKE (CONT'D)
          You're here to see... Ros?

                    GEMMA
          Yeah.

                    LUKE
               (confidentially)
          Gemma you should know, before you
          got here -

Ros appears from the back office.

                    ROS
          Hi. You want to come with me?

She leads Gemma away. Luke watches them go. Ros talking to Gemma.

               ROS (CONT'D)
          There is still the outstanding
          complaint.

                    GEMMA
          All doctors get complaints. And
          as I said on the phone there is
          no reason I can't come back -

                    ROS
          I thought we'd go somewhere more
          private?

They turn to go into the meeting room.

INT. SURGERY. MEETING ROOM. DAY

They walk in to find Simon. His coat is laid across
the chair nearby. Gemma stares at him.

                ROS (CONT'D)
      Simon called me just after you
      did. He told me what happened
      last night, and I thought perhaps
      the best thing would be for you
      to speak somewhere more neutral.
      To work this out.
                (beat)
      So no one else is caught up in
      the middle.

Simon and Gemma stare at each other.

                ROS (CONT'D)
      I'll be around if you need me.

                SIMON
      Thanks.

She goes. Closes the door behind her. They look at
each other.

Gemma goes to the water cooler, gets a cup and
drinks some water.

                SIMON (CONT'D)
      Kate says her dad won't help.
      He's going to cut me out. I
      assume you'd spoken already? If
      he didn't do what you wanted
      you'd go to the council, tell
      them about the conflict of
      interest.

                GEMMA
      Yeah. He's going to give the
      project to a new developer. And
      then when it's finished and sold,
      he'll pay me back every penny. In
      the meantime, he'll cover my

  expenses. I'll keep the house.
  Get the savings back.

     SIMON
  It's my project. I did all the
  work.

     GEMMA
  You're not as good looking as you
  think.

Gemma walks the room - she prowls.

     SIMON
  What was that, this morning?
  Leaving Tom on the doorstep.

     GEMMA
  Did you tell him?

     SIMON
  It's not fair, putting him in
  that position.

     GEMMA
  He has a right to hear the truth.
  I thought that you would want to
  do that yourself, but fine, you've
  had your chance.

Gemma puts her finger into her thumb again, there's
now dried blood on the side of her hand. Not a lot,
but it's starting to be noticeable.

     SIMON
  Please can we just try to -

     GEMMA
  Either you leave, or I tell the
  police that you forged my
  signature on the mortgage.

Gemma goes to Simon's coat.

     SIMON
  What are you doing?

>   GEMMA
> I bought all your clothes. In
> fact anything from the last two
> years came out of money that I
> earnt. You can't argue with that.

She reaches into the pocket of his coat. Takes out
his wallet.

>   GEMMA (CONT'D)
> This.

She puts the wallet on the table. Then takes out
his car keys.

>   GEMMA (CONT'D)
> Your car's mine.

She takes out his phone.

>   GEMMA (CONT'D)
> And this.

She keeps it in her hand.

>   SIMON
> I'm not leaving. Kate doesn't
> want to. And I can't live far
> from Tom so we're just going to
> have to start to talk.

>   GEMMA
> You have to leave.

>   SIMON
> I'm not going anywhere.

>   GEMMA
> Simon...

She suddenly lifts her arm and smashes the phone
against the table.

>   SIMON
>   (quietly)
> Gemma...

                    GEMMA
        What? You've got another one.

She picks up a chair and uses the leg to smash it
again, over and over.

                  ROS (O.S.)
        Gemma... can we speak to you?

Just after it's done, she looks up to find Ros at
the door, with another doctor, Martha.

                    GEMMA
        No.

                    ROS
        Simon explained what happened this
        morning with Tom, and I can see
        that you're... I called Martha,
        asked her to come and see you.

                    MARTHA
        Hi Gemma -

                    GEMMA
        Why?

                    ROS
        I really think the best thing for
        us all would be to -

                    MARTHA
        I just want a word -

                    SIMON
        Before you do something you
        regret.

                    ROS
        We think it'd be really good for
        you to see somebody that's not
        us, that you trust...

                    SIMON
        I don't know what happened with
        Tom this morning but when he was

there on the doorstep he looked
terrified.

                    GEMMA
     You... Tom?

For the first time Gemma's listening. Engaged.

                    GEMMA (CONT'D)
     Why are you talking about Tom?

A moment. The idea's in the room now. They're
suggesting she might be a danger to him.

                    GEMMA (CONT'D)
     Is that why you want...?

Gemma grabs her keys and makes to go, but Ros
doesn't move, blocking her way.

                    GEMMA (CONT'D)
     Are you going to stop me from
     leaving?

                         ROS
     Of course not, Gemma.

                    GEMMA
     Move!

Gemma walks out of the room.

INT. SURGERY. CORRIDOR. DAY

And Gemma's walking, at pace, down the corridor.
Behind her, Ros follows.

                         ROS
     Gemma!

Gemma doesn't stop.

                    ROS (CONT'D)
     Gemma!

EXT. SURGERY. DAY

Gemma walks out of the surgery - as she does, Poppy
runs over.

>   POPPY
>   Doctor Foster!

>   POPPY'S MUM
>   Poppy! The doctor's busy.

Gemma stops for a moment.

>   POPPY
>   They took it off! Look!

She waves her arm around. Simon comes out of the
surgery doors.

>   GEMMA
>   That's good, but you have to be
>   careful, it's better but it's not
>   quite -

>   POPPY
>   (singing)
>   *Doctor Foster went to*
>   *Gloucester* -

>   GEMMA
>   (slightly too sharply)
>   No.

>   (now calmer - softer - aware that Simon's
>   behind her)
>   No, Poppy, it's not Doctor Foster
>   any more. I'm getting divorced.
>   And changing my name is what you
>   call a silver lining.

>   SIMON
>   Gemma...

Gemma stands. Smiles to Poppy's mum.

>   GEMMA
>   Bye.

She leaves, keeps walking. Simon keeps following -

                    SIMON
          Stop. And think.

She unlocks her car. Then puts her hand in her
pocket for something else.

                    SIMON (CONT'D)
          Work this out, before it all gets
          worse.

                    GEMMA
          Do you want your car keys?

Gemma holds up his car keys.

                    SIMON
          What?

                    GEMMA
          Fetch.

And she throws his car keys up on to the roof of
the medical centre, then turns and gets in her car.
Starts it, reverses out and away.

INT. HIGHBROOK SCHOOL. RECEPTION. DAY

The headteacher, Mrs Walters - efficient, principled
and careful, is talking to Gemma.

                    MRS WALTERS
          I've just had a call from your
          husband. He requested that I
          didn't release Tom.

                    GEMMA
          My husband and I aren't together
          any more. So unless you honestly
          think there's a safeguarding
          issue, or that I'm drunk, or
          mentally unwell, or an urgent
          danger to my son, then you have
          to let me take him, right now.

CUT TO -

EXT. HIGHBROOK SCHOOL. DAY

Gemma walks away with Tom from the reception
towards her car. They get in and drive away. They
turn left out of the drive. As they disappear,
Simon's car speeds in from the right.

INT. HIGHBROOK SCHOOL. RECEPTION. DAY

Simon's car drives right up to the entrance and
parks suddenly. Simon gets out. Mrs Walters walks
towards him.

> SIMON
> Is she here?

EXT. PARMINSTER RINGROAD. GEMMA'S CAR. DAY

Gemma is driving home. Tom's in the passenger seat
next to her.

> TOM
> You say I have to go and knock on
> a door cos that's where Dad is
> and as soon as it's opened you
> drive off. Inside there's that
> girl. Everyone says she's a slut.

> GEMMA
> Don't use words like that -

> TOM
> She is though. I'm not stupid
> I can guess what's happening but
> you don't tell me anything.

Gemma doesn't reply.

> TOM (CONT'D)
> If you don't, I'm going to open
> the door -

He goes to open the door.

> GEMMA
> Okay.

He's about to, when Gemma suddenly turns the wheel.

We see from outside, as the car suddenly turns off
the ringroad, on to a track that runs across a
field. dust flies up, as Gemma keeps her foot down.

INT / EXT. FIELD. GEMMA'S CAR. DAY

The car continues at speed, along the track, until
they're a long way from the ringroad, and the town.

It feels in the middle of nowhere.

With another skid of dust, the car stops.

> TOM
> What are you doing?

> GEMMA
> You wanted to stop.

Gemma opens the door and gets out.

EXT. FIELD. DAY

It's a bleak, English field. No one around. Cold and
cloudy.

Gemma stands a little distance from the car. Tom
also gets out, and goes round to confront her.

They look at each other.

                    GEMMA
          So what do you think's going on?

                     TOM
          Other families they spend time
          together, you get in so late,
          I want to talk to you but then
          you just say you're so tired. The
          other mums, they do things for
          their children, packed lunches,
          take them places -

                    GEMMA
                   (quietly)
          I do all those things.

                     TOM
          Buy them new clothes at the
          weekend, and they love the dads.
          But you just work. You work all
          the time.

Gemma looks at him.

                 TOM (CONT'D)
          So I think Dad got sick of it and
          went to have sex with that other
          girl. And now you both hate each
          other and want to get a divorce.

                    GEMMA
          You think it's my fault.

                     TOM
          Dad has fun with me. We do stuff.
          He's there.

                    GEMMA
          He has time. He doesn't earn the
          money.

                     TOM
          It's not all about money, Mum.

A moment.

                    GEMMA
        You like Dad.

                    TOM
        Yeah.

                    GEMMA
        You don't like me.

                    TOM
                  (pause)
        No. Not at the moment.

Gemma goes to the boot of the car, and opens it.

                    TOM (CONT'D)
        See you're not even talking to me
        now, you're just ignoring me -

Tom continues to talk. We see, from inside the
boot, Gemma opening her doctor's bag and reaching
inside.

                    TOM (CONT'D)
        You know, you're supposed to
        spend time with your family? Not
        just think about yourself, or
        work, to do what you want to -

Gemma grabs something from the bag and turns.

Tom looks at her, shocked. In her hand are the
scissors, from Episode One.

                    TOM (CONT'D)
        What you doing?

Close on Gemma's eyes - dark. Hidden.

CUT TO -

INT. FOSTER HOUSE. HALLWAY. DAY

Simon comes down the stairs and out of the front
door. He's halfway through a conversation on his
other mobile (to Kate).

> SIMON
> (on phone)
> She didn't say anything to anyone
> at school about where she was
> going so I haven't got a clue
> where...

EXT. FOSTER HOUSE. DAY

> SIMON (CONT'D)
> (on phone)
> She's got him but I don't...

Gemma swings into the drive as Simon comes out of
the house.

Simon sees Gemma's car heading towards him. He
moves out of the way.

> SIMON (CONT'D)
> (on phone)
> Okay. She's here.

Gemma gets out. She looks windswept, mad, her hand
now has a bandage round it.

> SIMON (CONT'D)
> Where's Tom?

Gemma walks past him, and into the house. He
follows her inside.

INT. FOSTER HOUSE. KITCHEN. DAY

This is real. Rough edges.

We follow Simon through the front door, down the hall, and round the corner, into the kitchen.

Gemma sits at the breakfast bar, on a stool, adjusting her bandage.

> SIMON
> Where is he?

Simon looks at her, unsure.

> GEMMA
> Becky's.

> SIMON
> Becky's at work.

> GEMMA
> Not any more.

> SIMON
> So if I call her...

Gemma gets off the stool, and goes and pours herself a drink. Rum and Coke.

> GEMMA
> Do you remember when we went to
> Devon? Tom was about three, and
> we went to that causeway to get
> to the island, and on the way
> back, the tide had started to
> come in but you said let's do it
> anyway, and you lifted him up on
> to your shoulders, and held my
> hand and paddled through the
> water. That was fun.
> (beat)
> You destroyed it all.
> (beat)
> I wasted fourteen years of my
> life when I could've been with

>   someone better. Who do I go to
>   for justice? To make this fair.

>   SIMON
>   I honestly thought if I could
>   just get us in a position where
>   we had money, and Tom was a bit
>   older.

>   GEMMA
>   You are so stupid.

> Simon picks up his phone and dials Becky's number.

>   SIMON
>   Okay, well maybe my mistake was
>   even trying, maybe I should've
>   come to you straight away, said
>   I know we're married, but I'm
>   fucking someone else.

>   GEMMA
>   Why did you do it? I still don't
>   understand.

> He puts the phone to his ear. It's ringing.

>   SIMON
>   Because we're all animals,
>   sometimes we can't control our
>   biology, we fall in love when we
>   shouldn't, we have sex with the
>   wrong people. I'm sick of saying
>   sorry cos it happens to people
>   all over the world, all the time,
>   people just deal with it, this
>   kind of thing happens a lot.

>   GEMMA
>   You haven't.

>   SIMON
>   What?

>   GEMMA
>   You've never said sorry.

The phone's picked up at the other end.

> SIMON
> Becky, it's me. Is Tom there?
> Gemma said he's with you.
> (beat)
> Okay.

He hangs up. Gemma drinks her drink.

> SIMON (CONT'D)
> (to Gemma)
> Where is he?

> GEMMA
> Neil said that all men cheat,
> it's just most of them get away
> with it. Is that true?

> SIMON
> Where's Tom?

We're on Gemma. Drinking. A very slow push in on her.

A sense of foreboding as she drinks. Her face giving away very little.

A moment. Close on both of them.

Closer and closer on her. We're thinking - who is she? This woman we've been watching for five weeks now. What has she done? What is she capable of?

> GEMMA
> You've taken everything away from
> me, my respect, my job, money -

She holds out her hand. A small clump of brown hair.

> GEMMA (CONT'D)
> Could it be after all that, when
> you made everyone think that I
> was mad so that I'll be removed
> from my son -

                         SIMON
          What's that?

                         GEMMA
          His hair. It came off in my hand.

Simon looks at her, horrified.

                    GEMMA (CONT'D)
          Could it be that I decided that
          I'd rather do something to
          protect him from having to grow
          up to be someone like you?

                         SIMON
          What do you mean?

                         GEMMA
          Because if it's true that all men
          are entirely led by their desire
          to fuck anything they want, then
          why would I want him to grow up
          to be like that?

She puts the hair on the counter.

                    GEMMA (CONT'D)
          Everyone will ask, who made her
          do it? How was this allowed to
          happen? And where were the
          neighbours and the friends?
                       (beat)
          It'll be the only thing that this
          town is known for.
                     (genuinely)
          Maybe I am mad.

He goes towards her.

                    GEMMA (CONT'D)
          You really think that I could do
          that?

He stares at her.

                         SIMON
          I don't know.

                    GEMMA
          Exactly. Simon, he's so beautiful
          and you don't deserve him.

Gemma's eyes are full of tears - at what she's
done.

He steps back, distraught. Unsure what to do...

                    SIMON
          Should... I should...

He cries, against the wall...

                    GEMMA
          Through all of this, you've had
          that look like you're about to
          smile, even when things were
          serious - I don't think you ever
          got what you did. The horror of
          losing it all. And when you slept
          with her, you killed the person
          that I love and the son that I
          was going to bring up. The me
          that I was starting to like.
          Everything that I wanted and
          worked for, and loved, died.

Simon looks up at her, about to attack her. He
picks up the hair on the counter.

He's distraught, and staggers away from Gemma,
towards the front door.

He opens it -

EXT. FOSTER HOUSE. DAY

- and Tom's standing there, about to come in.
Carly's in the background with her car.

                    SIMON
          Oh god -

Simon grabs Tom and hugs him. Tom pushes him away
and heads inside. Simon follows him inside and
closes the door.

> SIMON (CONT'D)
>
> Mate —

INT. FOSTER HOUSE. KITCHEN. DAY

Tom walks through into the kitchen. Simon follows.

> TOM
>
> Mum said that she had to spend
> time with you. I had to wait with
> her friend Carly.

> SIMON
>
> Okay... well... your mum and me,
> we have to have a conversation
> about a lot of things, so maybe
> the best thing -

> TOM
> (crying)
> Mum says that you had sex with
> Kate Parks for two years and hid
> it from her and me. That you
> spent all of our money.

Simon looks at him.

> TOM (CONT'D)
>
> Is that true?

A moment. Simon thinks about more lies. He could.
He could claim Gemma was mad.

> SIMON
>
> Yeah. I...
> (neat - no excuses now)
> Yeah. I'm sorry. I'm so sorry.

> TOM
>
> Why?

Tom looks at him, desperate not to cry. Looks at
Gemma, sat drinking, not looking at them. Then goes
upstairs. A moment, and the door slams.

> SIMON
> (to Gemma)
> I didn't want to tell him, like
> that.

> GEMMA
> Then you should've been better.

> SIMON
> I thought he was dead. You made
> me think...

Simon stands opposite Gemma.

He's sobbing, crying now - he's half-distraught,
half-furious. He picks up the hair.

> GEMMA
> It's my hair.

> SIMON
> It smells of him.

> GEMMA
> I smell of him.

Simon's making a strange noise. He's primal now -
full of... something. Hate, or animal revenge. He
hates this woman. He grabs her by the neck, then
the face and pushes her, holding her tight... we
don't know what he's doing - he doesn't know what
he's doing.

He's pushing her against the glass doors, harder
and harder.

> GEMMA (CONT'D)
> This is it. This is what it felt
> like. Now you understand.

> SIMON
> He's my son!

>   (beat)
>   He's. My. Son.

Simon lets go, turns, walks away for a moment... we
think he's calming down, then suddenly he comes
flying back at her, pushing her hard, into the glass
doors.They crack, as she hits them, don't smash,
but her legs give way, and she <u>slumps</u> to the floor.

A moment. He can't believe what he's done...

CUT TO -

EXT. FOSTER HOUSE. DAY

Carly is stood outside the house. She's smoking.

>   CARLY
>   (to herself)
>   Shit.

She has seen Kate get out of her car. Kate sees
Carly.

>   KATE
>   What are you... you know them?

Anna runs across from her house.

>   ANNA
>   What's happened?

>   KATE
>   What do you mean?

>   ANNA
>   He just called me!

Anna doesn't stop - just heads straight through the
front door. Kate follows, then Carly.

INT. FOSTER HOUSE. KITCHEN. DAY

She sees Simon sitting on a stool, Gemma on the
floor. Anna goes straight to her. Her face has blood
on it, as her nose is bleeding. Gemma's still
conscious, just -

                    SIMON
     I hit her...

                    ANNA
     Have you called an ambulance?

                    SIMON
     No.

                    KATE
     Is she alright?

                    ANNA
     Just stand outside. Both of you.

                    CARLY
     Where's Tom?

                    SIMON
     Upstairs. I told him to stay
     there.

                    CARLY
     I'll stop him coming in.

                    ANNA
                  (to Carly)
     And call an ambulance.

                    SIMON
     And the police.

                    ANNA
     What?

                    SIMON
                  (sad, guilty)
     Call the police as well.

Simon gets up and goes outside. Kate looks at the
scene, and follows him. In the background Carly

calls an ambulance. Anna is close to Gemma, whose
eyes are opening.

ANNA
(to Gemma)
It's alright. Can you sit up?
Come on, you're going to be
alright.

Close on Gemma... fading consciousness...

A sense of detachment. Chaos around her - Carly
speaking to Tom on the stairs. Anna's talking to
Gemma, trying to help but we don't hear it -

Through the open door, Simon listens to Kate, who's
screaming at him, wanting to know what happened.

Tom gets past Carly, and runs down the stairs, to
her, and stops, shocked... Gemma reaches out to
him. Takes his hand.

Then closes her eyes, exhausted.

FADE TO BLACK.

INT. FOSTER HOUSE. BEDROOM. DAY

BLACK. Then -

The alarm goes off, on the bedside. 6.30 a.m.

Gemma is curled up in the double bed. She turns on
to her front. The overhead shot we've seen so many
times. But now she's on her own.

CUT TO -

INT. FOSTER HOUSE. KITCHEN. DAY

An identical shot to the one in Episode One. Gemma
in the kitchen with Tom eating his breakfast. Gemma
grabs her keys and bag and has a last sip of coffee.

> GEMMA
>
> Ready to go?

> TOM
> (getting off the stool)
>
> Yeah.

EXT. FOSTER HOUSE. DRIVEWAY. DAY

There's only one car in the drive now. Tom opens
the passenger door to get in. Gemma closes the
front door of the house, and goes round to the
driver's side.

As she does, she sees Anna saying goodbye to Neil
across the road. They both notice her. Anna waves,
kind.

Gemma smiles a little, and then gets in her car.

INT. G56 SOLICITORS. ANWAR'S OFFICE. DAY

Anwar looking thinner, and quite ill, hands the
divorce papers to Gemma. She signs them, then gives
them back. He signs them.

They look at each other and smile.

CUT TO -

INT. SURGERY. BACK OFFICE. DAY

Ros and Gemma stand opposite each other at a table.
It's formal. Not much trust between them now.

> ROS
> He's withdrawn the complaint. No
> reason not to come back. And I
> don't like being in charge. Can't
> do the spreadsheets!

Gemma glances at her. Too soon for that kind of
relationship.

> GEMMA
> You should have this.

She puts the doctor's bag on the table.

> GEMMA (CONT'D)
> Don't want any confusion.

> ROS
> Keep it. Just for a while. See
> how you feel.

Gemma looks at it. Not sure.

> ROS (CONT'D)
> Gemma...
> (beat)
> I just didn't want to hurt
> anyone.

EXT. SURGERY. DAY

Gemma comes out of the surgery, where Tom is
waiting. She is still holding her bag.

They walk off, towards town...

EXT. PARMINSTER TOWN SQUARE. DAY

Gemma is sat outside a coffee shop with a coffee.
The doctor's bag is at her feet.

She drinks. Looks at the people walking past.
Couples. Families. She's still detached from them
all. She's thinking... unresolved. Unsure how to
move on now. What to do next.

She can see across to a newsagent where Tom is
looking at computer magazines, serious. He looks
older somehow now.

Gemma then sees Kate walking right past her, only
three months later, clearly pregnant now, but
dressed differently.

Kate comes across.

                    KATE
          How are you?

                    GEMMA
          Good.

                    KATE
          We're moving to London.
               (beat)
          Simon wanted you to know but
          obviously, he's not allowed to
          call so. My parents are pleased
          as well, actually. New start.

Gemma nods. Awkward pause. Kate decides to leave.

                    KATE (CONT'D)
          Bye.

She walks away, towards the road. As she does, Tom
comes out of the shop with a magazine he's bought.
Gemma smiles. He sits across the table from her to
read it.

                    GEMMA
          Do you want to sit here?

Tom looks at her, sighs, then gets up and moves to the chair next to his mum, without really looking at her. Then he continues to read.

She makes a decision and kisses his head. But he doesn't respond and it feels awkward.

Gemma then turns and watches as Kate goes to the road. A small second-hand car pulls up. A world away from Simon's old car. Simon gets out, unshaven, and opens the door for Kate.

He looks somehow older now, but less harried, less naive, and more sober.

Gemma watches them together.

Simon looks up, he sees her.

They make eye contact, at a huge distance. She doesn't flinch. She keeps on looking.

They stare at each other.

He looks at Tom. She turns to look at Tom too. (Tom doesn't notice all this. Doesn't see his dad.)

Gemma and Simon look back at each other. As they stare, maybe there's even a flicker of love, still there...

He looks away. Shuts the car door now Kate is in, hurries back to the driver's side, gets in, and the car drives off.

Gemma drinks her coffee, looks at Tom.

On the page Tom's got open, there's a advert for a video game - it features very prominently an image of a woman with few clothes on in a sexualised pose. Tom doesn't seem to notice it, particularly. But it's there.

                    GEMMA (CONT'D)
          Are you alright?

                         TOM
                  (a little annoyed)
             Yeah, I'm reading.

She turns and looks at all the people walking past.
instead.

Happy families - all out at the weekend.

Couples, kids, laughing, enjoying themselves.

Suddenly a scream.

                       PASSER-BY
             We need a doctor!

Gemma's already out of her seat, and running across
the square, cutting through the crowd of people and
kneels to examine the man. She looks at the wife.

                        GEMMA
             My name's Doctor Gemma Foster.
             Are you his wife?

                        WIFE
             Yes.

                        GEMMA
             Call nine-nine-nine, tell them
             it's a cardiac arrest.

Tom's run across and is right there. Gemma looks up
at him.

                   GEMMA (CONT'D)
             Tom, I need my bag!

But he's already got it. He gives it to her.

                   GEMMA (CONT'D)
                  (affectionate)
             Thank you.

They share a quick smile - complicit again.

Then he stands back, and watches, actually
impressed as his mum works.

He's never seen his mum like this before.

A doctor.

CUT TO BLACK.

Cast in order of appearance

Dr Gemma Foster	SURANNE JONES
Simon Foster	BERTIE CARVEL
Tom Foster	TOM TAYLOR
Gordon Ward	DANIEL CERQUEIRA
Luke Barton	CIAN BARRY
Julie	SHAZIA NICHOLLS
Ros Mahendra	THUSITHA JAYASUNDERA
Nick Stanford	PETER DE JERSEY
Carly	CLARE-HOPE ASHITEY
Susie Parks	SARA STEWART
Poppy	TYLA WILSON
Isobel	MEGAN ROBERTS
Becky	MARTHA HOWE-DOUGLAS
Neil	ADAM JAMES
Anna	VICTORIA HAMILTON
Jack Reynolds	ROBERT PUGH
Helen Foster	CHERYL CAMPBELL
Bridewell Nurse	CHARLOTTE McKINNEY
Chris Parks	NEIL STUKE
Andrew Parks	CHARLIE CUNNIFFE
Kate Parks	JODIE COMER
Daniel Spencer	RICKY NIXON
Anwar	NAVIN CHOWDHRY
Belinda	BESSIE CURSONS
Dr Stevens	JOHN WEBBER
Lilly	SAMANTHA BEST
Julie	SHAZIA NICHOLLS
Mary	ELIZABETH RIDER
Isobel	MEGAN ROBERTS
Martha	HEATHER BLEASDALE
Poppy	TYLA WILSON
Mrs Walters	HELENA LYMBERY

Crew

Stunt Coordinators	ANDY BRADFORD
	GARY CONNERY
	RAY DE HAAN
Stunt Performers	TANYA BRASS
	ZARENE DALLAS
	RAY DE HAAN
	IAN KAY
Production Coordinator	ANNA GOODRIDGE
Production Secretary	TIM MORRIS
Production Runner	EUAN GILHOOLY
Script Editor	LAUREN CUSHMAN
Production Accountant	ELIZABETH WALKER
Assistant Production Accountant	LINDA BAIGE
Casting Associate	ALICE PURSER
Casting Assistant	RI McDAID-WREN
1st Assistant Director (eps 1–3)	KRISTIAN DENCH
1st Assistant Director (eps 4&5)	DEAN BYFIELD
2nd Assistant Director (eps 1–3)	SEAN CLAYTON
2nd Assistant Director (eps 4&5)	CHRISTIAN RIGG
3rd Assistant Director	JAMES McGEOWN
Floor Runners	ALEXANDRA BEAHAN
	SOPHIE KENNY
Location Manager (eps 1–3)	KAREN SMITH
Location Manager (eps 4&5)	BILL TWISTON-DAVIES
Assistant Location Manager	ELENA VAKIRTZIS
Location Assistant	COREY MORPETH
Camera Operator	JEREMY HILES
A Camera Focus Puller	JAY POLYZOIDES
B Camera Focus Puller	PIOTR PERLINSKI
2nd Assistant Camera	ANDRES CLARIDGE
Camera Trainees	CAROLINE DELERUE
	CLARE SEYMOUR
DIT	DYLAN EVANS
Script Supervisor	ALANA MARMION-WARR
Grips	BRETT LAMERTON
	BEN FREEMAN
Gaffer	MARK TAYLOR

Best Boy	DANNY GRIFFITHS
Electricians	SIMON ATHERTON
	JAMES KENNEDY
	GUY MINOLI
Standby Rigger	ROB ARMSTRONG
Sound Maintenance Engineer	GIDEON JENSEN
Sound Assistant	MATT FORRESTER
Art Director	ADAM MARSHALL
Standby Art Director	SUSIE BATY
Assistant Art Director	GEORGIA GRANT
Set Decorator	HANNAH SPICE
Props Buyer	ANTONIA TIBBLE
Props Master	NICK WALKER
Standby Props	DAVE ACKRILL
	EDDIE BAKER
Dressing Props	DAVE SIMPSON
	SAM WALKER
Art Department Assistant	LOTTIE McDOWELL
Art Department Trainee	ANNA CZERNIAVSKA
Standby Carpenter	RONALD ANDERSON
Special Effects	SCOTT McINTYRE
Costume Supervisor	NADINE DAVERN
Costume Assistants	JEN DAVIES
	RUTH PHELAN
Costume Trainee	ELIZABETH WEBB
Make-Up Supervisor	KATIE PICKLES
Make-Up Artist	ALANA CAMPBELL
Make-Up Trainee	SIMONE CAMPS
Medical Advisor	DR RACHEL GRENFELL
Publicist	CHRISTOPHER DUGGAN
Communications Manager	CHARLOTTE INETT
Picture Executive	VICTORIA DALTON
Picture Manager	JULIAN WYTH
Stills Photographers	DES WILLIE
	ED MILLER
	LIAM DANIEL
Legal and Business Affairs	BELLA WRIGHT
Financial Controller	DENIS WRAY
Assistant to Executives	TROY HUNTER
Head of Production	SUSY LIDDELL

Post Production Supervisor	BEEWAN ATHWAL
Post Production Paperwork	ILANA EPSTEIN
Assistant Editor	OLIE GRIFFIN
Dialogue Editor (eps 1–4)	TOM DEANE
Dialogue Editor (ep 5)	IAIN EYRE
Sound FX Editor	JIM GODDARD
Dubbing Mixer (eps 1, 2&5)	STUART HILLIKER
Dubbing Mixer (eps 3&4)	FORBES NOONAN
Title Music 'Fly' by	LUDOVICO EINAUDI
Online Editor	OWEN HULME
VFX	SASCHA FROMEYER
Colourist (eps 1–4)	AIDAN FARRELL
Colourist (eps 4&5)	COLIN PETERS
Music Supervisor	IAIN COOKE
Composer	FRANS BAK
Title Design	PETER ANDERSON STUDIO
Casting Director	ANDY PRYOR CDG
Sound Recordist	BILLY QUINN
Hair & Make-Up Designer	JOJO WILLIAMS
Costume Designer	ALEXANDRA CAULFIELD
Editor (eps 1–3)	TOM HEMMINGS
Editor (eps 4&5)	RICHARD COX
Production Designer	HELEN SCOTT
Director of Photography (eps 1–3)	JEAN-PHILIPPE GOSSART
Director of Photography (eps 4&5)	JOEL DEVLIN
Line Producer	CHRISTINE HEALY
Executive Producer for the BBC	MATTHEW READ
Executive Producers	ROANNA BENN
	JUDE LIKNAITZKY
	MIKE BARTLETT
	GREG BRENMAN
Producer	GRAINNE MARMION
Director (eps 1–3)	TOM VAUGHAN
Director (eps 4&5)	BRUCE GOODISON

for BBC
© Drama Republic Limited MMXV

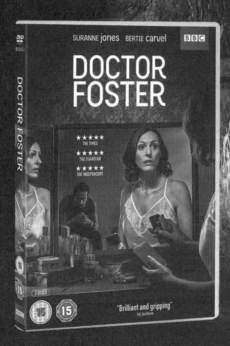